SPINNING OUT

David Stahler Jr.

SPINNING OUT

chronicle books · san francisco

Library of Congress Cataloging-in-Publication Data

Stahler, David.

Spinning out / by David Stahler Jr.

p. cm.

Summary: Frenchy and Stewart, two Northern Vermont high school seniors, try out for the school
musical, "Man of La Mancha," but when Stewart is cast as Don Quixote he soon becomes obsessed with
his role and Frenchy must try to overcome his own demons to help his friend stay grounded in reality.

ISBN 978-0-8118-7780-0 (alk. paper)

[1. Schizophrenia—Fiction. 2. Mental illness—Fiction. 3. Emotional problems—Fiction. 4. Friendship—
Fiction. 5. High schools—Fiction. 6. Schools—Fiction. 7. Theater—Fiction. 8. Vermont—Fiction. 9.
Wasserman, Dale. Man of La Mancha—Fiction.] I. Title.

PZ7.S78246Sp 2011

[Fic]—dc22

2010039392

Book design by Amelia May Anderson.

Typeset in Requiem.

Manufactured by C & C Offset, Longgang, Shenzhen, China, in February 2011.

10 9 8 7 6 5 4 3 2 1

This product conforms to CPSIA 2008.

Chronicle Books LLC
680 Second Street, San Francisco, California 94107

www.chroniclekids.com

*For all those who suffer from
the wounds that can't be seen.*

ACT ONE:
EXPOSITION

CHAPTER ONE

"Come on, pass it over."

I glanced down at the joint in my hand, watched its thin line of smoke curl up around my wrist, before handing it off to Stewart.

"Sorry." I felt like telling him that it wasn't me who always hogged the joint, but I couldn't muster the energy. I wasn't especially high—not yet, anyway—but it was Monday morning. And I was replacing one fog with another before heading off to school.

The pit stop. That's what we called our morning layover. Stewart would pick me up at quarter after seven on his way past my house. We'd drive a half mile down the mountain, then turn off into a field that looked out over the valley where the village lay and park along the tree line. We'd only been back at school for four weeks, but it had become part of the routine. A "tradition," Stewart called it. To me it was just a habit.

September was almost over, and the colors were bursting from the maples all around us. It was a good year for the leaves—even for northern Vermont—with lots of red, a little gold mixed in, all shimmering in the cold against the early slant of sun. Best of all was the mist that hung below us in the valley—a thick September mist that always slipped in those first cold nights of fall, flooding the hollows by morning, turning the valleys into lakes of white that glowed under the blue sky. It was so goddam beautiful, you almost didn't need the pot.

I'd tried making the point last week, but Stewart would have none of it.

"It's not a matter of need, Frenchy," he'd scolded. "Just a matter of enhancement." He repeated the line, quietly, more to himself than anyone. I wondered if he was pondering its meaning or storing it for posterity.

I watched him take a drag, his third since squirreling the joint away from me. He had a way of smoking—pulling hard, then opening and closing his mouth four or five times in rapid succession, biting at the air—that I found both cool and revolting at the same time. It was like he was eating the smoke, devouring it.

Seeing me watch him, he offered it back. I shook my head. To be honest, I was getting tired of the whole thing. It would have been fine if we could've stayed here in the field, but Stewart wasn't one for skipping. He was just one for enhancing. Not me. Pot made school longer. And more boring.

"Do those fuckers *ever* turn?" he asked.

I followed his gaze across the valley to the opposite ridge, where the wind turbines stood, twenty of them all in a row, their blades glinting against the sunrise. At three hundred feet tall, they loomed over everything, a phalanx of metal towers plopped down by a bunch of power company suits from Boston or New York or who-the-hell-knows-where. They'd offered our poor little town a shitload of money to install them, an offer—in spite of serious resistance from quite a few people—the slim majority couldn't refuse. But it came at a pretty steep price. Two years later, half the town still hated the other half.

It was kind of funny how the battle lines had been drawn. Not the way you might think. Sure, there were the hippie types who loved the wind towers because they were all into clean power and that kind of shit, and there were plenty of locals who were pissed off about a bunch of rich assholes coming in and taking over their ridgetops. But a lot of the natives didn't mind them. Most people around here don't have much money, and the idea of saving a few hundred bucks on their taxes made them come around pretty fast. Actually, the people most against the towers were ones like Stewart's family, who'd moved here from out of state. Flatlanders, we called them. And even though a lot of them were pretty crunchy, a lot of them were pretty rich, too, and they didn't want their piece of backwoods paradise ruined by a giant row of steely eyesores.

Stewart's parents had led the charge against the turbines, donating a pile of money to fund lawsuits that ultimately went nowhere. It wasn't a big deal—the Bolgers had quite a bit of dough—but nobody hated the wind towers more than Stewart and his family.

"I saw them turning the other night. Before the storm," I offered.

I pretended to hate them too, because of Stewart, but at this point I really had a hard time giving a shit. Sometimes I even thought they looked kind of cool, especially after the morning pit stops.

"Those fuckers need to come down," he muttered. He said that every day.

"We better get going," I said.

Stewart looked at his watch and nodded. He took one more drag, then bent down and carefully put out what was left of the joint before placing it in an Altoids tin. Sticking the tin in his pocket, he looked up at me and grinned. I snickered. He was quite a sight, all tall and gangly with his thrift-store hipster garb, long hair, toasty eyes, and cheesed smile. Rising, he started to say something, then jerked his head to the side and whirled around, as if someone had goosed him from behind.

"What?" I said, even though I knew what was coming.

"Did you hear that?" he said. "I heard someone."

"Oh, Jesus Christ. It's nobody. We're all alone. Same as always."

He nodded, but I could see the echo of fear still on his face. I took one last look down into the valley, then walked past him toward the car.

"Hey, Frenchy!" he called out. "We're getting low. Better talk to your man."

I hesitated, then turned around. "Don't you want to take a break?"

He just frowned.

I knew that look. "All right."

"Thanks, pal." His grin returned as he joined me.

"Oh," he said when we reached the car. "I almost forgot." He pulled a wadded piece of paper from his pocket and tossed it over the hood at me. While I unrolled it, he ducked into the dinged-up Volvo his parents had given him last summer. Something was up.

I'd noticed the neon green flyers at school—they'd been hanging everywhere since the first day back—but it was funny seeing one of them out here in the field, the paper soft and crinkled, the words a collection of cut-out letters that made it look more like a ransom note than an announcement:

ATTENTION ACTORS
Gilliam High School Fall Musical:
Man of La Mancha
Audition! Audition! Audition!
Wednesday, Sept. 30, 3:00 P.M., Auditorium

A breeze rose, fluttering the paper in my hand. I crumpled it back up and got in. Stewart didn't look at me as he started the engine.

"So what the hell's this all about?" I flicked the wad into his lap.

He picked up the neon ball and held it out before him, regarding it for a moment as if it were a precious jewel.

"We're going. You and me."

I burst out laughing. I didn't think I had smoked very much, but it was hitting me hard all of a sudden. Through the windshield I noticed the blades on the far towers had started to turn, all twenty turbines spinning in perfect synchronicity.

"You're joking," I said, rubbing my eyes.

He glanced over at me with a mischievous grin.

"Frenchy," he said, "we're all over this mother."

This time we both burst out laughing. But behind those halfbaked lids, I could see it in his eyes—he wasn't kidding at all.

ᴸᴵᴵ CHAPTER TWO ᴵᴵᴸ

"Frenchy, Frenchy, Frenchy." Stewart giggled as we drove into Gilliam. The school sat on a hill on the far side of the village.

"Stewey, Stewey, Stew," I shot back. He hated when I called him Stew.

"What makes you so special, anyway, *Gerard Paquette*?"

"What do you mean?"

"The nickname, Frenchy. I mean, half the people around here are French."

"That's French-Canadian to you, asshole. And stop driving like my goddam grandmother. We're going to be late for school."

He waved off the insult. "Just answer the question."

"Christ, Stewart, look at me."

With Quebec just to the north of us, there are a lot of locals with French roots, but I really look the part—short and rugged, thick black hair, dark eyes. I started shaving in eighth grade. Now I practically have to hit the razor twice a day to avoid looking homeless. Classic Canuck.

"I don't know," I said as we neared the school. "I don't even remember when people stopped calling me Gerry. Everyone calls me Frenchy. Even my teachers. Even my mom."

"Wish I had a cool nickname."

"There's nothing cool about being Frenchy."

"It's the jokes, isn't it?" Stewart said.

"You mean like how many dumbass Frenchmen does it take to screw in a lightbulb?"

I stuck out my tongue and conjured up the most moronic face I could muster. Stewart burst out laughing.

"You'd think in these enlightened times, people would know better."

Stewart's face darkened. "There's nothing enlightened about these times, Frenchy. Barbarians!" he shouted, gesturing at the town. "Barbarians all around us."

"Watch where you're going, for chrissake!" We'd started to drift over the center line. Stewart pulled back into his lane, glancing around to see if anyone had noticed.

"Don't worry, Frenchy. I know who you really are. Smarter than the lot of them. You should be in the honors courses. I keep telling you."

"You mean like you?" I said as we pulled into the school lot. "No thanks. I don't have a quarter the work you have. I just collect my easy As and coast. That's intelligence, if you ask me."

"Maybe you're right," he said, parking the car.

"Yeah, maybe," I whispered. I glanced up at the visor mirror. My red eyes squinted back at me.

We popped in a few drops of Visine, got out of the car, and headed across the lot through the bright morning sun.

"Shit, I don't even care," I said as we climbed the front steps. "Let people think what they want. They're going to anyway. Besides, once you get stuck with a nickname, that's it. You might as well learn to like it. That, or move to Alaska. Try to get rid of it, try to make people stop calling you what they want to call you, and they just end up thinking you're an asshole."

He nodded and gave me a sad sort of smile as we paused in the lobby, then parted ways until lunch.

"Off to AP Chem," he said with a wave, then headed down the hall.

"Try not to blow anything up," I called after him.

He flashed a peace sign above his head, turned the corner, and disappeared.

"So it's just a joke, right?" I said.

We were tucked away in our usual spot in the corner of the cafeteria, me and Eddie Edward shoving subsidized Tater Tots down our low-income gullets while Stewart munched on the organic, bullshit hippie fare his mother always packed for him.

"What's just a joke?"

"This audition business. Another one of your pranks?"

Stewart was known for his pranks. Putting teachers' cars into neutral and pushing them to the other end of the parking lot after school, slipping Ex-Lax brownies into cafeteria bake sales, squishing a dead mouse between the pages of a book on rodents in the library—stupid shit, I know. But that was the whole point. Stewart fancied himself an anarchist.

"What do you mean, *my* pranks?" he retorted. "You're my accomplice. They belong just as much to you. And don't forget, the cricket job was your idea."

Last year for Halloween, we went to a pet store over in Burlington and bought two hundred crickets. The guy behind the counter gave us the once-over, but Stewart convinced him they were for his pet snake. A few days later, we smuggled them into school and—as Stewart put it—"liberated" them. Within days they'd spread to every part of the building, their chirping permeating the walls. They were resilient suckers, too. Walking down an empty hall in the middle of May, you could still hear a lonely cricket or two calling from some hiding spot.

I laughed. "That was a good one."

"The best."

"So that's what this play business is all about?"

Stewart flashed a quick smile, then went back to surveying the scene.

"Tina got a boob job this summer," he said.

"Really?" Eddie Edward said, his eyes widening as we all watched Tina Rutherford walk by with her tray. Eddie Edward was a sweet kid but kind of a dingbat. He would believe just about anything you told him, which was why Stewart let him sit with us at lunch. Everyone called him Eddie Edward. Compared with that nickname, Frenchy didn't sound so bad.

"Jesus, Eddie, don't be a moron. Stewart's talking shit again."

"Oh," Eddie Edward said, his face falling.

"No. Consider the matter closely," Stewart said as Tina headed back to her table in her tight-fitting shirt. "Far more ample than last year."

I had to admit, they did look bigger. "They probably just grew. Girls don't get boob jobs. Not around here."

"One can always dream," Stewart said.

I told you he was into enhancement.

"Stewart," I pressed, "the play's a big deal. It's not like dumping a bunch of crickets in the library."

The fall musical was one of the few things our school truly excelled at. Half the county showed up to the performances, packing the auditorium. Hell, I even went once. Okay, twice.

"Besides, I hear those auditions are supercompetitive. I don't know shit about acting, and I'm pretty sure you don't either."

Stewart grabbed my arm. "Look at this place," he said, turning me toward the crowd. "Everyone in this room, everyone in this goddam school, is acting. Believe it. Besides, like you said, it's just a prank. Come on, it's senior year! We're due."

"Yeah, well, pranks are one thing," I said. "Crashing a school function with a spectacular display of public humiliation is something else altogether. Life's humiliating enough already."

"Frenchy, my swarthy little friend, the problem with you is that you're a worrier. You've got to stop with the worrying."

"Frenchy?" Eddie Edward laughed. "He doesn't worry about shit. That's why everyone loves him."

Stewart turned back to me with a grin. "Yes, well, Edward, I guess that goes to show what a good actor Frenchy really is after all."

I shot him a dark look and went back to my lunch. Fucking Stewart.

"Frenchy," Stewart said, watching me toss an entire chicken nugget into my mouth, "when are you going to stop eating that crap? It's no good for you. You're only seventeen and already halfway to fat-ass."

"Bite me," I said, instinctively reaching down to my stomach. I actually had put on weight lately.

"No, bite this." He pushed his green-and-beige-colored wrap in my face.

"Get your bean-sprout-veggie-burger-eating ass away from me," I said, knocking his hand away and trying not to smile.

"Eat it!" He laughed as he jumped up, practically tackling me as he tried shoving his sandwich into my mouth. With my extra heft, I got the better of him, though. Before he knew it, I had him in a headlock.

"Eat this!" I hollered back, squishing a Tater Tot against his sealed lips.

"Frenchy!"

I looked up to see the assistant principal, Mr. Ruggles, glaring at me.

"Knock it off!"

"Sorry, Mr. Ruggles." I let go of Stewart. I wasn't too worried. I knew the look was all for show. Ruggles liked me because I never gave him a hard time, even when I got in trouble.

"You too, Bolger," he added.

Stewart jumped to his feet. "You saw that, didn't you?" he shouted, trying not to laugh. "You saw him try to taint me with his vile filth! Detention! Detention!"

Mr. Ruggles frowned. He came over, handed me a note, then turned and walked away as the bell rang and everyone scrambled to their feet.

"What's that?" Stewart asked, glancing over my shoulder.

I opened up the stapled note. "Bryant." Shit, I'd forgotten.

"Another Gerry session, eh?"

"Yeah." I kept my head down, my eyes on the note. "I gotta go."

"I'll bring your tray up," he offered, taking it from the table.

"Thanks." I crumpled up the piece of paper and shoved it in my pocket.

"No problem. Hey, I've got a guitar lesson after school," he said. "Can you get a ride with someone else?"

"Sure. I'll get home somehow."

"Cool. Come up to the house after."

I nodded, then turned and left the cafeteria. As I headed toward Bryant's office, I could feel my stomach clench as all the Tater Tots and nuggets fused into a toxic ball of sick. I guess Stewart was right about that garbage after all.

It was my fourth time in Mr. Bryant's office, a tiny room tucked away in the corner of the guidance department. The place was sparsely furnished—a few nice prints on the wall, a bowl of candy and a worn baseball beside the computer on the desk, a set of Venetian blinds covering the window, a Red Sox cap perched on top of a bookcase. At least there wasn't any couch. That's what you usually see in a shrink's office.

To be honest, I didn't know if Mr. Bryant was an actual shrink or not, but he was my "school-appointed counselor." Whatever, the guy seemed to know his shit. I admit I'd been a little rattled to be called in that first week of school, but it was to be expected after what had happened last summer. Besides, it got me out of math.

Mr. Bryant sat across from me, quiet, a sliver of smile on his face. This was how things usually started. Sometimes the silence lasted several minutes.

"Glad we finally connected, Gerry," he said.

Bryant was the only one who called me Gerry. Probably because he was a Gerry too. Hence "the Gerry sessions." His term, not mine, which I thought was pretty funny. He tended to crack little jokes like that—one of his therapist tricks to loosen me up, I'm sure. It was about as animated as he ever got. I swear, the guy must have been a Zen monk in a former life. Nothing seemed to bother him. I mean, I could set his desk on fire, and he'd probably just nod a few times, turn, and stare pensively out the window.

"Sorry I didn't make it before lunch," I said at last. "I forgot."

He waved off the apology. "How was your weekend?"

"One big fucking thrill."

I'd started swearing sometime during the second session, mostly just to see how he'd react. He didn't. So I kept on doing it. Why the fuck not?

"Maybe you could be more specific."

"You know, sat around the old double-wide. Watched shitty movies on cable. Ate mustard sandwiches. Just your typical white-trash weekend."

Bryant laughed at the joke, even though we both knew it wasn't far from the truth.

"Did you see your mother this weekend?"

"Some. She spent most of it at Ralph's."

Bryant nodded. "Okay. How about friends? Did you get together with anybody? How about Stewart? I mean, please tell me you stuck your head out of the trailer for at least ten minutes."

It was my turn to laugh now. "Yeah, I saw Stewart. He actually dragged my ass up Bald Mountain on Saturday. Last time I'll ever do that."

"Wouldn't want to get too much exercise, now, would you?"

"Hell, no. I might strain a muscle."

"You're pretty tight with Stewart, aren't you? I always see you together."

"We're neighbors."

"I was looking over both your schedules this morning. Is it hard, him being in the advanced classes when you're not?"

Ah, here we go, I thought. *Tricky.*

"Hard for him, maybe," I quipped. "Not for me."

Bryant raised his eyebrows. He knew what I was getting at. "I see you did quite well on your PSATs last year. One of the highest scores in the school."

He saw me stir.

"Didn't know that, did you?"

This was a new side of Bryant. The tranquillity was still there, but the questions were coming faster, the voice with a hint of edge. *So that's the way it is,* I thought. *Game on.*

"Got lucky, I guess."

He snorted. "You didn't have to take that test."

I shrugged. Then my curiosity got the better of me. "Did I score higher than Stewart?" Stewart had never told me his scores.

He ignored the question. "You're going to be graduating in a few months. Got any plans?"

"So that's why I'm here. To talk about my future, huh?"

There was a long pause as he looked at me. *Shit,* I thought. I'd walked right into that one. I knew it, and so did he.

"You know why you're here," he said at last.

I rolled my eyes. "I was wondering when we were going to get around to it."

"Around to what?"

I shot him a look. He knew. He just wanted to hear me say it. More therapist bullshit, I'm sure. I just thought it was mean.

"My father," I said. "About him blowing his fucking head off."

He wanted to hear me say it? Fine. I'd say it.

Bryant flinched. It was just an instant, but it was enough. *That'll show him*, I thought.

He nodded. "I'm sure you miss him."

"Of course," I snapped. "But it's nothing new. Nothing I wasn't used to."

"He had a pretty long deployment, didn't he?"

"I guess. And then when he got back . . . "

Bryant finished the thought for me. "He wasn't the same."

I didn't say anything. I just stared down at my hands, my fingers all twisted around one another. My nails were dirty.

"How do you feel about what he did?"

I shrugged.

"You feel *something*," he said. "In fact, you probably feel a whole lot of things, right? Sadness. Anger." He paused. "Shame."

I jerked my head up. "Fuck you," I said, as nasty as I could.

It didn't faze him, of course, not this time. The bastard.

"It's an honest question."

I didn't answer.

He gave me a little smile and nodded. "I think that's enough for today."

"That's it?" I was usually there for half an hour. I glanced at my watch. "We've still got twenty minutes."

"It's okay. It was a productive ten minutes. We'll go longer next week."

"Fine." I stood up to go.

"Oh, by the way," he said. "I think we'll start meeting after lunch like this from now on."

"Why's that?" I asked, pausing in the doorway.

"You're more interesting to talk to when you're not stoned."

CHAPTER THREE

It took me a while to get home. I had to walk the first three miles to the base of Suffolk Heights. Normally I didn't mind. I used to walk everywhere before Stewart got his car. It's one of the few acceptable forms of idleness. Not much to do, except maybe think. But I didn't want to think today. I was still riled up from the Gerry session—in fact, I almost skipped the last two periods of school entirely—and all I wanted was to put one foot in front of the other and forget about everything. So I trudged along, working my steps into a rhythm that turned into a song in my head, and just stared around at the leaves. It was a nice day—sunny but with the slightest chill in the air, the kind that lets you know it's not summer anymore.

Once I got over the bridge and started up out of the valley, one of the farmers who lived up on the Heights pulled his truck over. I jumped into the back for the rest of the way. My old man had worked for him in high school, so he knew who I was. He'd even offered me a job a couple months ago, but I turned it down. Who wants the hassle?

He gave me a smile through the back window as I settled down onto the bed liner, but behind it I could see the sadness in his eyes. I hated that pity crap. It was one of the worst things about the whole situation. If you're going to pity someone, okay. Fine. Just don't let them see you doing it. It won't do anything but make them feel like shit.

Ten minutes later he stopped in front of my place. I jumped down, hollered thanks, and gave him a wave as he continued up the hill and out of sight. The house stood back from the road about fifty feet. It was nothing special, believe me—a yellow double-wide trailer with no real features except for a satellite dish bolted to the front and a pair of black vinyl shutters framing the kitchen window—but I knew plenty of kids who lived in worse. Mom and I both did a halfway decent job of keeping it tidy, probably as a tribute to my father more than anything else. The old man had been a neat freak. Army guys usually are.

The house—or rather the freezer full of Pizza Pockets and ice cream—beckoned, but I didn't go in. My mother wouldn't be home from her job as a dispatcher at the state police barracks in St. Johnsbury for a few more hours, and I suddenly didn't feel like leaving the sunshine for the trailer's darkness. Besides, it was almost 3:30. Stewart would be done with his lesson pretty soon, and I had matters to attend to.

I crossed the road and trotted fifty or so yards back down the hill before turning into the driveway of a house that had seen better days. Drifting by the beat-up Camaro, I traced a line along its dusty side with my finger, then skipped up the broken steps and rapped on the door. It took a while, but the door finally opened.

"Hey, Ralph," I said, staring up at the tall, scrawny figure.

Ralph—cheesy-mustached, mullet-headed, tight-jeans-from-God-knows-how-long-ago-wearing Ralph—was scrogging my mother.

I'd ascertained this painful fact a couple weeks ago. (I'll leave it to you to figure out how.) When confronted, Mom admitted it had been going on for a while, right around the time I'd started back in school. I was pissed off at first. After all, my father had only been gone for a few months. And of all the men within a fifty-mile radius, it had to be this douche bag. But I got over it a few days later. I mean, I wasn't crazy about it, but it was better than listening to my mother sob every night like she had all summer. And as for Ralph, yeah, he was a douche bag, but he was a lovable douche bag in his own pathetic way. It was almost impossible to hate the guy. Believe me, I tried.

Besides, as I'd discovered long before I learned he and my mother were doing it, Ralph had other uses.

"What's up, bro?" Ralph said.

Ralph always called me bro. A weird thing to call a kid when you're banging his mother, but whatever.

"I need a bag. A quarter."

Ralph raised his eyebrows. "I just got you one two weeks ago. Don't tell me you've gone through it already."

"I told you before, Ralph—it's not for me. It's for a friend."

Technically that was true, though I'd certainly had my share. I could see him hesitate.

"Look, man," I said, "I'm trying to do you a favor. You want the business or not?"

"Yeah, yeah. Come on in."

"I can't stay long," I said, following him into the living room.

"Whatever, bro," he said, disappearing down the hall to the back room where he kept his stash.

The room smelled of cigarette smoke but not of weed. I guessed Ralph refrained from smoking pot in the house now that he was with my mother. Maybe she'd gotten him to stop altogether.

I flopped onto the couch and looked around the dumpy old place Ralph had inherited from his mother—complete with the same dirty wallpaper she'd hung probably forty years ago, the same pair of faded Sears portraits of Ralph when he was five years old on top of the TV, the same kitschy knickknacks on the shelves he still hadn't put away in the two years since she'd died—but it was definitely neater than it ever used to be. My mother's doing, no doubt. In fact, I noticed one of our mugs sitting on the coffee table in front of me. It was one I'd given her for her birthday about five years ago. *World's Greatest Mom!* it said. Lame, I know, but I was only twelve at the time. What the hell did I know?

It felt strange seeing the cup here in a different setting, this lost and lonely thing surrounded by alien artifacts. But then, the more I stared at it, the more it seemed like it was the only right thing, like everything else around it—the newspapers, the ashtray, the living room, the house—was wrong and out of place. Still, I didn't like it. I reached out with my toe and gave it a little kick. It tumbled off the side of the table, fell onto the threadbare carpet, and popped into three clean chunks.

Ralph reappeared as I was picking up the pieces.

"Sorry, Ralph. It got knocked over."

"Whatever, bro," he said, clearly not giving a shit. I wondered if he even knew the mug wasn't his. I put the pieces back on the table and stood up.

"Fifty, right? I'll bring the money by tomorrow."

"Yeah, okay." He looked around the room as if he'd forgotten something, as if he were trying to figure out where he was. "So is this for that Stewart kid, or what?"

"No," I lied. "It's for someone else. Someone at school."

He nodded, but he didn't look at me. I don't think he believed me.

"Okay, that's cool." He held out the bag of weed, a generous quarter ounce, then drew it back as I reached for it.

"Just be careful, Frenchy," he said. "Don't go smoking too much. It's not good for a kid your age to smoke too much, right?"

I reached out and took the bag with a snort. This time, he let go.

"Yeah, thanks, Ralph. Thanks for the concern." The guy had only been selling me pot since I was fifteen. "You're a fucking compassionate soul."

His face reddened. He hesitated again.

"You're not going to tell your mom, are you? You know, about all this?"

"You mean that I buy pot from you?" I asked, trying not to laugh. "No, Ralph, I don't see that happening."

I could see the relief on his face. The poor dumb shit.

"Thanks, bro." He held out a fist.

I touched his fist with my own. "No sweat, bro."

As I started to leave, he stopped me.

"You want a bag for yourself, Frenchy?" he asked. "I could fix you up a little something. No charge."

Remembering his earlier concern, I shook my head. Typical Ralph. God bless him.

"No thanks, Ralph. I'm good."

ᴊᴅ CHAPTER FOUR ᴊᴅ

I hoofed it back up the hill. A quarter mile or so above my place, a dirt road turned off to the right. The green sign at the turn spelled it out: *Shangri La, PVT*—private road. The Bolgers lived at the end, a few hundred yards from the main road. It was a big house. A nice house.

I stopped in first at the workshop—a copper-roofed, cedar-shingled building beside the garage—and poked my head through the open doors, blinking against the shower of sparks flashing from the center of the room.

Stewart's dad was hard at work, acetylene torch in hand. He paused on seeing me, then lifted his visor and killed the torch.

"Hello, Frenchy," he said, wiping the sweat and smoke from his eyes. He didn't smile, but then he never did. A bit of a cipher, he played it close to the vest like my old man had. It was the one thing they had in common.

"Hey, Mr. Bolger. What's shakin'?"

"Living the dream, Frenchy," he murmured. "Living the dream." His usual joke. Probably the only one he had.

Stewart's dad had cashed out four years ago from some big software company he'd started down in Boston, retiring early to start his new career as a metal sculptor. He'd been working hard ever since to break into the craft-fair circuit—without much success. Glancing at the freakish jumbles of cobbled-together scrap metal cluttering up the shop, it wasn't hard to figure out why.

"Good for you, Mr. Bolger. So what're you making, anyway?" I always made a point of asking about his work.

He stepped back to survey the mass of wire and steel. "It's called Spider's Dream."

It looked like a giant birdcage that had been stepped on, but what the hell did I know about art?

"Oh, yeah. Yeah, I can see that," I said, but he'd already flipped the visor down and gone back to work.

I crossed the driveway and bounded up the steps onto the front deck, then rang the set of chimes by the door, knocking for good measure. Mrs. Bolger's face appeared in the window, smiling at me through the glass. This was her little game. It was kind of goofy, but sweet too. I just smiled back, waved, and waited until she finally opened the door.

"Frenchy, hello!" she gushed in an airy voice. She always sounded out of breath, as if she'd just come back from a run or something. Maybe she had asthma.

"Hi, Mrs. Bolger." I slipped past her into the kitchen.

The house was bright and warm, filled with the buttery glow of hardwood and tasteful lighting. I closed my eyes and breathed in all the usual aromas—spices, garlic, the scent of Mrs. Bolger's patchouli. And then there was that other familiar smell.

"Have one, Frenchy," Mrs. Bolger said. "I just took them out of the oven."

I opened my eyes to see her standing there with a plate of cookies. Stewart's mother was always making cookies—healthy, organic cookies, made with molasses and oats and shit. They were also delicious, especially when Stewart and I would come back from a "walk in the woods" with a serious case of the munchies. No wonder I was getting fat.

"Thanks, Mrs. Bolger." I grabbed a handful. "Is Stewart done with his lesson?"

"Yes. Clark, the teacher, left about ten minutes ago," she said, watching me stuff a cookie in my mouth. "So how was school?"

"The usual thrill. How about you? How's life at Shangri La?"

Her face tightened. "Fine." She glanced up at the ceiling. "Stewart's been a pain lately. Another one of his phases. You know how he can be, Frenchy. Sometimes I just . . ." Her eyes started to glisten. I looked away.

"Frenchy!"

I turned to see Stewart bounding down the staircase. Thank God.

"Hey, man." I reached out to slap his upheld hand.

"Lucinda," he said, turning to Mrs. Bolger, "Frenchy's going to stay for dinner. Okay?"

Lucinda and Phil. Stewart called his parents by their first names. I think he always had. And I always flinched when he did it. I just couldn't get used to it, not even after four years. If I spoke to my mother the way Stewart spoke to his parents, I'd get slapped faster than you can say "Mylanta." And as for my father— well, let's just say I'd have gotten a major dose of military discipline if I'd ever dared mouth off to him.

"Of course, honey," she replied. "We'd love to have you, Frenchy. We miss having you around."

I'd practically lived with the Bolgers after my father died. After a few weeks I had to go back home, though. It was doing a number on my mother. Of course, she hadn't hooked up with Ralph yet.

"How was the lesson?"

"Great. I learned a new lick. Come check it out," he said with a wink. Don't ask me how, but he knew I'd been to Ralph's.

I followed him up the stairs to his first room. Stewart had two rooms to himself. The room looking out over the mountains had been his mother's sewing room until Stewart decided to make it his study. He'd turned it into a nice little pad, with a desk along one whole wall—some far-out cherry table his father had rigged up for him with all kinds of baskets and shit underneath—where he kept his computers and some of his books.

Stewart had lots of books. Especially the smart kind—you know, history books and others on politics and the environment. They bored the crap out of me, I'll admit it. I never actually read any of them, but I had to listen to Stewart and his parents go on about them all the time, always in this sort of nasty, cynical tone, like they were arguing, even though they all were on the same side.

The one thing they didn't talk much about was the war. At least, not in front of me, since my father had been in Iraq, not to mention what had happened after he got home. I wasn't all gung-ho Mr. Patriot or anything like that—not like my father— and in fact, I'd grown to hate a lot about the whole goddam affair. But my hackles still rose when one of them slipped and made some comment about American atrocities and killings, and blood for oil, and the big bad wolf du jour. Old habits die hard, I guess. Everyone's hackles were raised these days; it was impossible really to talk about anything. The whole thing sucked.

Stewart's bedroom had a king-size futon and a kick-ass flat-screen TV mounted on the far wall. Compared to my room, it was fairly spare. Of course, his room was twice as big. Go figure.

It had been a couple weeks since I'd been here, and right away I noticed a difference.

"Whoa. Look at this place."

For someone who was supposedly an anarchist, Stewart was a bit of a neat freak—everything in its place, a world in order—especially when it came to his rooms. It was the one thing about him my father always approved of. But Dad wouldn't have liked this.

The bed was unmade, clothes littered the floor, a few drawers had been left half open, and the TV was on, with some nature show glowing mutely on the screen. Weirdest of all was the scattering of dirty dishes, some piled on the bureau, some on the nightstand, a few even on the floor. It was the kind of thing Stewart would normally never abide.

"Dude. This looks like my room," I said. Almost, anyway. Mine was worse.

Stewart glanced around and shook his head a little. He seemed almost confused. "It's a bit messy." He turned to me. "It's a conscious choice. A matter of will. I'd become a prisoner to my own self-imposed walls of rigidity. Got to break free."

"That's your excuse, huh? Me, I'm just lazy."

He laughed. "So you are, Frenchy. It's one of the things I like about you."

"Have your parents noticed?"

"My mother knows better than to come knocking around my room. As for the Picasso of Steel, as long as I make it into Harvard or Yale and don't interrupt his studio time, he doesn't give a fuck what I do. They're both clueless."

"You should be nicer to your parents, Stewart. They practically worship you."

"Hey," he said, whirling back around. "You get a chance to visit old Ralphie this afternoon or what?"

"Yup." I pulled the bag from my shirt pocket and tossed it to him.

He snatched it from the air and held it up, feeling it gently, testing its weight and fullness, like he was Weed Inspector #7 or something.

"Good old Ralph." He took a long sniff of the bag.

"Yeah, good old Ralph," I muttered. "By the way, I told him I'd pay him tomorrow."

"Sure, sure. Help yourself."

I went over to a jar on the top of the dresser, removed the lid, and tipped it toward me for a better look. Even with permission, I always felt weird poking around the jar full of cash. Stewart had quite a little hoard in there, some his parents had given him but most he'd made himself by selling shit on eBay and places like that. As much as he derided "capitalist pigs," Stewart could be quite the entrepreneur when he wanted to be.

I spotted a fifty-dollar bill in the mix and fished it out.

"So, what about that new lick?"

He made a face. "There isn't one, really," he said. "I didn't have a very good lesson. In fact, I think I'm going to quit."

"Really? What for?"

Stewart had started playing two years ago. He was actually pretty good. Of course, he was good at everything he tried, but he took the whole guitar thing pretty seriously. At least he used to.

He shrugged. "I want to focus on other things." There was a pause. "You disapprove?"

I looked up at him. "No," I said. "Whatever, man."

"Thanks, Frenchy."

I just shook my head. Stewart's messy bedroom, his quitting guitar: It was just like the mug I'd broken back at Ralph's—the familiar turned upside down, things out of place. It just wasn't right, none of it.

We both stared at the TV a moment.

"How'd it go with Bryant?"

I could sense him trying to feel out my mood.

"Whatever. Same old stuff."

Stewart nodded. "You got to be careful about those shrinks. They'll try to do all kinds of shit to you. Next thing you know, they'll have you doped up, walking around like a fucking zombie."

Thinking about our morning pit stops, about *all* our herbal adventures over the last two years, I had to shake my head. Then I burst out laughing. I just couldn't help it.

"Yeah, we wouldn't want that."

Stewart was sharp. "Pot doesn't count," he said. "It's natural."

"Oh, right. Natural." I snorted.

Then suddenly it just came out. Before I could stop them, the words rushed out:

"Ralph and my mother are having sex."

There was a long pause. I could see Stewart looking me over, trying to figure out what to say.

"Ouch, dude," he said at last.

"Yeah."

"It doesn't mean anything," he said.

"Yeah," I said again.

"People need companionship. It's been a tough few months," he continued.

"Yeah," I repeated. I was starting to sound like a goddam broken record. "Thanks, anyway."

"I know what you need." He clapped me on the back. "You need a good walk in the woods."

By this, of course, Stewart meant going out behind his house to smoke a bowl. It wasn't exactly what I needed—I needed Ralph to stop banging my mother—but I figured it wouldn't hurt.

"Let's go," I said.

"Excellent," he said, his face lighting up with glee. He turned and left the room. I followed him across the hall into the second room. It was more cluttered than usual but not as bad as the first.

While Stewart fished his bowl from its hiding place, I glanced over at some of the papers and shit on his desk. And that's when I saw it. Right there on the desk in a Netflix sleeve: *Man of La Mancha*. I was about to ask him what the hell it was doing there when he hollered out.

"Think fast, Paquette!"

I turned just in time to catch the plastic shopping bag flying toward my face.

"What's this?" I asked, weighing the bulky bag in my hands, feeling something soft beneath the plastic.

"Just something I picked up," he said. "Yesterday. In Burlington."

Burlington was an hour and a half away, the only real city in Vermont. Stewart and his parents went there every couple of weeks to shop in expensive stores and eat in nice restaurants and generally get back to their downcountry roots.

"So open it up, already," he said, watching me.

I untied the knot and looked in.

It was a coat. A peacoat, to be exact, like what the sailors used to wear, black and woolen, as soft as anything. I pulled it out and looked at the tag by the collar—Emerson Mills.

"Holy shit," I whispered. It was a two-hundred-dollar coat.

"It's going to be winter soon. Figured you could use a new jacket. Your old one's a piece of crap."

"Dude, you serious?" I held it up before me. "It's just like yours."

Stewart laughed. "You said last year you wanted mine. I was going to give it to you, but I got too attached. Then I saw this."

"Great," I joked. "Now we can be twins. The Hippie and the Canuck."

He grinned. "Something like that."

Now that the initial shock was wearing off, I could feel my face getting red all over again. Fucking Stewart. He did shit like this from time to time. He knew I could never afford it on my own. But I figured, if the shoe were on the other foot, I'd do the same for him. That's what friends do, right?

CHAPTER FIVE

We slipped downstairs, out the back door, and made for the woods at the far end of the backyard. The afternoon was clear and cold, so I wrapped my new coat tight around me, inhaling the sweet smell of new wool and autumn leaves.

We stuck to our traditional route, drifting along the path between the trees until we reached the smoking rock. The large, flat stone was our accustomed destination. But that wasn't why it was the smoking rock—we'd named it that long before we ever started getting high. I still remember the morning we made our way out here for the first time. It was November, our freshman year, and we hadn't known each other very long. There'd been a hard frost the night before, and with all the leaves gone, the sun shone down warm and bright on the rock. Its black surface was just sucking up the heat, and in the morning cold of the woods, the melted frost rose in a curtain of steam along the rock's entire length right before our eyes. We just looked at each other in awe—this was first-class mystical shit, a holy moment amid the dead leaves and gray, barren limbs. That was where we bonded, I guess you could say, right there before the smoking rock.

We packed the bowl and got right to it. It was all very methodical. Efficient, almost. Of course, Stewart engaged in his little theatrics, bringing the pipe to his mouth with a flourish, flicking the lighter above his head before applying the flame, drawing loudly, making a production of the holding and exhalation—like it was some ritual or something, like it was goddam performance art. Sometimes it amused me, usually I ignored it, but today it annoyed me. I wasn't in the best mood to begin with, and now all I could think about was that movie on his desk. I was about to get pulled into something, I could feel it.

We finished up, shot the shit for a while, and then left the rock, taking the path farther out onto a loop that roughly traced the perimeter of the Bolgers' land. Neither of us spoke as we made our way along, each wrapped in a warm, fuzzy glow under the autumn colors. The sun was breaking fast for the horizon by the time we reached the far point.

A muted buzz sounded from Stewart's pocket. He pulled his cell out, glanced at the screen, and rolled his eyes.

"Lucinda wants to know when we want dinner." He keyed a quick reply and shook his head. "It's like the fifth text today. I never should have taught them how. My father's even worse. You're lucky, Frenchy."

"Quit your bitching. At least you have a cell phone. I've been bugging my mother for months, but she says we can't afford it. I keep telling her there's this little thing called the twenty-first century."

Stewart laughed. "Come on, let's go."

We turned to head back. I felt more relaxed now, but there was still that kernel of angst keeping the bliss at bay. I'd been hoping to leave it behind in the woods, but it had followed me.

"So you're really serious about trying out for the musical?" I asked. We were getting close to the house now. I could see all the glass shining at the end of the path.

"Why not?"

"The last time I was in a play, I was a fucking cucumber in the fourth-grade nutrition pageant."

"So what? That's the beauty of it. We'll go to the audition, fucking ham it up, and blow everyone's minds. They'll be talking about it for months."

"So it is a prank, then. A joke. Right?"

"Dude, when am I serious about anything?"

We both came to a stop. I had him.

"Don't give me that bullshit. I saw that movie on your desk. There's something else going on here. You're serious about this thing, aren't you?" I reached out and pressed a finger against his chest.

His face turned dark red. He shook his head and pushed my hand away.

"So what?" he said at last. "Look at us, Frenchy. Everyone thinks we're a pair of clowns with all the stupid shit we do."

"We *are* a pair of clowns. That's the fucking point. We don't give a shit about anything. Everyone has their thing. That's ours."

"Look, it doesn't even matter. We're not going to get parts anyway. Not real ones. It's just something to do. And it's a good musical, Frenchy. I've seen it, like, ten times now. There's something about it," he said, his eyes drifting off. "I don't know. It's good, you know? It's just good. Really good."

"Hey, if that's what you want, then go for it. But don't drag me along," I said. "I got enough shit to deal with right now."

"Maybe you need a distraction, Frenchy," he said, his eyes snapping back. When I didn't answer, he kicked the ground. "I knew you were going to be this way," he muttered. "I knew you were going to. I knew it. I knew it."

Fucking Stewart.

"Oh, really? Is that why you got me the jacket?" I grabbed the front of the peacoat. "A bribe? Something to get dumb old Frenchy to go along?"

I had a hard time not wincing at the look of pain that crossed his face. And the confusion, the fear. The same look he'd had this morning and all those other times, jumping at whatever he thought he'd heard. I hated it. And then it suddenly hit me. I'd seen that look somewhere else before. I'd seen it on my old man's face during those long, horrible days after he'd come home.

Stewart turned and ran off toward the house. I didn't run after him.

I made my way back slowly, trying to push my buzz aside. All it was doing now was amplifying the nasty vibes welling up, making it hard for me to sort out what had been said.

Mrs. Bolger smiled as I came in through the back door. If she knew anything was amiss, she didn't show it. I tried to give her my best smile in return, but my face felt a little numb, like somebody else's face had been glued over my own, and not very well at that. I couldn't reach the stairs fast enough.

Stewart was in his study, standing at the window. The sun was dipping behind the valley's rim, behind the string of wind towers that rose and fell with the ridgeline, a row of black silhouettes against a clear gold sky.

He didn't turn as I came up beside him.

There was a momentary glint as a few of the tower blades caught the waning light. I wondered how many hours Stewart had spent staring through the window at those hated towers over the last couple years.

"I can hear them," he murmured. "Sometimes."

"All the way from here, huh?"

That was one of the complaints people had against the wind towers—that they were noisy. And when the wind got ripping, it was true, they were pretty loud. I'd heard them a few times, down at the school, in town. But not on the Heights. Not this far away.

He closed his eyes. "In my head," he whispered as the last sliver of sun ducked behind the ridge.

The room was warm from the afternoon sun, but a shiver ran down my spine anyway. "Right." I glanced back at the open door. "Look, I'm sorry. You know, about before."

Stewart nodded.

"It's just, I really don't want to be in that play. I don't even want to try out, that's all."

He brought his hands up and covered his face.

"Listen," I said. "I'm going to go. Mom will be home from work soon, and I should be there for dinner and all. How about another night? Maybe tomorrow, okay?"

"Sure." He lowered his hands. His eyes were still closed. I took a few steps backward, turning halfway across the room. I'd almost made it to the door when he stopped me.

"Take the movie," he said. "Watch it. Just watch it."

I hesitated, then grabbed the DVD from the desk and slipped it into my pocket.

"All right," I said. "I've got it. Okay?"

Stewart nodded, but he didn't turn around. He just kept staring out the window.

"I'll pick you up in the morning," he said.

"Thanks." I hesitated once more in the doorway. "And thanks again for the coat."

I headed for the stairs without waiting for a response.

I dodged Mrs. Bolger with a few quick apologies, then booked it out of the house and down the driveway, not bothering to look back to see if Stewart was up at the window watching me. I knew he was. I shoved my hands in my coat pockets and walked faster into the fading light, clutching the disc all the way home as the air bit at my cheeks and nose. It was unseasonably cold, even for northern Vermont, and I knew there would be a hard frost tonight.

By the time I reached my house, it was still light outside, but inside it seemed like night already. A double-wide trailer wasn't a particularly bright place to begin with, but it was mostly due to the shades—my mother had a thing for keeping them closed. It's because she was paranoid from her job. Working as a police dispatcher, taking all the emergency calls and working with the state troopers, seeing the scumbags they brought back to the barracks with them—she knew just what kind of sick fuckers were out there. I thought she was too paranoid, though. You can pull all the shades you want; it's not going to stop someone who's really out to get you. And even if you block out the dark, you end up blocking out the light, too. Besides, there was already plenty of darkness inside. My father had seen to that.

There was a message on the machine from my mother—she was going to be stuck late at work but would bring home pizza.

Fine by me. It saved me from having to make dinner for the two of us, like I usually did when she worked the day shift. Suddenly I had a couple extra hours on my hands, and as I grabbed a bag of chips from the kitchen to stuff my face with, it occurred to me what I should do.

"Goddam it," I muttered, fishing the DVD from my coat pocket. Sitting down to watch a musical after a shitty Monday was the last thing I felt like doing, but after what I'd said to Stewart, I figured I owed him. Guilt sucks.

I stuck *Man of La Mancha* in the DVD player, flopped onto the couch with my bag of chips, and settled in. I wasn't looking forward to it at all. The idea of people breaking into "spontaneous" song and dance annoyed the crap out of me, and the songs are always so corny I wanted to barf just listening to them. And even *they* wouldn't be so bad if they didn't go on forever. I mean, by the third or fourth verse I'm like, okay, I get it already.

At least I'm still high, I thought as the movie started.

I say all this merely to give you some context, so you'll understand just how shocked I was to discover that I actually liked the damn thing. Maybe it was the mood I was in. The kind of day I'd been having, the kind of life I'd been having. Maybe my guard was down. Maybe it was the pot. Maybe it was Sophia Loren with her big, beautiful boobs. All I know is that by the time it ended, I was sort of starting to think that musicals weren't so bad after all. At least not this one.

As it turned out, I already knew some of the story. It's mostly about Don Quixote. You know, the crazy old knight who attacked the windmills? He's from La Mancha, which is some place in Spain, hence the title. I was a little confused at first, because the movie actually starts out with this guy named Cervantes—who happens to be the actual author of the book *Don Quixote*—getting thrown in jail by the Spanish Inquisition. They're going to torture him and his servant or something. Anyway, he's screwed, especially when the other prisoners grab up all of his shit and threaten to burn his manuscript containing his life's work. He's in a bad spot: He's not rich or anything, but he's a bit of a dandy. They're a bunch of hardened criminals and whores and dirtbags, and they're screwing with him just for the hell of it, telling him they're going to put him on trial and then punish him. But Cervantes is a pretty sharp dude, and before long he's got them eating out of his hand. Being an actor and all, he puts on a play with the help of his servant about these two characters he's created—Don Quixote and his sidekick, Sancho Panza.

Most of the movie is about the two of them having crazy adventures, though from time to time it cuts back to the dungeon, where Cervantes has to keep scrambling to keep the prisoners' attention so they don't take everything he's got. The bad part is that there's some guy who calls himself the Duke, who's pissed off about *something* and seems to have it in for Cervantes. There's always a Duke, isn't there? Lord knows I've met my share.

Yeah, there were plenty of songs, and some of them were gag-inducing. Others weren't too bad, though. Some were even pretty funny. There were a lot of funny parts, actually, and I don't think it was just the pot. I laughed hardest when I saw old Don Quixote charging the windmills on his pathetic old horse. No wonder Stewart liked the story.

Oh, and did I mention Sophia Loren is hot? Actually, I don't know what she looks like now, but she sure was a babe forty years ago. She plays this tavern wench named Aldonza, who's also a bit of a whore. But Don Quixote calls her Dulcinea and tells her she's a first-class lady, and he's so good, she almost believes him. I wondered who our school would get to play *that* part.

It wasn't all fun and games, though. Actually, it's a pretty sad story. I don't want to spoil it too much in case you decide to see it for yourself, but I can tell you that it doesn't end well. Or does it? It's kind of hard to say. Those are the best kinds of stories. I will say that I felt bad for Don Quixote, all caught up in his delusions of grandeur, with everyone laughing at him and bullying him. Crazy or not, he strikes you as a better human being than all of them put together. But I felt even worse for poor old Sancho. At least Don Quixote was crazy. I mean, it was something he could fall back on when things got rough. Sancho had nothing except old Don, and he was pretty goddam worthless.

Anyway, when it finished, I felt so odd—sort of wired, with this strange feeling that everything around me was suddenly both less real and less awful. You know how a good movie can do that to you? I mean, you know it's not real, but somehow it makes your own life feel more dreamlike, more like a movie, at least for a while.

Then my mother came home.

I could tell right away she'd had a bad day, even worse than mine. Her days usually are. I can always tell. It's the eyes—red and swollen from crying during her drive home.

She dropped the pizza box onto the counter with a sigh as I came into the kitchen. Seeing me, she gave me an exhausted smile. I hated that smile—it was a guilty kind of smile, trying to cover up all the shit that had followed her home.

"I'm sorry, sweetie," she said. "Janice had a doctor's appointment that went late, so I had to cover the first part of her shift,

then a bunch of calls came in, and the boys were out, and . . ."
She sort of drifted off. I opened the fridge, grabbed a beer, and
handed it to her. She smiled again, only this time it was for real.

"Thanks, Frenchy," she said, popping the top and taking a sip.

"Tough day at the office, huh?"

"There was a girl," she said, then faltered.

"What happened?" I hated asking. Sometimes she'd tell me,
sometimes she wouldn't. I liked it better when she didn't.

"There was a little girl," she whispered again. It was all she
could manage.

I went to the cupboard and got a couple plates while she wiped
her eyes on her sleeve. She set her beer down and took the plates
from me.

"Pizza's still hot. Go wash your hands and we'll eat."

"Right," I mumbled.

I hated washing up. It meant I had to go into the bathroom,
where the hand soap was—my mother wouldn't get any for the
kitchen sink (that's where dish soap belonged, and dish soap was
for dishes, not hands)—and I hated using the bathroom sink. It
meant I had to stand right where he stood, look into the mirror
just like he did the night he did it. It meant I had to stare at the
reflection of that cheap-ass imitation painting of the fuck-ugly
flowers covering up the stain on the wall behind me as I looked
into the mirror.

My aunt had spent a whole day cleaning, but some stains
don't come out, no matter how hard you scrub.

I kept my eyes closed in the bathroom and washed my hands
by touch alone. All the songs, all the energy I'd felt from the
movie, all of it was gone, chased away by reality. It was Monday
all over again.

Stewart picked me up the next morning at the usual time. As far as I could tell, everything was back to normal. One of the advantages of being a guy, I guess—sometimes it's more peaceful for everybody if you pretend you don't have real feelings. Or maybe Stewart was just playing nice because he still wanted me to try out with him tomorrow.

It had been cold last night like I thought it would be—dipping down into the teens—and the grass was crunchy underfoot as I dashed from the trailer in my new coat. The frost was still thick on his car, with just a tiny circle scraped away on the windshield in front of him, so that once the door was shut, I felt like I'd closed myself into a crystalline egg, the morning light pale and opaque around me. I didn't like heading down the mountain blind, with just Stewart's little peephole to show the way, but I stayed quiet. After all, I was just along for the ride.

Neither of us said much on the way to the pit stop, but we never did anyway. It took a bit of enhancement to stir us from our morning stupor.

He waited until after we were well enhanced before asking, waited until I was all full of brotherly euphoria before putting me on the spot.

"So, Frenchy, did you watch it last night? Did you? Huh? Huh?" he said, all in my face.

I tried my best not to answer him, to look just past him and keep my eyes focused on the wind towers, standing silent and still in the frigid distance. But as scenes from the movie flashed through my mind—Don Quixote charging the windmills on his crappy old horse, he and Sancho Panza and Aldonza fighting off the thugs at the inn, Cervantes squaring off in the dungeon against the Duke—the slightest smile sneaked out before I could stop myself.

"I knew it," he crowed. "I knew you would. So, what did you think? Pretty good shit, huh? You liked it, didn't you?"

He was babbling now. I let him go. Times like this, it was better just to let it run its course. And he seemed more jacked up than usual, in a way that set me a little on edge.

"Yeah," I said at last, when he'd finally settled down. "It was pretty good."

"I knew you'd like it," he said. "It's got something, doesn't it? This sense of hope."

I started. He saw me and broke out laughing. "You felt it too!" he shouted, pointing. "I knew you would, Frenchy. Imagine having that, every day, for two months. Two months, dude!"

I shook my head. "You're crazy."

"So you'll do it, right? Tomorrow afternoon, we're there, right?"

Fucking Stewart. He never gave up when he really wanted something.

"Yeah, I guess," I said, still staring past him at the wind towers. I winced. That was it. I'd said it. There was no going back. A wave of fear and excitement all mixed together washed over me.

Stewart clapped me on the shoulder and nodded, quiet in victory. Then he followed my gaze to the horizon.

"Those fuckers have got to come down," he said.

I laughed. Mixed up as I was, it was good to know some things didn't change.

ACT TWO:
RISING ACTION

CHAPTER SIX

"Let's go, let's go." Stewart took me by the arm, walking so fast with his long, gangly legs I had to practically trot down the hallway past the trophy cases to keep up.

"What about the auditions?" I asked. It was twenty past two. Tryouts were at three.

"Don't worry. We've got plenty of time."

"So where are we going?"

"We have to get ready." He let go of my arm to slip through the crowd of students making for the exit. "Just follow me."

I had a sneaking suspicion what "getting ready" entailed.

"I don't think it's a good idea, Stewart," I said, catching up to him.

"Of course it is. We'll take a little drive, have a few tokes of the good stuff. Just the thing you need to relax."

"Fuck, Stewart, it's the last thing I need. What if I tweak out?"

"You won't. You'll do great. Trust me."

I could tell by the way he was walking and talking that he was nervous too. Maybe even more than me. It was an odd thing to see. Of course, it only made me more anxious.

We followed the pack out into the parking lot and then headed for Stewart's Volvo in the far corner. As we drew closer, I heard him groan at the sight of the group gathered around the cars parked beside his own. We both slowed our pace.

It was the Pokers.

That was what Stewart called them, anyway—the dickheads who had made a point of hassling us since freshman year.

Our school had two kinds of hicks: good hicks and evil hicks. The good hicks wore canvas trousers and steel-toed work boots and liked to listen to country music while driving around in their old pickup trucks, drinking cheap beer with their chubby girl-friends. The evil hicks wore black heavy-metal T-shirts, sported low-hung baggy jeans, and played angry-sounding hip-hop music really loudly on the stereos of the lamely tricked-out shitboxes they called their cars. Though they were really just hicks, they fancied themselves "gangstas," which, in the hills of northern Vermont, was just plain sad.

Needless to say, the Pokers fell into the latter category.

"Hey, faggot, where's your faggy little dress?" one of them called out to Stewart as we approached.

"Look at the little sperm-burpers!" another cried.

"Bag-lappers!"

And so on.

That was their schtick—the "gay" thing. I don't know, maybe it was because Stewart had long hair, or maybe they couldn't get the idea of two guys hanging out together. The poor kids weren't particularly imaginative in their bullying. I'll give them one thing, though—they never actually touched us. Mostly they were annoying. Sometimes I found it downright funny.

Stewart didn't. It really got to him. Even now, I could see him whiten and pick up the pace, stepping around a pair of Pokers making a halfhearted attempt to block us from Stewart's car. He never looked at them. Just kept his eyes on the ground, his mouth screwed back in silent rage.

I stopped in front of the pair, looked them in the eye, and waited. I'd known most of these guys my whole life. Some of us had even been friends back in middle school. Funny how things change.

They glared and glared, nostrils flaring, before finally stepping aside to let me pass. It was the same old dance—just like with Stewart's mother at the door, only a nasty version with zits.

"Come on, Frenchy." Stewart's voice sounded strained.

"What's the rush, queerbait?" one of the Pokers—a pug-faced moron named Scott—called out. "Got a date with your homo buddy here?"

"Actually, Scott," I said, "we've got to hurry so we can get back in time to try out for the school musical."

Everyone burst out laughing. I glanced over at Stewart, waiting by the car. Even he managed a grin.

"Besides," I continued. "Stewart and I broke up. There's a new love in my life."

"Oh yeah? Who, fairy?"

"Why, you, of course," I said. "You're much better looking. And even though everyone says you have a tiny pecker, don't worry—I like them that way."

The Pokers practically fell over screaming in delight, like it was the funniest thing they'd ever heard. Everyone except Scott, that is. He looked all pissed off and kind of confused. I think he thought I was serious or something. To be honest, I don't know why I was egging him on. He could have easily kicked the shit out of both Stewart and me at the same time. I guess I was wired over the audition. All that nervous energy had to go somewhere.

"Shut the fuck up, asshole."

"Okay, Scott," I said, walking to the car. "Just let me know if you change your mind."

I blew him a kiss and then hopped in the Volvo. Stewart had already started the engine. He pulled out as fast as he could, then gunned it toward the exit, weaving around several cars trying to back out. Looking through the rear window, I could see Scott yelling at his fellow Pokers.

"That was funny, Frenchy," Stewart said a few minutes later as we headed through town. "Good stuff, good stuff."

He laughed a few times, but it was a nervous laugh, all high-pitched and fake sounding.

"You shouldn't let the Pokers get to you."

"I know, I know," he said, his eyes blinking like crazy. "I really shouldn't. They shouldn't be assholes, though. They shouldn't be pricks. Why can't everybody just leave each other alone?"

"They're just Pokers."

"Right you are, Frenchy." He waved a hand in front of his face. "Put it away, put it away."

He took a deep breath and closed his eyes, which freaked me out a little since we were heading toward a curve.

"Stewart," I said. His eyes snapped open. "Let's get this show on the road."

He nodded and reached up, pulling down the visor above me. A big fat joint fell into my lap. He turned left and we headed out of town. Thirty minutes to go.

CHAPTER SEVEN

The stage was flooded with light, making the rest of the auditorium seem even darker than normal. In the shadowy back of the auditorium where we entered, the quiet had a thick, heavy feel to it, the voices down front dampened despite the crowd of kids gathered under the lights.

"All right, Frenchy," Stewart said, putting a hand on my shoulder, "let's give them a show to remember. No fear."

He whispered "No fear" again, quieter.

I giggled. "No fear," I whispered back.

I followed Stewart slowly down to the stage, drifting past row after row of empty seats. I felt like I was diving, submerging into some deep underwater cavern, its bottom illuminated by a few rays of sunlight cutting through the roof, shining down onto the grinning multitude of sea monkeys just grooving out in their own little sea monkey world. It was pretty fucking magical.

I held back when we reached the stage, taking a seat in the front row, while Stewart climbed up onto the stage, a big grin on his face, oblivious to my withdrawal.

The stage was busy. Students were clustered in groups, chatting anxiously as they filled out forms, or flitted about, bristling with nervous energy. A middle-aged man doodled on a piano off to the side. I caught snatches of music I'd heard from the movie. The drama teacher, Ms. Vale, meandered among the students, beaming as she handed out papers and made small talk or offered words of encouragement, trying to put everyone at ease.

For a teacher, she was a hottie: short blond hair, tight blouse, long skirt, all young, urban, and chic. She'd joined the staff my freshman year, and I'd been in awe of her ever since. So had Stewart. She came up to him with a warm smile. He didn't seem intimidated at all. In fact, they started chatting as if they'd spoken before, as if they were old pals. It was really weird, and I suddenly wished I'd followed him onto the stage to hear what they were saying.

A second later, I got my wish. Stewart paused, turning in confusion, before spotting me in the seats below. With an urgent look, he waved me up. I stumbled to my feet and climbed onto the stage, my heart pounding as I stepped into the light.

"Frenchy, hello," Ms. Vale said, taking my limp, sweaty hand.

"Hello," I mumbled back, trying to smile. I felt like some goddam troll who'd just been released from his cage. I took a step back behind Stewart.

She cocked her head a little and gave a quick smile. "Perfect, perfect," she murmured, then turned and headed over to talk to a few new arrivals.

"What were you doing down there?"

"I'm too high, Stewart. Too fucking high."

"So what?" he said. "No one cares. No one even knows, so get it together. No fear, remember?"

"No fear, no fear," I began whispering to myself. *Christ*, I thought, *I'm starting to sound like Stewart.*

But just because you say it doesn't make it so. That's what my father used to tell me. *No fear, no fear, no fear.* It was too late—my tranquillity had vanished the moment I stepped onto the stage. Of course, it didn't help that most of the other kids had stopped talking and were now looking at us with a mixture of amusement and resentment. I could tell they were all wondering what the hell we were doing on their turf.

The theater crowd was a squirrelly gang—all artsy and dramatic, a weird combination of kids from other cliques. There were a few of the special ones—the popular, attractive, athletic, your typical well-bred all-American teen—mixed in with a random assortment of creative types from band, chorus, dance club, wherever. Then there were the techs, the ones who did lighting and set design. They were always goths. I think it was a rule or something. Anyway, stick them all together, add a dose of competition, and you've got the makings of a really intense scene. And I didn't even come close to fitting in.

"Hey, Stewart," a girl's voice said.

Stewart and I both turned to see Kaela Smith standing before us, her hands behind her back, leaning forward ever so slightly with an expectant smile, her eyes on Stewart. Kaela was a semi-goth, semi-cute junior who had hung out with us on a few occasions. She had a bit of a crush on Stewart, though he always seemed oblivious.

"Hey, Kaela, what's up?" he replied, his voice all smooth as he smiled with that silly-stoned grin. Fucking Stewart. All the nervousness I'd felt in him before seemed to have disappeared. "You trying out for the play?"

"Actually, I'm going to be stage manager." She waved the clipboard she'd been holding behind her back.

"Cool, cool," Stewart said. "That sounds, like, important."

"The stage manager is in charge of tech," she said with a shrug, blushing. "What about you? Come to join my crew?"

Stewart beamed and shook his head. "Nah. Frenchy and I are here to try out. We're going to be actors!" he added with a flourish, his voice rising so that both Kaela and I jumped a little.

"Oh." She gave me a quick glance.

There was nearby laughter, that sort of scoffing laughter that makes your teeth grate. And it was obvious it had been directed toward us. We all turned.

It was Quentin Bernard. Quentin was a fellow senior, a pretty boy who'd been awarded the lead role in just about every play since middle school. He'd made quite a splash in last year's musical, and ever since he'd been bragging about going to college for acting in New York. As if anybody gave a shit.

Kaela looked back and rolled her eyes. "Well, good luck, guys," she chirped, and she went back to the tech table.

Stewart and I were scribbling our names and other information on the forms, trying not to giggle, when Quentin sidled over to us.

"So you guys are really trying out, eh?" he said.

"Hell yeah," Stewart said. He started laughing. Then Quentin started laughing. It seemed like they were laughing for a really, really long time, like they were trying to outdo each other, like it was a goddam laughing contest. I just kept my head down and tried to concentrate on the form.

"That's great, that's great," Quentin said, like he was auditioning for an infomercial or something. "It's good to have new blood. Really, really good."

"Thanks, Quentin. I take it you're trying out as well?" Stewart said, mimicking Quentin's tone so perfectly I glanced back to see if it was really Stewart who had spoken. Then I turned to Quentin. A look of astonishment flashed across his face, but he recovered pretty quickly.

"Uh, yeah. *La Mancha* was my idea, actually. Ms. Vale loves it when we make suggestions."

"Good to hear," Stewart replied. "I've given her a few suggestions of my own."

Quentin's eyes widened. He glanced at me in confusion. I shrugged. I didn't know why Stewart was making shit up, but I knew he could mess with someone's head when he wanted to. I even felt a little twinge of pride—Stewart may have been rattled by the Pokers, but he certainly didn't seem intimidated by Quentin. Not like I would've been.

"Well, good luck. There are plenty of parts in this one, so you should get something. You two would make perfect prisoners in the Inquisitors' dungeon."

"Thanks, Quentin," Stewart cooed. "That means a lot. I look forward to sharing the stage with you."

Quentin's face darkened a shade. He scurried back to his friends. Stewart looked over at me with a sly grin.

"Not bad," I said, taking a deep breath.

"Oh, Frenchy, I'm just getting started."

"Okay!" Ms. Vale called out. "Let's get going, shall we? Circle up."

Everyone scrambled to join the ring at the center of the stage. I had no idea what was going on, but suddenly I was as excited as everyone else. It felt like Christmas Eve.

"First things first." She leaned into the circle to catch our eyes. "I want you to shake it out. Everyone's too nervous, and it's freaking me out. Shake your arms, shake your legs, get the nerves out."

There were a few titters, but all the kids started shaking their limbs—flinging their arms around, lifting their legs and kicking back and forth, shrugging their shoulders up and down really fast, making goofy sounds and faces. I glanced over at Stewart, who was dancing like an epileptic chicken. He stuck his tongue out at me and laughed.

"Come on, Frenchy, get loose!" he yelled.

I had yet to really move. I suddenly felt all stiff and self-conscious, even though no one seemed to be paying much attention to me. And the wilder Stewart got, the more frozen I felt. *Good Lord,* I thought, *what have I gotten myself into?*

Kaela saved me, God bless her. She crossed the circle and grabbed one of my arms and started shaking it, a shy smile on her face, then she grabbed the other arm and started shaking it even harder. Her touch was like a jolt of electricity, shocking me out of my stupor. Something broke inside of me, and before I knew it, I was wobbling and bobbling with the rest of them. I could just picture the grin plastered across my face as I moved. In fact, it was easier that way—to imagine myself outside of myself, watching from the side, like my body belonged to someone else, like it could be anybody else. *Maybe that's all acting really is,* I thought.

Kaela moved in a slow circle before me, throwing her head back and closing her eyes with a smile. Watching her, I got a funny feeling in my gut. She looked pretty good all of a sudden, and I wondered why I'd never noticed it before. She opened her eyes and caught me staring.

"Nice moves, Frenchy." She laughed. "Didn't know you had it in you."

"Me neither," I said. "Life's full of surprises, I guess."

She laughed again, and we kept on grooving until Ms. Vale called us all back to the middle of the stage.

We moved on to the next part of the audition, taking turns reading unrehearsed lines from the script. This was where the real audition began, and where things got truly weird.

"Here you go, Frenchy," Ms. Vale said when it was my turn. She handed me a sheet with some lines on it. "Try this."

I looked down at the page.

"Ms. Vale, I think there's some mistake here."

I figured I'd have one or two lines at most—a minor part— one of the random prisoners, just like Quentin said. But the high- lighted lines were all for Cervantes's servant, who also doubles as Sancho Panza.

She smiled. "No mistake. Give it a go."

It was strange to see the words on the page, having just heard them the day before yesterday. Compared with the movie, they seemed flat and lifeless. Stranger still was reading the lines in front of everyone, under the lights, feeling their heat and blinking back against their glare with my half-baked ember eyes. Beyond the stage, everything was black, as if the whole world had been snuffed out, leaving nothing but shadows.

"Not bad," she said, and handed me another sheet. "Now try this."

The next thing I knew, Ms. Vale had me reading all kinds of parts: the Governor, a crazy old dude who runs the trial; the Duke, that asshole who gives Cervantes a hard time. But mostly she kept coming back to the Sancho Panza character. By now, I'd come down a bit and was feeling pretty good. I even started to have fun. So I figured what the hell. I laid down the thickest Spanish accent I could muster and slapped my gut a few times. If Stewart could ham it up, then so could I.

But I was nothing next to him.

"Okay, Stewart," Ms. Vale called out. "You're next."

Stewart jumped onto the stage and slid into the spotlight with his arms stretched out.

"*Olé, amigos!* Let's do this!" he shouted, drawing laughs from the other kids. They all knew who he was, knew his reputation as a prankster, and were curious to see what he was up to.

Ms. Vale had him try a few of the Duke's lines to start, but almost right away she cut to the lead role, having him read for Cervantes, who for most of the play also acts the part of Don Quixote.

He took the sheet of lines and looked them over for a minute. Then another. Everyone watched, silent, wondering what he was doing.

"Whenever you're ready, Stewart," Ms. Vale said. She seemed as puzzled as the rest.

Stewart glanced up from the sheet, smiled, and tossed it aside. There was a collective gasp as it floated to the floor.

Then he began reciting lines from the page. And not just Don Quixote's lines. *All* the lines. I mean, it was scary. As he moved through the scene, I could see Ms. Vale getting more and more excited. Even the other kids were getting into it. The whole stage went quiet. Stewart had us all eating out of his hand.

A chill ran up my back, not just because he was so damn good but because it hit me that there was something much bigger going on. The curtain had been swept aside, the secret revealed. It was a trick, all right. How long it had been in the making, I didn't know.

All I knew was that I wasn't in on it. In fact, I suddenly felt like I was on the receiving end.

I wasn't the only one. Glancing over at Quentin, I could see his shock give way to glowering resentment. And his frustration only grew as the audition progressed. Sure, Ms. Vale also had him read some of the Cervantes lines—but only a few. And though he wasn't that bad, you could tell it was just a formality on her part. It didn't help that she kept having him read for the Duke, and when he went after Cervantes like the scene called for, the hostility was so real it was clear no one else could play the role *but* Quentin.

After that, it was time for the music.

With my voice all rough and husky, I've never been an amazing singer, but I can carry a tune well enough. Not that it really mattered—this wasn't the goddam opera or anything. I already knew from watching the movie that you just had to be able to belt it out, so it wasn't too bad. We all sang one of the songs from the musical with the accompanist, with Ms. Vale walking around from person to person listening in. We went through it over and over, until it started to get kind of boring. I tried to avoid her gaze as she came over to me, but I caught her smile from the corner of my eye, so I must've sounded okay.

We took turns singing solo with just the piano. I was a little shaky at first when it came around to me, but a wink from Stewart settled me down, and I managed to muddle through. Again, it didn't really matter. Everyone was cool, even when a few sucky kids sang. It was a pretty supportive group, actually. I admit, I was surprised.

You could sense everyone's ears perk up when it was Stewart's turn. After the way he'd spouted those lines, people were eager to see what he could do with the music. Ms. Vale had him sing one of the Don Quixote songs: "The Impossible Dream." It's supposed to be, like, the big hit of the play. You hear the damn thing ten times in the movie. It was my least favorite tune from the whole musical.

Then Stewart sang it.

There was a collective sigh as one of the most beautiful voices I'd ever heard burst over the stage. In my semi-stupor, I looked around, wondering if Stewart had rigged up some sort of sound system and was just lip-synching like a teenybopper icon at the Grammys. The voice—rich, resonant—didn't seem like it could possibly come from a goofball like him.

Hearing Stewart, it occurred to me that I'd never really heard him sing before, which was kind of weird. Then I realized I'd never heard lots of people I know sing. I don't know why. Where do people usually sing? Church, I guess, but I never went. Back in middle school people sang some, but that wasn't real singing—that was just the dull mumblings of a bunch of dorky preteens.

Not this. This was real singing. This was, like, *American Idol*–quality shit.

I guess I shouldn't have been surprised. Stewart was good at just about anything he tried. Still, it's an odd sensation to see a new side of someone you thought you knew pretty well.

They even clapped for him when he finished, me right along with them. Not as his friend, just one of the crowd. Maybe that's why the whole thing bugged me. It was no longer the two of us against the rest of them, crashing the audition for a cheap laugh. It was only him, basking in his newfound glory. Just the way he wanted it.

"Ms. Vale?" he said when everyone stopped clapping. "Can Frenchy and I sing 'Man of La Mancha'?"

She looked over at Franco, the piano player the school had hired to serve as accompanist. He was a huge man who dwarfed the electric piano in front of him, playing it the way a two-year-old would—slapping the keyboard nonchalantly with his meaty hands, staring absently up into the dark recesses of the auditorium. Amazingly, the guy never made a mistake.

Franco shrugged and nodded. "Got the music right here," he grunted.

"Actually, it's a fine idea." She pulled out a couple sheets of paper. "Come on up, Frenchy."

I hesitated, a bit confused. Wasn't "Man of La Mancha" the name of the play? Besides, I'd already done my singing.

"Come on, Frenchy," Stewart yelled, giving me a malicious grin.

A few kids joined in on Stewart's call, but I could see the rest screw up their faces. Their hospitality had finally reached its limit. Though we were both upstarts, they'd indulged Stewart—he at least had obvious talent—but this was too much.

"Ms. Vale, it's getting kind of late," Quentin muttered.

I could see her crinkle her nose, inwardly debating which way to go. I jumped to my feet. *Screw Quentin*, I thought. *Screw all of them.*

"All right," I said in the most reluctant voice I could summon.

I grabbed the lyric sheet from Ms. Vale and bounded over to Stewart. As soon as the music started, I recognized the tune—it was the very first song Don Quixote and Sancho Panza share while riding across the plain. Stewart sang first, picking up the tune as Franco finished the melody and started over. There was no question which part he was going to sing:

I am I, Don Quixote,
The Lord of La Mancha,
My destiny calls and I go,
And the wild winds of fortune
Will carry me onward,
Oh whithersoever they blow.
Onward to glory I go!

Then it was my turn:

I'm Sancho! Yes, I'm Sancho!
I'll follow my master till the end.
I'll tell all the world proudly
I'm his squire! I'm his friend!

And so on. There's really not much more to it than that. But we made the most of it, bellowing out the lines. Out of the corner of my eye I could see the kids who'd been glowering a moment ago laugh in spite of themselves. Only Quentin continued to glare.

We finished to even louder applause than before. It was one of the weirdest feelings of my life: That energy I'd felt after watching the film, the sense of power, the sense of possibility, the strange beauty of the world—it all came back, standing there under the lights.

I was so giddy that I hardly noticed when the audition ended shortly afterward. Aside from a brief sense of relief as I stepped out from under the stage lights and plunged back into the quiet darkness of the auditorium, I don't even remember leaving. I just remember Stewart and me crossing the parking lot, exchanging high fives, laughing the whole way to the car. The Pokers were long gone now. Everything was good.

We drove around and smoked another joint, still laughing. Then we went for pizza and laughed some more, rehashing the exercises, the lines and songs, re-creating the various looks of surprise and frustration on Quentin's and the others' faces, reminding each other once more just how luscious Ms. Vale truly was. Then he took me home, and we continued to laugh all the way up Suffolk Heights.

Ralph was there when I got back—sitting beside my mother on the sofa watching TV—but I didn't give a shit. His hair was slicked back, his shirt was tucked in, and his hands lay folded in his lap, like some delinquent stuck in church on a Sunday morning. He squirmed a bit when I showed up, but I just smiled and said good night and headed off to my room, still riding the wave of euphoria.

It wasn't until I shut the door that it all came crashing down.

I learned long ago that you don't change your mood; it changes you. And as I stood there in the flickering glow of my shitty old computer monitor, reality ambushed me once again, springing from the shadows. I closed my eyes and shivered, then collapsed onto the bed.

I still don't know why it hadn't occurred to me before. Not on any real level, at least. I guess I'd just been so focused on the audition itself, then so caught up in its aftermath, that I hadn't considered one important fact:

I might end up with a part. A real part.

I know. It's pretty stupid. Pulling the pillow over my face, I relived the audition from start to finish, this time free from the hazy cocktail of smugness and weed. It was quite startling. From the moment Stewart introduced me to Ms. Vale to the ridiculous folly of our duet, it all added up. I groaned and writhed on the mattress, hoping that in my pot-addled state I'd mistaken the crowd's annoyance for adoration, snide humoring for genuine enthusiasm. They weren't laughing *with* Stewart and me, they were simply laughing *at* us, and I'd just been too cheesed to realize the difference. That had to be it. I hoped and prayed myself to sleep that that was it. Fucking Stewart.

Chapter Eight

I didn't say a word the next morning when Stewart picked me up. He was pretty quiet himself, tapping a snappy beat on the steering wheel as we headed down the hill. Maybe he was just wrapped up in his own excitement, or maybe he could tell I was freaked out and had enough sense to back off—either way I was grateful for the silence. When we reached the pit stop, I was so nervous I took one hit too many, so that by the time I got to school, all I wanted to do was squeeze myself into a second-floor locker and shut the door.

Somehow I made it to lunch without falling off the roller coaster, though by the time I sat down at the cafeteria table with my daily dose of poop-on-a-tray, I was so exhausted from the effort I could barely carry on a conversation. So I just listened to Stewart talk circles around Eddie Edward with the usual slew of insults and outrageous lies, and kept my head down. Only when the bell rang did Stewart turn to me and speak.

"So you'll meet me outside the drama room after school, right?"

"What for?"

He gave me a semi-disgusted look. Apparently I'd missed something.

"The posting of the parts. Just like Ms. Vale told us at the end of auditions yesterday. Remember?"

"Already?"

He shrugged. "That's what she said. I've got a good feeling about this, Frenchy. Don't you?"

"Yeah, can't wait."

I knew the worst was true before I even reached the drama room. I could tell by the faces of the kids as, one by one, they peeled away from the bulletin board outside the door and flitted past me in the hallway. No one said a word, but I could see the looks of surprise or resentment or amusement—sometimes all three mixed together—as they passed. By the time I reached the board, the only one left was Stewart, standing before it, as still as a statue, his hands clasped before him, his head slightly bowed as if in prayer. I could hear him murmuring under his breath, and at first I thought maybe he *was* praying, but as I reached him, I realized it wasn't prayer. It was lines.

Don Quixote's lines.

Sure enough, there it was, right at the top: Cervantes/Don Quixote—Stewart Bolger. And right below it: Sancho Panza—Gerard Paquette.

"Fuck!" I reached up with both hands to grab my hair. "Fuck, fuck, fuck!"

Stewart turned to me with a smile. "I know. It's wonderful, isn't it?"

"No, Stewart, it's not wonderful. It's not wonderful at all."

His face fell. "What are you talking about, Frenchy? This is awesome. You were made for the role."

"I was made to be your sidekick?"

He shook his head. "That's not what I meant."

"Look, Stewart, I don't want a big part. It's a lot of work, a lot of responsibility. I mean, fuck!"

Before Stewart could reply, the door opened and out came Ms. Vale. Seeing us, her face lit up.

"Oh, boys, I'm so pleased," she said, locking her door. "Congratulations, seriously!"

I mustered the best smile I possibly could, which was pretty tough considering I felt like I was about to puke.

"Thanks, Ms. Vale," Stewart jumped in. "You won't be disappointed."

"I know," she replied. "I have to admit, Stewart, when you approached me a few weeks ago about this, I was a skeptical. But you blew me away at the audition. You both did. You're a great team."

She shouldered her bag and glanced at her watch.

"See you Monday. First rehearsal's always one of the best. Two forty-five sharp."

"Right," Stewart replied, avoiding my gaze as Ms. Vale walked away. I could see his face turn bright red.

I waited until she'd left, then grabbed him by the shirt and threw him against the wall. He felt light. He felt like nothing.

"You set me up, you asshole. You had this planned from the start!"

I could see the fear on his face. It was the same look he got whenever the Pokers came calling.

"Easy, Frenchy. I didn't think it would really turn out this way. I mean, it's pretty unbelievable, if you think about—"

"That's bullshit," I said, cutting him off. "You lied to me. Just admit it."

When he hesitated, I tightened my grip and pushed hard against him so that he gasped and looked away. One or two kids—freshmen, I think—rounded the corner. I gave them an ugly look and they beat it.

"Okay!" he said at last. "I'm sorry. I should have told you. But if I had, you never would've gone for it."

"You're damn right I wouldn't have. And I won't now."

A look of shock crossed his face. "What do you mean?"

"I'm not doing it." I let go of him and started walking away. "Find somebody else to be your Sancho. I don't need this shit!"

"But I do!" he shouted after me. When I didn't stop, he caught up to me and grabbed me by the shoulder. I whirled around so fast he jumped back and held up his hands.

"I need this, Frenchy. Seriously, you don't know how bad."

"Why? What's so important about this stupid play?"

"Him." He hesitated and looked away. "I get to be Quixote."

"You mean you get to be crazy?" I said. "So do it. I'm not going to stop you."

"No!" A stormy look crept into his eyes. "I need you, too. I can't do it without you, Frenchy. You're the only one who knows."

"Knows what?" I said. "What the hell are you talking about?"

"Please, Frenchy," he said, his voice all shaky, like he was about to start crying. "Please just do it. I'll do anything you want. I'll pay you if you want. You know, like a job? Like a professional actor."

"I don't want any money." I took a couple steps back, then turned to go.

He reached out again as if to stop me. "Then just do it because we're friends," he begged. Wisps of hair had come loose from his ponytail; his hand still hovered between us.

I shook my head. He wasn't supposed to be like this. He wasn't supposed to make *me* be like this.

I gave him the finger and walked away. This time he didn't try to stop me.

"Frenchy!" a voice cried out as I headed down the front steps.

I turned to see Kaela in the doorway. She came out to the top of the stairs.

"Congrats! Just heard the good news."

"Thanks. It's a dream come true, really."

She laughed. "Come on, now. You'll be great. You rocked that audition. Both of you did," she said, tucking her hair behind her ear. "I'm just glad I don't have to deal with Quentin as the lead this year. He's insufferable enough as it is."

This time I laughed. "I'm sure you know how to handle a guy like that."

"That's right. As stage manager, I outrank you all. Don't you forget it." She narrowed her eyes and gave me a sly smile.

"I wouldn't dream of crossing you." I held up my hands.

She glanced around. "So where's Stewart, anyway?"

"Yeah, him," I said. "He's inside somewhere. Probably still gazing at his name on the casting sheet."

She nodded. "Well, I'm going to go find him. See you on Monday?"

I hesitated, then nodded and gave her a quick salute. "At your command, Madame Stage Manager."

She blushed a little, returned the salute, then went back inside. I watched her go, then headed for home.

Stewart didn't even slow down when he drove by me a half hour later as I trudged along the road. He knew I needed to walk, and that if I walked, I'd get over it.

And so I walked all the way home. I tried not to think, but I couldn't help it. Even worse, the music started coming, the rhythm of my steps dragging it from my brain the way it always did when I used to walk home, only now it was those goddam songs from the play. I'd sung them and heard them so much yesterday that they were stuck in my head. Musical numbers—they're evil that way. No matter how fast I walked, I just couldn't escape them. Especially that one. It kept coming back, over and over:

I'm Sancho! Yes, I'm Sancho!
I'll follow my master till the end.
I'll tell all the world proudly
I'm his squire! I'm his friend!

Fucking Stewart.

For the second morning in a row, there were no words as I got into the car and plopped back against the seat. Neither of us spoke until we passed the field that looked out over the valley.

"No pit stop this morning?" I asked, forgetting myself. I'd planned on giving him the silent treatment all the way to school.

"No," he said, glancing at me with a smile. "No more pit stops."

He had such a loopy grin, I couldn't help laughing.

"Yeah? Why not?"

"Don't need them. Not anymore."

"Okay." I knew he wanted me to play along. And so I did. I couldn't help it. "And why is that?"

"Because I have Sancho." He turned to look at me. "Right?" he said, still staring.

I shook my head and sighed. "Yeah, whatever. Just watch the goddam road."

He turned back and slapped the steering wheel.

"I have Sancho," he murmured. "And I have Don. That's all I need."

As we came around the bend, the view opened back up. It was a dark morning, and the blades of the wind towers scraped the hovering clouds.

Stewart pointed across the valley. "Those fuckers," he said, pausing for dramatic effect, "those fuckers have got to come down."

We laughed all the way to the bottom of Suffolk Heights.

CHAPTER NINE

"I thought we were all done with the pit stops."

It was Monday morning and cold as hell. The frost was heavier than last Monday, the valley fog thicker than ever. When we pulled into the field, even the sky seemed bluer, the leaves an even richer, deeper red than last week. Of course, at that point I didn't know what Stewart had in store for me, had no clue I'd be wrapped up in this whole business of the play. It's funny how things can change so fast. I don't like it much.

"We are, dude," Stewart said, getting out of the car. "This is something else."

I dragged my ass out of the passenger side and watched him walk to the back of the Volvo. I could only wonder what he was up to this time. We hadn't spoken all weekend, which was fine by me—I was still a little pissed off with him over the whole audition thing. I mean, I'd gotten used to the idea, but I'd been just as glad when he didn't call.

"Went to Boston this weekend." He spread his hands over the trunk.

"Boston, huh?" I said. "Wow."

I'd been to Boston only once, last spring, when my mother and I went to pick up my father at Logan Airport. We never actually made it into the city, though. After an eighteen-month deployment, the old man wasn't in the mood for any detours.

"Lucinda was so psyched about the play, she wanted us to celebrate."

"Wow," I said again. "That's great." I didn't bother to mention I'd spent most of my weekend watching Ralph sit around on our couch scratching his nads.

"How about you? Was your mom excited?"

"Totally." A bald-faced lie, since I hadn't actually told her yet. I almost did a couple times, but with the douche bag hanging around, it just didn't feel right.

"That's awesome," Stewart said, gazing down at the trunk. I couldn't tell if he believed me or not. "Anyway, I got something when I was down there."

He opened the trunk and pulled out a long, thin box covered in wrapping paper, complete with ribbon and a bow. Fucking Stewart.

"Here you go," he said, handing me the box. "I even wrapped it for you."

"Thanks," I said, even though I knew his mother had really done the wrapping.

"Wait!" he said as I started to pull at the ribbon. He went back to the trunk and retrieved an identical box.

"I got one too," he said.

"So what's this all about?" I said. "Hasn't there been enough scheming?"

"Just a little something for the occasion," he said with a grin. "It's our first day of practice, after all."

"Oh yeah," I snorted. "Thanks for reminding me."

"Look, I know you were pretty upset about how this all came about, and you have every right to be," he said. "I thought about it all the way down to Boston. I should've told you. I should've trusted you. So consider this a peace offering. It's not a fucking bribe," he added.

I blushed and felt myself shrink a little in the wool jacket. It still had that new-coat smell.

"No, you were right, what you said last week," I replied. "I wouldn't have given it a chance. I wouldn't even have gone to the audition. But thanks anyway."

He laughed. "So open it already."

"All right, all right." I slipped the ribbon off and tore the paper. Stewart unwrapped his too. Underneath was a plain white box. I could see him waiting for me to open it.

Inside was a cane, about three feet long, polished and straight, with a marbled wood grain and a beautifully carved handle. Stewart's was the same, though with a slightly darker finish.

"Wow, a cane," I quipped. "Just what every seventeen-year-old needs."

"Yeah, well, check this out, smart guy." He gripped the handle of his cane, gave a little twist, and pulled.

The long, thin blade flashed against the sun as he pulled it from the body of the cane. I tried mine. Sure enough, the sword slipped right out. Holding it out before me, I could see my eyes reflected in its polished steel.

"It's really a sword," he said. He swept his blade around, batting mine aside with a loud *clink!* so that I almost dropped the goddam thing.

"Yeah, I can see that," I said, taking a step back. "What a . . . cool gift."

I was going to say "weird gift," but I didn't want to seem ungrateful. Besides, it *was* kind of cool. I reached out to test the edge. The next thing I knew, my thumb was laid wide open.

"Good fucking Christ, this thing's sharp!" I shouted, staring down at the blood welling up and running into my palm.

Stewart grimaced at the sight of my thumb before letting out a nervous sort of giggle.

"Yeah, I forgot to tell you," he said. "I spent a few hours sharpening them last night. The factory edge is dull as shit."

"Maybe there's a reason for that," I growled. I stuck my thumb in my mouth and did my best to ignore the metallic, salty taste of blood.

Stewart didn't reply. He was too busy slicing his sword back and forth before him in an arc, like he was one of the goddam Three Musketeers or something. His blade whipped through the frigid morning air, sending out a high-pitched whistle that made me wince. I returned mine to its scabbard and leaned on the cane, pulling my thumb out to check on it. It hadn't stopped bleeding.

"I can't believe your parents let you buy these things." I went over to the open trunk and grabbed a paper towel from the roll inside to wrap around my thumb.

"Oh, they were back at the hotel when I got these," he said, interrupting his imaginary battle to glance over at me. "They think they're just canes. That's the beauty of it, Frenchy. No one knows. Just you and me."

"Great. You got a Band-Aid?"

"Check the glove box," he said. "No, they never would've gone for it," he continued. "They're fucking pacifists. They don't approve of weapons. Not even one like this. This is a rapier, a distinguished weapon. A gentleman's weapon. The kind Don Quixote would have."

"And what about Sancho?"

"No, Sancho's a peasant. He'd have, like, a fucking club or something. But you're no ordinary Sancho, are you, Frenchy? You're a cut above. You're, you know, *special*."

"Special, huh? I've heard that one before."

Plunking down in the passenger seat, I rummaged through the crowded glove box while Stewart returned to his mock battle.

I finally found a Band-Aid under all the crap, and even though it was pretty old and beat up, it worked well enough. I could still taste the blood in my mouth. I could even feel my pulse beat in my throbbing thumb. I'll say this for the cut—it sure as hell woke me up.

When I got back out of the car, Stewart was going at it with renewed frenzy, drifting farther out into the field, slashing at the air as he faced the tower-lined ridge across the valley.

"You're going to break a sweat if you don't watch it," I called out.

He didn't reply, and as I drew closer, I could hear him murmuring. I wondered if he was rehearsing lines again.

He stabbed forward with one final thrust, then whipped the sword back, holding it upward, straight before him.

"How do you like that, fuckers?" he muttered.

"Hey!" I said. He whipped around and looked at me, still panting. "We're going to be late."

He sheathed his sword, glanced down at his watch, and nodded.

"Right you are."

"Just keep away from me with that thing," I said as we made our way back to the car. "You're fucking dangerous."

"No fear, Sancho," he replied. "No fear."

"Like my bandage?" I said, holding out my wrapped thumb.

Mr. Bryant glanced up from his desk. It was the first time either of us had spoken since he'd invited me to sit down. I don't know how many minutes had passed, but it was more than a few. I always felt like there was some unspoken challenge to see who would speak first, like those stupid staring contests I used to have with my older cousin Luc. I never won those things.

"I noticed that when you came in," he replied. "Hurt much?"

"Nah," I said. "Well, maybe a little."

It was still throbbing a bit. By the time I got to school, the Band-Aid was pretty soaked and threatening to slip right off. My first-period teacher had a fit when she saw it and sent me straight to the nurse, muttering about pathogens or some odd shit, like I had the goddam plague or something. The nurse was pretty cool, at least. She clucked over me a few times as she carefully cleaned the cut and applied a pair of suture strips to close the wound.

"You should probably have stitches," she said as she wrapped a few layers of gauze around the whole thing for good measure.

"Stitches are for wussies," I replied, suddenly sounding like my old man. I winced as she tightened the wrap.

Between the cut and the thought of our first rehearsal, I'd been on edge all morning. I don't know; maybe I just wasn't used to spending the first part of school unenhanced. When you're high all the time, it starts to become ordinary. Then it's the straight world that seems bizarre. Whatever the reason, I'd been too nervous even to eat lunch, and now, in the quiet of Bryant's office, it was starting to catch up with me.

"Can I have one of those?" I asked. Mr. Bryant always had a well-stocked bowl of candy next to the baseball on his desk. I'd never taken one before. Didn't want him to think he could get to me that way.

"Help yourself," he said, leaning over to push the bowl a few inches my way.

I grabbed a handful of mini Hershey bars and dug in.

"Oh, you'll get a kick out of this," I mumbled between bites. "I'm going to be in the musical."

Bryant chuckled. "That's what I heard. A lead role. Congratulations."

"That's right. Sancho fucking Panza. Pretty funny, huh?"

"I don't think it's funny at all," Bryant said with a smile. "I think it's wonderful. Good for you, Gerry."

"Yeah, thanks." I finished the last Hershey bar, then grabbed a few caramels.

"*Man of La Mancha*'s always been one of my favorites. I can't wait to see how this production turns out."

"Me neither," I quipped.

"So what made you decide to go for it?"

I shrugged. "Stewart, I guess. It was his idea."

"I wondered when I saw he'd been cast too. And as Cervantes, no less."

"Yeah, he's all hopped up to play Don Quixote."

"And what about you? How do you feel about being Sancho Panza?"

Ah, here we go, I thought. *Nice, Bryant. Nice.*

"I don't know. I'm a little nervous. I've never really been in a play before. Not a real one, anyway. But I figure it can't be that hard— you just pretend to be somebody else. Somebody you're not."

"Some people find that hard to do," Bryant observed.

"Really?" I shot back. "I thought pretty much everyone did it."

Bryant smiled. "What, pretend? Sometimes, I suppose. What about you? Who do you pretend to be?"

"Me? Nobody. I'm just good ol' Frenchy," I said, screwing my face up into the best dumbass look I could summon.

Bryant laughed, louder this time. "That's nice, Gerry," he said. "Good one."

"Goddam right," I said. I was cracking up now too. Must've been the chocolate.

The laughter faded and a new silence settled into the room.

"So what does your mother think? She must be proud."

I hesitated.

"Have you told her yet?"

"I'm going to. There just wasn't a good time this weekend, that's all."

"You sound like you're talking about a bad grade on your report card or something. Gerry, you scored a lead role in the Gilliam High School musical. That's a big deal."

I shook my head and looked away.

"Don't you think she'll be happy?"

"Yeah, I guess. It's just going to be a lot of work. I'm going to be stuck in rehearsals every day. I mean, who's going to make dinner?"

Bryant nodded. "I'm sure you'll work it out. It's only a month or two. What about your father? What do you think he would've said?"

"How the hell should I know? He probably would've said it was gay or something."

Bryant didn't reply. He just looked at me with that little Zen smile of his.

"I don't know," I said after a while. "Maybe he wouldn't have cared. He probably would've been glad that I was getting up off my fat ass and doing something. Even if it was gay."

"Do *you* think being in a musical is gay, Gerry?"

"Not really."

"Good." He paused. I could tell he was working up to something.

"You don't like to talk about your father, do you?"

"Not a lot to talk about," I retorted. "He was gone for a year and a half, came back for a few months, then offed himself. What else is there to say?"

"You don't even like to think about your father, do you?"

"Not much to think about." I could feel my heart starting to pound. I looked at my watch. Twenty minutes to go. Fuck.

Bryant nodded. "It's okay, Gerry. Something like this takes time. People go about it in different ways, at different paces. But you'll get there, eventually. You'll have to."

"Get where?" I said. "Go about what? I don't know what all this fucking psychobabble means."

"The grieving process. Coming to terms. Acceptance. Death is never easy. And in cases like yours, it's even more complicated. There can be other issues involved."

"Issues, huh?" My brain was buzzing now, but I couldn't get a hold of what was going on in there. It just sounded like one steady stream of static.

I could see Bryant's face start to shift. I cringed. I thought for sure I was going to see the old pity look, but it was just a general sort of sadness, one that wasn't only for me, and I wondered if that was even worse.

"I don't know, Gerry," I said. "I'd like to agree with you on this one. I'd like to be a team player, I really would. But the truth is, I'm over it. I'm even kind of relieved. I mean, he was messed up when he came back. Really, really messed up. And the sickest part of it all was that there was no help. No one did a fucking thing about it."

"Including you?" he murmured.

Our eyes locked. We stared in perfect silence as the seconds ticked by until I finally had to look away.

Chapter Ten

"Hey! You're going the wrong way." Stewart swung me away from the auditorium and down another hallway.

"We have practice, don't we?"

"Yeah, but it's not in there. Not yet. We're in Ms. Vale's room."

"Oh." For some reason, I suddenly felt better. Hanging out in a classroom seemed somehow less intimidating than going right up onto the stage.

"Jesus, Frenchy, it's a good thing you've got me looking out for you. I'm surprised you can even get yourself dressed in the morning."

"It's a challenge sometimes." My head was still buzzing a bit from the Gerry session. Bryant had backed off after our little staring contest. We spent the rest of the time talking about my childhood and that sort of crap, but I'd been sufficiently rattled.

"Hey, did you get a chance to go over your lines this weekend?" Stewart asked. He'd given me a paperback copy of the script when he dropped me off from school last Friday. He'd ordered two copies from Amazon after the audition and had them overnighted.

"A little." Actually, I hadn't touched the script. I was still too pissed off. In fact, I'd thrown the goddam thing in my bedroom trash can as soon as I got home, though I'd come around enough by Sunday night to fish it back out.

"Got to work on those, Frenchy," he scolded.

"Blow me."

Normally he would've laughed at something like that, but not today. He just sort of shook his head and frowned. I suddenly got the feeling that this was going to be a long seven weeks.

The drama room was a pretty far-out place. The usual corpse-colored cinderblock walls were obscured by a collection of bizarre posters, bohemian tapestries, and multicolored flags. Six-foot-tall puppet masks hung on either side of the whiteboard like sentinels. Not only that, the cheap-ass linoleum floor had been carpeted over. Lamps illuminated each corner of the room, playing off the decorations to give the whole place an almost decadent feel, like some exotic den.

There were a few kids there already, seated around a group of tables that had been pushed together to form a large square. Like last week, their expressions were all different: curious, annoyed, friendly. No one seemed indifferent to our arrival. The only thing that made it bearable was the fact that most of the looks were directed Stewart's way. I was pretty much ignored. Life of a side-kick, I guess. Fine with me.

Stewart stopped before the table. I had to pull up to not run into him.

"Everybody ready?" he shouted. Everyone's faces went blank. He continued, in full Stewart fashion. "Well, I am. Man, am I psyched!" He let out a whoop so loud, half the kids jumped in their seats.

I could tell everyone was thinking what I'd just been thinking: It was going to be a long seven weeks.

Amid a few eye rolls and titters, he took a seat, and I sat down next to him, though at this point the other side of the table was looking pretty good. Then Kaela came in with a couple of her gothy tech friends. Seeing us, she skipped right over and sat next to Stewart.

"Hey, sweetie," she said. She liked to call people sweetie.

"Hi, Kaela. Good to see you here." Ever since we'd shown up, the place had gone silent, and he seemed glad to talk to someone.

I tried to muster up the courage to say something, but Kaela was totally focused on Stewart. So I just sat there like a retarded monkey as they chatted away.

"Hey, where's Ms. Vale?" Stewart asked, looking around.

"She's on her way," Stacey McGovern said, striding in with Quentin Bernard at her heels. "She told everyone to sit tight."

Stacey had been given a lead role: Aldonza, the barmaid-slash-prostitute who Don Quixote worships by the name of Dulcinea. It wasn't a huge surprise—Stacey had already been the female lead in the last two musicals and could really sing. And she was hot and popular and good in school, a real diva, basically—the Gilliam High School equivalent of a movie star. But I just couldn't buy her in the role. She was luscious but not in an Aldonza kind of way, all husky and busty and dark. Stacey was too pert, too blond, too coldly pure.

Stewart didn't seem to share my skepticism. I could see his eyes light up the moment she came into the room, just like Don Quixote's had the first time he saw Aldonza—a look of untainted adoration. And now Stewart would be confessing his undying love and service to her just about every day. Maybe *that's* why he'd wanted to do the play so badly. I snuck a quick glance at Kaela. She was frowning. She'd noticed the look too.

Stewart jumped up from his seat and hurried around the table, meeting a startled Stacey at her chair. He pulled it out for her and beckoned. "My lady?"

Another round of giggles spread across the table. Stacey's face reddened as she sat down with a prim smile. Quentin gave Stewart a nasty stare before plopping down beside her.

Kaela, meanwhile, continued to glare.

"So, you ready?" I said, leaning toward her. She pulled her gaze away and, seeing me, flashed a smile.

"I'm ready. Got my crew assembled and everything. Question is, are you?"

"Hell, no. In fact, I still don't know what I'm doing here."

"At least you've got Stewart," she said, glancing back at him still hovering over Stacey.

"And you," I said. "I mean, we're going to be seeing each other every day."

"Yeah, well, it's a long season. I'm sure you'll be sick of me by the time it's over."

"As long as you don't drop a stage light on me, I'll be fine." I winced at the stupid joke, but she laughed as Stewart rejoined us.

A few more kids came in, followed at last by Ms. Vale, who marched in with a smile, balancing a stack of books with one arm and holding a steaming paper cup in her other hand.

"All right," she said, setting everything down at the head of the table before dropping into her swiveling director's chair. "Let's get this show started. Is everyone here?"

"Check," Kaela said, brandishing her clipboard.

"Excellent." Ms. Vale took a sip of her drink before continuing. "I want to start by telling you how excited I am. I absolutely adore this musical, and I want to thank Quentin for suggesting it this summer."

She paused for the brief smattering of applause. Quentin offered a smile in response. A very meager smile.

"This is probably the most talented cast I've worked with in my time here at Gilliam, and I have no doubt this will be a performance people will never forget."

Everyone glanced at one another with quick grins.

"But we have a lot of work to do if we're going to be ready for our premiere. It's only seven weeks away. Seven weeks, people."

Smiles faded, faces paled. I felt a twinge in my stomach.

She proceeded to cover the rules: which people were expected to show up when and where, at what point people were expected to have their lines memorized, that sort of thing. She used words like *expectations, commitment, accountability.*

Normally this is where I'd start rolling my eyes and stop paying attention, but for some reason, I didn't. In fact, I found myself buying it. The whole thing. Maybe it was because I was falling half in love watching Ms. Vale's beautiful lips move as she spoke in earnest tones and gazed into our eyes, or maybe I was just so freaked out, anything to hold on to was a relief. Then it occurred to me: Maybe I *was* ready for it. Maybe Stewart had been right. Maybe I did need this. It made sense, I figured—it was in my blood. My father had answered the call to service, to discipline and dedication. And now it was my turn. Of course, he'd served in the army and then the National Guard. He'd gone to war—two wars, actually, both in the Gulf. Me? I was in a fruity play.

"Okay, here are your scripts," Ms. Vale said, patting the pile at her side. "You're welcome to purchase your copies if you want to keep them, otherwise I'll need them back."

She began passing them around the table. When she got to Stewart, though, he gave his back.

"Actually, Ms. Vale, I already got a copy ahead of time. It's okay, it's the same version. I wanted to get a head start on the lines."

"Okay," she replied, a little surprised. But she quickly recovered with a smile. "Well, I admire the dedication."

"Frenchy's got one too," Stewart added, clapping me on the back.

I smiled back and gave a sheepish nod. At this point, the other kids were all staring at me with a hint of murder in their eyes. I couldn't blame them. I turned and glared at Stewart while Ms. Vale continued around the room.

Fucking suck-up. I did my best to project the thought. He just gave me a confused sort of look, as if to ask what my problem was, followed by a grin.

Ms. Vale finished handing out the scripts, and from there things took off. Day one of practice was what she called a read-through, which is basically just what it sounds like—all of us assuming our parts, reading through the whole script from start to finish. It took most of the afternoon, though skipping the songs helped. We'd work on those next, she said.

I did all right. No worse than anyone else. Ms. Vale didn't say much as we plodded along, though she took a million notes. Stewart, big surprise, stole the show, reading with gusto, sometimes not reading at all but reciting from memory. Slowly, I could feel the others coming back around, especially the girls. Kaela blushed as Stewart intoned Quixote's declarations of love and praise to Dulcinea. Even Stacey's iron jaw seemed to slacken a little when he hit a particularly potent line. Ms. Vale just gave a demure smile every time Stewart got going, but you could tell she was pleased.

Poor Quentin. I never thought I'd feel sorry for the guy, but I had a front-row seat to his own private hell. I could see his face flash from one kind of bitterness to another as we moved deeper into the script. I bet he never imagined when he proposed *Man of La Mancha* that it would turn out this way. Every time Stewart spoke, they were *Quentin's* lines Stewart was speaking, *his* part Stewart was playing. It had to suck big-time.

And part of me did feel sorry for him. But not much. *Life is full of surprises*, I wanted to tell him. *Most of them nasty. Better get used to it, pretty boy.*

Chapter Eleven

It was after five o'clock by the time Stewart dropped me off. I grabbed the gift box with the cane in it from the trunk and hustled to the door. My mother would be home pretty soon, and I wanted to have dinner ready. I figured I'd make tacos. Tacos were quick and easy, and I was pretty beat. I'd never stayed at school that late before. Not even for detention.

The TV was blaring when I stepped through the door and into the kitchen, which was kind of weird since my mother's car was still gone. Then I saw a pair of feet dangling over the edge of the couch and got really freaked out. Everything slowed down and turned all nasty, like a bad dream or one too many hits off the old bong. I slipped the cane from its box and drew the blade out as I stumbled around the corner.

It was Ralph. The douche bag was reclining across the entire length of the couch, right hand on the clicker, left hand in his pants, scratching his balls like he'd been doing all weekend.

The sight of me popping out, sword in hand, caught poor Ralph by surprise. He tried scrambling to his feet and ended up falling backward over the couch with a strangled, girly yelp. As tweaked out as I was, I had a hard time not laughing.

"Fuck me, Agnes!" he hollered. "You scared the shit out of me, Frenchy!"

"I scared *you?*" I shouted back. "This is *my* house, Ralph! What the hell are you doing here, anyway?"

He shrugged. "I don't know. Your mom invited me to dinner."

"Jesus, you were here, like, all weekend. It's only Monday."

He shrugged again. "Your mom said to come over, so I did."

I suppose if I had to live in that run-down shitbox he'd inherited, I'd want to spend as much time as possible somewhere else too. But why did that have to mean *my* house?

"Yeah, well, dinner's not until six o'clock." I could still feel my heart pounding. "Don't tell me you've been here all day."

He looked away, uncomfortable, but I didn't give a shit. *Let him squirm*, I thought.

"I didn't have nothing to do."

"Yeah, that's because you're a fucking loser, Ralph. A first-rate fucking loser."

His face dropped. He looked like a dog that'd just been kicked. I was about to apologize when he caught sight of the sword. His eyes opened wide.

"Whoa!" he whispered. "Where'd you get that, bro?"

"It doubles as a cane." I sheathed the blade. I didn't feel like telling him where it had come from.

"Yeah, yeah. That's pretty sweet." He came around the back of the couch for a closer look.

"It is, isn't it?" I said, letting him check it out.

He drew the sword out partway and gave a low whistle.

"You could really fuck somebody up with this thing." He closed it back up.

"Yeah, I suppose," I said. "Just don't tell Mom."

He gave me a conspiratorial smile. "Chicks just don't understand, do they? Don't worry, Frenchy. I ain't going to say a thing. Bros before hos."

"Good lord," I said, shaking my head. "And while we're at it, don't go in my room when I'm not here. Ever."

"No sweat," he said, raising his hands and breaking into a stupid grin. "A man's room is his castle. That's my motto. No one goes in my room either, unless it's to . . ." He hesitated. "Well, you know."

I snatched the cane from his hands and gave him the nastiest look I could. Fucking Ralph.

"Hey, Frenchy," he said. He knew he'd upset me. "Want to smoke a joint before your mom gets home?"

"No thanks." For all the pot I'd smoked over the last couple years, I'd never smoked at home, not even outside. I'd go off into the woods or up the road; hell, I'd go anywhere, but not on Paquette soil. It wasn't so much because my mom worked for the state police. It had to do with the old man, mostly. Even with him on the other side of the world, slogging it out in some arid hellhole, I hadn't been able to shake the idea that he was watching somehow, keeping an eye on the place. And now, well . . .

"I got to make dinner," I said, and headed off to my room to stash the cane.

"Dinner?" he called after me. "I'll make dinner!"

I stopped and turned.

"You? You'll make dinner?"

"No sweat, bro."

"Since when do you know how to cook?"

"I was a prep cook at the Rory Inn for two years. I went to culinary school."

"*You* went to culinary school?" I stifled a laugh. I tried to picture the douche bag in a chef's hat and apron.

He glanced down at his feet. "For a semester," he muttered before looking back up. "So, what are you making?"

"Tacos. Think you can handle it?"

He gave me a look of mild disdain, then headed for the kitchen.

"You'll have to thaw some hamburger out," I hollered after him. When he didn't reply, I followed him into the kitchen. He'd already found the taco kit in the cupboard and was getting the hamburger out of the freezer to defrost in the microwave. I watched him as he proceeded to grab lettuce and a green pepper from the refrigerator—along with an onion and a tomato from the hanging basket near the sink—and begin chopping everything up. It was weird watching him go at it with a knife. I had to admit—he had skills.

"So how come you didn't make yourself useful this weekend?" I said as he chopped and diced away.

"I have to cook for myself all the time," he said. "I figured if she'd wanted help, she would've asked. Isn't that how it works?"

"Yeah, I suppose," I murmured, looking down at my thumb. It was starting to throb again. Against the whiteness of the gauze, I could make out the slightest trace of blood.

I got Ralph a few things he needed, then he kicked me out. ("Go watch some TV or something, bro.") I was kind of glad not to have to make dinner, what with my cut and all, but a part of me was annoyed. I didn't like anyone telling me what to do in my own house, let alone that moron. Besides, it was my job to make dinner, my responsibility, not his.

Anyway, my mother came home to the sight of Chef Ralph going at it in the kitchen and, sure enough, thought it was the sweetest thing. That's what she said as he handed her a beer— "the sweetest thing."

I had to admit, the tacos were damn good. I don't know what he added to the package of seasoning mix, but they were the best fucking tacos I ever had. I'd wolfed down six of the things and was on my way to making a seventh when my mother turned to me with a grin.

"Oh, I almost forgot. Something interesting happened at work today."

"Yeah? What?" I glanced over at her, suspicious. Usually when she said that, the something wasn't so much interesting as it was horribly bizarre. Like last year when some drugged-up nut job stumbled into the barracks with his dick stuck in the end of a plastic bottle of vegetable oil. (I'll leave it up to you to figure out what it was doing there.) The poor bastard panicked and decided that, instead of waiting for things to settle down, the best solution would be to cut the bottle off with a butcher's knife, a tricky proposition even for a sober person playing with a full deck of cards. Apparently the results weren't pretty, though the troopers cracked jokes about the "Crisco Kid" for months afterward.

But this time she didn't have that macabre gleam in her eye. At first I thought it was because she was still all giddy over Ralph making dinner, but it turned out to be something else.

"Jeanie told me you're in the fall musical. She said Liz told her you got a lead role!"

Shit. Liz was playing Antonia, Don Quixote's niece. I'd completely forgotten our mothers worked together.

I could see from Mom's expression that she was pretty psyched. I glanced over at Ralph. He just seemed sort of confused. A pretty typical look for him, actually.

"Yeah," I finally mustered, "Stewart talked me into it."

"That's right. He has the lead role, Jeanie said. Both of you together."

"It's not a big deal or anything."

"Of course it is." She leaned over to touch my arm. I tried not to pull it away. "My baby's going to be onstage." She was still beaming.

"Musical?" Ralph said, still puzzled. "Does that mean you have to wear a leotard or something?"

"No," I snapped, though in the back of my mind I suddenly wasn't so sure. "It's just a play with songs in it. That's all."

"Ralph!" my mother said. I could see her face darken.

"What?" he mumbled through a mouthful of taco. Poor dumb bastard, he didn't have a clue. "All I'm saying is that it sounds kind of gay."

"Yeah, well, you're gay!" I yelled.

"No, *you're* gay."

"Hey, at least I'm actually doing something with my life. At least I'm not sitting around on the couch all day with my hands in my crotch, watching TV like a loser."

"No, you're just prancing around on the stage with that weird buddy of yours."

"Oh, fuck you, you fucking douche bag."

"Boys!" my mother hollered, slamming her hands down on the table so hard a little milk sloshed out of my glass. "Quiet! Both of you!"

Ralph and I exchanged glares while my mother dropped her face in her hands and shook her head.

"It's been a long day," she said at last. "I'm tired. I'm going to bed."

She didn't look at either of us, but I could see her eyes had the same dull look to them that I'd seen last summer.

"Frenchy, could you clean up the kitchen for me, please?"

"Sure," I whispered.

"Thanks, sweetie." She came over and kissed me on the head before turning to Ralph. "Thanks for making supper, Ralph. I'll call you later."

"Yeah, okay," he murmured, his shoulders slouched, staring down with that same hangdog look he'd given me earlier. He got up from the table, grabbed his jacket, and shuffled out, closing the door softly behind him.

My mother and I looked at each other for a moment. She tried to give me a smile.

"Don't listen to him."

"I won't."

"It's a good thing, what you're doing."

"Yeah, thanks."

"I'm sure your father would . . . you know."

I nodded, then started gathering the plates. She nodded too. When I looked back up, she was gone.

ᴄɪ|ᴌ CHAPTER TWELVE ᴌ|ᴌ·

"Got any eights?" I asked.

"Dammit," Kaela said, tossing me a card. "What do you have, ESP or something?"

"Just lucky, that's all," I said with a grin, laying down the pair.

We were in the corner of the drama room. Most of the cast were spread around the room, chatting in small groups while the rest clustered around Franco at the piano. The first full week of rehearsals was drawing to a close. They weren't really rehearsals, actually. It was music week, and we were hard at work getting the songs down. Most of us, anyway.

"Glad this week is almost over."

"Come on, it's not that bad. You don't even have that many songs, not compared to Stewart. Poor guy's in just about every number."

"You kidding me?" I said, watching him standing beside Franco, singing away. "He's at the center of attention. Right where he likes it. I'm just glad I've got you to keep me company. I don't think the others appreciate Stewart and me crashing the party."

She blushed a little. "Give me a seven. I know you have one."

I handed the card over.

"Don't worry, Frenchy. No one here cares. Except maybe Quentin. Oh, and Stacey, the bitch," she muttered. "In fact, most people think it's pretty cool. It's nice to have some new blood. Not only that, lots of kids in school are talking about it. You're a bit of a hit."

"Well, they should wait until opening night." The very thought tied my stomach in a knot. "Still, I guess it's better than just being that dorky scrub who lives up on the Heights and pulls stupid pranks. Or even worse, the kid whose father blew his head off in his trailer. No one wants to touch that one."

She froze as soon as the words came out of my mouth. *Idiot*, I thought. What the hell was I thinking?

"Looking for a jack here," I finally murmured. "Help me out?"

"Go fish." I could see her eyes start to glisten. I had a real way with women.

"What's up with that guy?" I said, nodding toward Franco, where he sat in the far corner, perched in front of his electric piano, pounding away with his sausage fingers. "I stuck around at the end of practice a few times to see if he'd leave, but he never got up. He just kept on playing."

"Maybe he lives here," she said, breaking back into a smile.

"I bet he does. I can see him walking around the halls at night, eating old candy bars and stale crackers from the vending machines, sleeping under his bench, waking up early to sneak a shower in the boys' locker room."

Kaela burst out laughing. Everyone turned to stare. Even Franco stopped playing.

"Sorry," she said to the group, glancing over at me with a look of chagrin.

"Get ready, Frenchy," Ms. Vale called out, with the slightest glare. "You're up in five."

"Sure thing," I answered as everyone went back to business. Kaela and I looked at each other. I could see her trying to stifle another round of laughter.

"She's quite the taskmaster," Kaela murmured.

"Yeah, well, the hot little Nazi routine works," I said. "I know those songs backward and forward at this point. I can sing them in my sleep. In fact, last night I think I actually did," I added, seeing Kaela start to laugh again. "Even worse, I started singing them in class the other day. That went over well."

"Threes?" She giggled.

"Go fish."

She drew a card.

"By the way, what are you doing here?" I asked. "You don't need to subject yourself to this."

She shrugged. "A good stage manager's involved with every part of the production." Her eyes narrowed. "Besides, somebody's got to keep you out of trouble."

"Good luck with that."

"Don't worry. Next week we'll be moving to the theater, and we'll all be working straight out. I'll be starting set construction, and you'll be busy blocking."

"What's that mean?"

"Blocking's when you actually start playing out scenes on the stage. There's a lot to it—you have to figure out where you're going to stand when you say a line, what you're going to do when you say it, where you come in and out. That sort of stuff."

"Sounds hard."

"Just do what Ms. Vale tells you to do and you'll be okay."

"Don't worry. I'm used to following orders."

"Hey, Renny," I shouted, "get me some nails!" We were nearly a week into blocking, and already the beginnings of the set were coming together backstage.

"Sure thing, Sancho," Renny said. The tech, a sophomore who wore the same pair of skinny black jeans every day, scrambled to fetch the clinking coffee can.

"Thanks, man."

"Do you need anything else?" Fitch—another one of the techs—said, popping out from behind a nearby curtain.

"No, I'm good for now."

"Hey, Frenchy," Fitch said, "tell Renny that joke you told me before practice about the two monkeys. That was the fucking funniest thing I've heard all year."

"Boys!" Kaela barked. Renny and Fitch whirled to see her glaring at them, her hammer raised. "I believe you two have a riser to paint. Get to it and leave Frenchy alone. He's helping me right now."

The two jumped, practically knocking each other over in an effort to escape.

"Man, you're almost as scary as Ms. Vale," I said, pounding another nail into the piece of plywood. She chuckled.

"Who do you think I learned from? Don't worry, your little fans will recover. It's kind of cute, actually, seeing them fawn over you."

"What can I say? I'm a celebrity now."

"It's only been a few days, Frenchy. Don't let it go to your head. Besides, you may have been pretty good in that last scene, but it's not your acting skills that's spurring the hero worship."

"Yeah, then what is it?"

"It's that you're actually deigning to work on set construction. Most cast members act like a bunch of prima donnas and don't even talk to techs, let alone lift a hand to help out."

"I actually feel more comfortable pounding nails than singing."

"Stop it," she said as we lifted another sheet of plywood. "I've been watching you out there on the stage. I can see it in your eyes. Hear it in your voice. Admit it—you're becoming a total theater geek."

"Why not?" I said, grinning. "I've been every other kind of geek." We started nailing the new sheet to the frame. "So where'd you learn to be so handy, anyway?"

"Dad's a carpenter." She wiped the sweat from her brow. "I've been handling tools since I learned to walk. Always been a bit of a tomboy. It's served me well, for the most part. A little hard on the love life, though."

"Hey, there's nothing sexier than a woman with a power tool in her hand."

She shook her head and laughed.

"Sancho!" a voice called out. "Sancho, where are you?" It was Stewart.

"Back here!"

Stewart pushed the curtain aside. He snatched the hammer out of my hand and handed it to Kaela.

"Come on, man, we need you out there. Let's go!"

I turned to Kaela and shrugged. "Duty calls."

"Go for it," she said.

"Listen," Stewart said as we headed toward the stage. "I think the problem last time was that you were a touch late on the third line. And maybe rethink how soon you turn after Aldonza comes in. It's got to look more natural. And another thing—"

"But Ms. Vale said it was fine," I cut in.

"Yeah, yeah," he muttered, as if he hadn't even heard me. "Anyway, I'm thinking about changing my entire approach to the lead-in on the song. What do you think about me holding the very first note for an extra five seconds? And maybe sing it in a falsetto. Yeah, I think that would work."

I stopped and watched as he kept going, babbling away, not even realizing I was no longer beside him. It wasn't the first time that week he'd done that.

And that was just the start of my troubles with Stewart.

It wasn't that Stewart wasn't good. From day one, while we all had our eyes glued to the script, he knew his lines. Hell, he knew everyone else's lines. And when he was in the middle of a scene—especially in the Don Quixote scenes—everyone paid attention, even the kids who didn't need to. Whether it was as Cervantes or as Don Quixote, he seemed to disappear. Stewart Bolger would disappear, and a stranger would take his place.

"That's acting!" Ms. Vale cried out one day after Stewart finished a scene. "*That's* acting!"

When he was really on fire, we could practically feel the energy crackling around us onstage. And we could use it. He made everyone around him better, so much so that by the third day of blocking, anyone who'd had any doubts about Stewart playing the lead had come around. Even Quentin seemed to have resigned himself to the situation.

No, the problem wasn't that Stewart wasn't good. It was that Stewart was *too* good, that Stewart was *always* good, was always on. Everyone loved it. Everyone thought it was cool. Not me. I had to live with it.

By the end of the week, the play was the only thing he talked about. Every morning on the way to school, every afternoon on the way home, and every moment in between—at lunch, in the halls—it was all *Man of La Mancha*, all the time. Dissecting this or that kid's performance, analyzing his own performance, speculating on blocking changes Ms. Vale might make, wondering how the sets were going to come together, debating whether we should be working more on choreography—you name it, Stewart obsessed about it. He even roped me into practicing on the weekend, luring me over that Saturday with the promise of dinner, since Ralph was taking my mother out to the Wellboro Diner. I humored him for an hour or so, but he could tell I was getting tired of it toward the end, so he suggested a movie.

"Not *Man of La Mancha*," I said.

"I know." He raised his hands. "I've got *Hamlet*."

"*Hamlet?*" I said. "You serious?"

"Figured I should broaden my theatrical horizons with a little Shakespeare."

"Great," I moaned.

"Dude, it's a classic."

"It's fucking boring."

"How the hell would you know?"

"Because I read the goddam thing last year."

"Yeah, when?"

"I was bored one day, so I read it. Some dumbass forgot his copy in the library."

"Oh," Stewart said, crinkling his brow. "I think that was me."

We looked at each other and cracked up.

"Come on," he said. "Kate Winslet's in it. You're always saying how hot she is."

"Fine," I muttered.

"Hamlet was an actor, you know," he said as we settled down to watch.

"Hamlet was crazy."

"No, he wasn't," Stewart shot back. It was the voice he usually used with his parents when they had their stupid arguments around the supper table. "He was just pretending. Besides, crazy people don't know they're crazy. Hamlet wonders if he might be."

Was that really true? I saw my father, staring into the bath-room mirror on a hot night in June while I lay sleeping in the next room. I thought I'd gotten the image out of my head, but all of a sudden it was back. *To be or not to be*. Fucking Hamlet.

"Yeah, whatever." I didn't feel like arguing. "Either way, he ends up dead. That's all that matters."

For the most part, I went along with Stewart's obsession. I was into the play, too. But after a while, the intensity started to get on my nerves. It made me wonder whether I was committed enough, if I was enjoying the whole "experience" enough. I knew I could never match Stewart, but for some reason I felt like I should. I'd never felt that way before, and it pissed me off.

A part of me missed our pit stops, our walks on the outer loop, our back-road detours. I missed being stupid and fun. I even tried to get Stewart to partake one afternoon on the way home, producing a joint as we made our way out of town. Stewart always kept the bag, but I'd been able to scrape one together with what was left of my own little stash.

"Come on, let's just take a break," I said. "We've been going all week."

Stewart did a slight double take at the sight of the joint. He took it from me, brought it to his nose, and gave it a deep sniff before smiling. Then he rolled down the window and tossed it out.

"Hey! What the hell?"

"Sorry, old friend. Purity is the name of the game now. I tainted myself for too long. As did you."

"Whatever happened to enhancement?"

"You're lucky you've got me, Frenchy," he said, ignoring my anger. "We're on a journey now. Distractions won't do."

"Yeah," I muttered. "We wouldn't want any distractions."

During the second week of blocking, he backed off the production talk, only to start a new obsession—Stacey McGovern, a subject even more annoying, if you can believe it.

We were well into the play and had gotten to the part where Don Quixote attempts to woo Aldonza, whom in his madness he names Dulcinea. But Aldonza has other ideas, at least at first. So, it seemed, did Stacey, who was game enough during the scenes to engage Stewart but broke character as soon as they were done. Stewart, meanwhile, did his best to hold her attention, following her around, striking up conversation, going out of his way to ask her questions. She humored him, for the most part—he'd gotten to be pretty popular with the other actors. But when cast members clustered around him during breaks, she always found an excuse to slip away.

Stewart, unfortunately, refused to see it. All the way home, he'd chatter on about how beautiful she was, how delicate. Like a rose. A rose! Apparently roses have perfect asses, too, from the way he talked. I couldn't argue with him there, but then he'd go on about how in love they were, how their passion for the stage united them, how maybe they would go to the same college, maybe both be actors, blah, blah, blah. I kept my mouth shut at first, but after a few days of that bullshit I couldn't help myself.

"Dude, she isn't into you," I snapped as we headed over the bridge and started up the Heights.

He scrunched up his face, then shook his head a little.

"Trust me. She isn't."

"A noble jest. But I know for a fact she is."

"No, she isn't," I insisted. Normally I'd just roll over with a "whatever," but for some reason I suddenly couldn't let him get away with it. "She walks away whenever you come over. And she doesn't laugh very much at your jokes. Sorry, dude."

"She's just being Aldonza," Stewart said. "You know how the wench plays hard to get. But in the end, she can't help being charmed by Don Quixote."

"I'm not talking about the play, Stewart. I'm talking about real life."

"I know," he said, drawing out his words. "But there are things you don't notice. She has confessed her love for me more than once this week."

"She has? When?"

"There are secret looks, ones that only we share. I know she cares."

"Yeah, right."

"You just don't understand women, Frenchy. When's the last time you had a girlfriend, anyway?"

"Eighth grade. Same as you, asshole."

"Well, maybe it's your time too. What about Kaela? You two have been hanging out quite a bit." He flashed me a quick grin.

"She's cute," I admitted.

"She is," he said, adding, "Of course, she's no Dulcinea."

"Yeah, well, neither is Stacey."

"Not yet," Stewart whispered.

Chapter Thirteen

It took a few days, but as the third and final week of blocking rolled around, Stewart finally cooled on the whole Stacey business. Whether I'd managed to talk some sense into him or he'd decided to keep his infatuation to himself, I had no idea. Frankly, I didn't give a shit. It was just nice not having to listen to him carry on like some pathetic horndog.

But then other things started happening. Weird things.

On Tuesday, Stewart stopped in the middle of a scene. At first, I thought he'd forgotten his line.

"'The Enchanter may confuse the outcome, but the effort remains sublime!'" I whispered, prompting him from the script.

He didn't answer. He just looked around, kind of dazed.

"Stewart?" Ms. Vale asked. Everyone was starting to glance at one another.

He snapped his head up. "What about costumes? We need costumes, don't we?"

There were a few snickers. Stacey McGovern gave a disgusted sigh.

"Well, Stewart," Ms. Vale explained, "we don't really worry about those until we get closer to the actual performance."

"It's called dress rehearsal," Quentin shouted. More laughter.

Ms. Vale whipped her hand up for silence. The laughter stopped.

She brought both hands up to her head, the tips of her delicate fingers spread out, disappearing into her hair so that it was pushed back a little. She was thinking. She always did that when she was thinking.

"Still, it wouldn't hurt to have a few props, I suppose," she finally said. "In fact, it can be quite helpful during blocking."

Stacey and Quentin gave each other an eye roll.

"Props?" Stewart said. He paused for a moment, then slipped right back into the scene. We moved along. It was forgotten.

Until the next day's rehearsal, that is, when Stewart came into the auditorium with a duffel bag. He dropped it at the foot of the stage and began rummaging through it while the rest of us shot the shit, waiting for Ms. Vale. When I looked back, Stewart had a cloak draped around his shoulders, a silver mixing bowl on his head, and a set of fake glasses with a huge nose and mustache attached. Everyone laughed. I tried to, but I couldn't. They all thought Stewart was joking, but I could see his eyes behind those glasses, and I could tell he wasn't laughing either.

I hurried over and grabbed the fake glasses off his face. "What's with the Groucho Marx bullshit?"

He snatched them right back. "It's for Don Quixote," he said, putting them back on. I suddenly remembered how, in the movie, Cervantes wears a fake nose, beard, and wig to play the part of Don Quixote before the prisoners at the trial.

"It's just temporary," he added. "I'll get the real stuff later."

"Yeah, well, it looks stupid. And so does that fucking bowl on top of your head."

"It's supposed to be a helmet. I am a knight, after all."

"Yeah, I know what it's supposed to be, but it still looks dumb. And you're not a knight."

"Come on, Frenchy, lighten up," Quentin said. He'd been eavesdropping.

"Yeah, Frenchy, lighten up," Stewart said.

I turned to glare at Quentin, who had a big smirk on his face.

"Actually," Stewart went on, "I brought some stuff for you too, Frenchy." He went back to digging through his bag.

"No thanks," I said, and walked away. I didn't want to see what he might pull out.

Ms. Vale showed up, and we all mounted the stage. She stopped short at the sight of Stewart, then let out a snort of laughter, high and nervous, like a bird in a pet store. Stewart shifted uneasily.

"That's quite a look," she said.

"Props," Stewart said.

"Indeed," Ms. Vale replied, then clapped her hands. "All right, everyone, let's get going."

We didn't get far before a few of the kids started cracking up. We started over, then it happened again. Stewart reciting his lines in that getup killed the magic. He just looked silly. And the more serious he got—the more dramatic he got—the sillier he looked, and the more people laughed.

I could tell he was getting frustrated. And he wasn't the only one.

"Hey!" I hollered, turning to a pair of extras after, like, the fifth time. "Shut the fuck up! We're trying to work here."

They shrank back, cringing as if I were going to hit them or something. Too much for the theater crowd, I guess.

"Frenchy!" Ms. Vale warned.

"Yeah, sorry." I looked down at the stage, too scared to see whether she was glaring at me.

"Okay, Stewart," Ms. Vale said. "Time to lose the costume."

"But they're my props," he insisted.

She arched an eyebrow.

I came over and gave him a slap on the back. "Come on, man. There'll be plenty of chances for this shit later. Please, Stewart."

He sighed, removing first the bowl from his head and then the glasses, which rattled as he dropped them into the bowl. We all watched him quietly.

"Can I keep the cloak at least?" he asked.

"Fine."

He hopped down off the stage and tossed the bowl and glasses into the duffel bag. Ms. Vale had turned back to us and begun issuing new orders when Stewart interrupted her.

"Ms. Vale, how about a sword?"

"Excuse me?" She seemed more confused than annoyed, but I could feel my stomach start to clench.

"You know, as a prop. I mean, every knight needs a sword, right?"

"I suppose," she conceded. "We can get a foil for you tomorrow. How does that sound?"

"Great!" he said. Then he turned back to the duffel bag.

Oh no, I thought. I knew what was coming.

Sure enough, out came the cane. "Ms. Vale, how about this?" he asked. "Can I use this just for today?"

Ms. Vale hesitated. "Sure," she said at last. Now she was getting annoyed.

Stewart hopped back up onto the stage. "Too bad you didn't bring yours," he said, coming over to stand beside me. "Frenchy's got one too," he announced to the group before turning and giving me a quick wink. I stared down at the stage. It was the only place I dared look. For the rest of the rehearsal I had to listen to the click-click of the cane as he turned the handle's safety release off and on. Knowing what was inside the sheath made me shiver.

"What the fuck was that?" I said on the way home.

"What do you mean?"

"That bullshit with the sword. I kept waiting for you to whip it out and stab someone."

Stewart laughed. "Don't be silly, Sancho. There are no villains on our stage. We're all in it together."

"Ha, ha," I said. "I still don't like it."

"Well, what do you think I got them for? They're for Sancho and Don. I expect you to bring yours tomorrow."

"Blow me."

This time he laughed.

The next day Ms. Vale dug up an old foil—you know, one of those Three Musketeers–type jobs—from the props room. Stewart seemed satisfied and threw himself back into the play with the usual intensity. It didn't bother me as much at this point. I'd gotten sort of used to it. Besides, we were all working furiously to complete the blocking. It was really getting tough now—we were starting to do longer run-throughs (stumble-throughs, Ms. Vale called them) at the beginning of every rehearsal of scenes we'd blocked out the day before and were moving closer to the day when everyone had to be "off-book," with all lines memorized. I was pretty sure I knew mine, but I was scared to let go of the script. It was like having a little security blanket tucked in my pocket. Stewart, of course, didn't care. He'd been off-book since the first week. Next to him, we all looked like dummies. There he'd be, buzzing along, and it would come to one of us and we'd have to pause to find our place, or we'd stumble with a line, and then Ms. Vale would interrupt with a direction, and sometimes we'd have to start over.

Stewart took it in stride at first, but as the week went on, he grew more and more impatient with everyone. All it was going to take was one major screwup to make him lose it completely.

Unfortunately, that screwup turned out to be me.

I knew it was going to be one of those days the moment I opened the door and got into Stewart's car. Glancing over, I did a double take at the sight of the strange old man behind the wheel.

"Holy shit," I said. "Look at you."

"Morning, Sancho," the figure replied. "And a fine morning it is indeed."

It was Stewart's voice, but the man speaking didn't look like Stewart at all. He looked just like Don Quixote, the one I'd seen in the movie and in all the pictures Stewart was steadily accumulating on the walls of both his rooms. He had it down perfect—the wig, the mustache and beard, a prosthetic nose and set of ancient teeth, even the crazy eyebrows. And then there were the clothes—a beat-up-looking set of old armor, complete with battered helmet, leggings, tunic, and cloak. Topping it all off was a sword—not the chintzy foil Ms. Vale had given him or his cane sword but a real-life broadsword. The kind a knight would carry.

"How the hell did you do that?" I asked. "I mean, where did you get all that crap?"

"It's called the Internet, Sancho," he replied, his voice all nasal and lispy-sounding with the fake nose and teeth.

"Must've taken forever," I said, peering around to inspect the perfectly blended prosthetics.

"Three hours. So where's your costume?"

"What the hell are you talking about?"

"It's Halloween, Sancho. Where's your spirit, old friend?"

It was actually the day before Halloween, but the school was celebrating today since tomorrow was a Saturday. I'd forgotten all about it. Not that it mattered, since I never dressed up on "Halloween Day." Stewart always did. Usually his outfits were these dorky little hippie statements—"social consciousness–raising costumes," he called them. One year he dressed up as a walking recycling bin, though by fourth period the other kids had thrown so much shit in his costume that he was forced to abandon it. Last year he dressed up as a corpse wrapped in the Iraqi flag. That went over great. I usually avoided Stewart on Halloween Day.

"My spirit? Guess I'm saving it for the stage."

"Good idea," Stewart said, nodding grimly. "We need every bit we can muster."

I laughed. "I don't know, Stewart. You've got enough for all of us."

He shook his head and frowned. "If only that were true. But I can't do it alone. I can't carry the entire burden. I need you to help me, Sancho. Otherwise, we'll never make it."

"You need to fucking relax. That's what you need to do."

Stewart slammed on the brakes. I hadn't put my seat belt on yet, so I nearly went through the goddam windshield.

"Jesus Christ!" I shouted, sinking back into the seat. Shaking, I reached for the seat belt and put it on as fast as I could. The Volvo just sat there, right smack in the middle of the road. Looking out the window, I saw the pull-off where we took our pit stops. The leaves had all fallen from the maples so that I could see the field beyond and even make out the wind towers in the distance, intersecting the spreading limbs.

"How dare you make light of the production," he fumed, drops of spittle flying out onto the steering wheel. He wouldn't look at me.

"Okay, fine. Sorry. Just move before we get creamed by a logging truck or something."

Still staring straight ahead, he turned back into our lane and sped off down the mountain. He seemed to grow calmer as we reached the bottom, though with all that shit on his face, it was hard to tell.

"I just think you'd have more fun," I offered.

"I'm not doing it to have fun."

"Then why the hell *are* you doing it, Stewart?"

"Don't call me Stewart," he replied. He paused, then smiled before breaking into the musical's first song:

> I am I, Don Quixote,
> The Lord of La Mancha,
> My destiny calls and I go,
> And the wild winds of fortune
> Will carry me onward,
> Oh whithersoever they blow.
> Onward to glory I go!

He paused and looked at me. This was where I was supposed to come in—*I'm Sancho! Yes, I'm Sancho! I'll follow my master till the end!*—but I turned and looked out the window. I didn't feel much like singing.

Stewart got stopped on the way into the building—they made him leave his sword in the main office—and I didn't see him for the rest of the school day. I hid out in the library during lunch, scarfing down the bag of emergency chips I kept in my locker when the librarian wasn't looking. It wasn't so much the morning outburst that kept me away, though that had been pretty annoying. It was the costume. Already people were referring to us as "Sancho and Don"—something Stewart probably started—and with him in full regalia, it was only going to get worse.

But I still heard plenty about Stewart's costume. Kids all over school were discussing it, even the teachers. A few kids asked me about it, asked why I wasn't dressing up with him, but for the most part people forgot about me, which was fine. The talk was pretty divided. Some thought it was cool, others thought it was weird. A lot of people didn't know what to think.

Not the theater crowd. They gave him a standing ovation when he showed up late to rehearsal after persuading Ruggles to give him back his sword. Striding onto the stage, he gave a bow and a flourish and a tip of the old helmet as everyone laughed and cheered. Everyone was pretty punchy. It had been a long week. Hell, it had been a long four weeks between the music rehearsals and the blocking, and we were all pretty tired and stressed out and looking for some kind of release.

"Very nice, Stewart, very nice," Ms. Vale said, with a hand on her forehead. "Guess we know who'll be doing makeup."

"Makeup?" Stewart asked. "Whatever are you talking about? And who's this Stewart character you speak of?" He turned and looked behind him. The kids started laughing even harder.

"Okay, okay," she said, turning to the rest of the group. "Let's try to get this wrapped up today if we can. And don't forget—when we come back on Monday, we're off-book."

A ripple of murmurs washed over the ensemble. It was the news we'd all expected, but dreaded just the same.

Things started out well enough. Somehow, Stewart's transformation had cast a spell over everyone, and we moved through the scenes pretty efficiently. But it was too tough to hold on to. Before long, fatigue set in, coupled with nerves over the thought of going off-book. Some kids were already trying to do their lines without any help. I don't know what they were trying to prove, but it made for some moments of real confusion. Ms. Vale was very patient, telling them not to worry about it, giving prompts when needed, but I could see Stewart growing increasingly furious. So could everyone else, which only made them stumble more.

Then it got to my big moment.

There's a part in one of the final scenes—after Don Quixote's delusion has been punctured by the Duke and he's totally collapsed and turned into this weak, sick old man—where I go to his bedside and try to bring him back to his senses. It's a whole long bit with a bunch of singing mixed in. Anyway, I was already nervous about it—I knew we'd be covering it today—and with kids screwing up left and right, I kept praying Ms. Vale would call an early end to rehearsal to put me out of my misery, or at least delay it. No such luck. She was the kind who believed in soldiering on, no matter what.

It was a mess from the start. I kept screwing up the lines, my timing was off on the music—poor Franco had to keep playing the intro over and over again—and every time I messed up, I'd be so nervous that I'd start laughing or say something stupid. And there was Stewart, lying there in front of me, having to put up with my incompetence at close range, without being able to move or speak, without even being able to have his eyes open.

There was one line in particular—"Whether the stone hits the pitcher or the pitcher hits the stone, it's going to be bad for the pitcher"—I just couldn't get right. I kept saying "picture" instead of "pitcher," or mixing up the order of the phrase. It was like some goddam tongue twister in my mouth.

I think I was on my fifth try when Stewart's eyes flew open. Before I could finish, he reached up and grabbed me by the shirt. The next thing I knew, we were wrestling on the ground.

"Stewart, what the hell?" I shouted as he rolled on top and pinned a knee against my chest.

Behind the mask of Quixote, I could see the eyes, wide and wild. For a split second, I couldn't tell whose eyes they were. They didn't look like Stewart's. Then his hand snapped up and gripped my face and started squeezing. Stewart was a skinny guy but surprisingly strong. It took everything I had to pull his hand away and twist him off me.

I finally managed to kick him away. Quentin and another guy tried to grab him. He shook them off, but he didn't come after me again.

"Goddam it, Frenchy!" he screamed inside. "What's your fucking problem? I mean, how long have you had to learn this shit? Come on, even I can do it!"

He launched into my monologue, the words flying from his mouth at top speed, not bothering with pauses or inflection, singing the verses with equal tempo in a nasty sort of mocking voice. It made me shiver. But worst of all, even worse than him attacking me, was the look in his eyes—a haunted, desperate look. Like some wounded animal.

A circle had gathered around Stewart and me. No one looked at one another. They just stood, frozen, staring at Stewart with open mouths. I didn't say anything either. I just sat there on the stage, gasping for breath. Who was this strange old man yelling at me?

"Stewart!" Ms. Vale yelled. She'd been saying his name over and over, louder and louder, trying to get his attention before finally shouting it, her voice impossibly loud.

It worked. Stewart shut up. The auditorium went silent.

"I think," Ms. Vale said, digging her fingers into her hair, "we should call it a day."

Stewart glanced down at me. There was a loud ringing sound as he pulled his new sword from its scabbard, followed by a gasp from everyone else. With a cry of anguish, he stabbed his sword straight down into the wooden floor of the stage, then stormed off, muttering under his breath. Everyone watched him leave the auditorium. Except me. I just stared at the sword still swaying back and forth in the center of the stage.

The kids left without saying much, drifting off in twos and threes to quiet whispers, still in awe of the spectacle. Ms. Vale just stood there shaking her head. It was the first time I'd ever seen her look rattled.

She came over and helped me to my feet.

"Are you okay?"

I nodded.

She sighed. "Maybe I've been pushing too hard."

"It's not a big deal. Stewart and I fool around like this all the time. He just got a little carried away. He's very dedicated."

"He certainly is," she said, shaking her head again. She looked back at me and mustered a smile. "Well, try to relax this weekend, Frenchy. And don't worry about that monologue. We'll pick it up first thing on Monday. I'm sure you'll do fine."

She gave my shoulder a little squeeze, then went over to speak to a couple kids who hadn't left yet.

I went over to the sword. It was stuck in there pretty good—I had to twist it back and forth a bit to get it out. It left quite a mark in the stage. I rubbed a few splinters away with my shoe, then left the auditorium, sword in tow.

"Frenchy!" a voice called out. It was Kaela. She'd followed me into the lobby.

"Oh, hey." I paused to let her catch up. Pretty much everyone had left, and it was just the two of us. For a few seconds, we just stood there, quiet. It was kind of awkward, to tell you the truth.

"Can I give you a ride home?" she said at last.

"Sure." I was pretty glad for the offer, actually. It saved me from having to walk through town with a big-ass sword over my shoulder.

"Cool." She gave me a sideways smile and took my free arm in hers, and we headed out to the parking lot. A wave of giddiness overtook me, with her close like that. The sword slipped from my hand and clattered to the pavement. We both jumped.

I stared at it for a moment, listening to its fading ring. It was Kaela who finally reached down and picked it up.

"Jesus, this thing's heavy," she said, handing it back to me.

"Yeah. I don't know how Stewart can deal with carrying it around all the time."

"Maybe you just get used to it," she said as we reached her car.

We were quiet for the first part of the drive.

"So that was a crazy scene," she finally said as we crossed over the bridge and started up Suffolk Heights.

"Yup."

"Stewart's a pretty intense guy, isn't he?"

"Yup," I said again.

"I never realized he was that way," she said. "He always seemed so laid-back. You both did."

"It's mostly the play. All that pressure. But Stewart's always been intense in his own way," I said. "I suppose I am too. I worry about all kinds of shit. I don't know. Maybe that's why we're friends."

"But he's kind of different, though, isn't he?"

"I suppose. Guess I'm used to it."

"You're a good friend, Frenchy," she said. "I heard what you said to Ms. Vale before you left."

"Everyone's just tired. That's all."

"Yeah, well, it was good what you said."

"Thanks."

We pulled into my driveway and sat there for a minute with the car running.

"You want to come inside?" I said at last, trying not to cringe as I said it. It sounded so lame, at least coming from me.

She glanced at the house, and before she even spoke, I knew what she was going to say. There it was—that little look of fear. She'd heard the story about my father, of course. All the kids had. But I'd forgotten.

She scrunched up her face in apology. "I have to get home. My parents and I are going out for dinner."

"That's cool. And thanks again for the ride. You saved me a hell of a walk."

"Okay," she said, her voice still all apologetic. I grabbed the sword and jumped out to spare her any more embarrassment.

"Hey!" she called out, rolling down the window as I headed for the steps.

"Yeah?"

"There's a party tomorrow night, up at the old airport. All the techs are going. Want to come with us?"

"Maybe," I said.

"What's your cell phone number? I'll text you."

I hesitated. "I don't actually have one."

"Oh," she said. She looked surprised. Goddam cell phones.

"I mean, I had one. But I lost it. I'm sort of in between phones right now. You know how it is."

"Sure." She wrote something down on a slip of paper and held it out the window. I came over and took it from her. It was a phone number. "Here's mine. Call me if you need a ride."

She gave me a quick smile, then backed out of the driveway and headed down the hill. I tucked the number in my pocket, gave the sword a swing, and watched her drive away.

∎ CHAPTER FOURTEEN ∎

When I got inside, there was a note on the counter:

Hi, Sweetie—
Got a double shift tonight. (Covering for Jeanie.) But I have all day off
tomorrow. Am planning a special dinner for you and Stewart before trick-
or-treating—something to send you off in style. Don't worry—I called
Stewart's mother. It's all arranged.
Love you, Mom

I winced at the message. Stewart and I went trick-or-treating every Halloween. We'd gone our freshman year as a sort of joke—being in high school and all, it was kind of ridiculous—but we had so much fun, it just sort of stuck. But after today, I couldn't imagine Stewart coming over for dinner, let alone us going out trick-or-treating. I wasn't even sure I wanted him to.

I laid the sword down on the table and went to the fridge. I was starved from skipping lunch, so I made a sandwich and gobbled it down. After that, I ran out of ideas. I thought about watching TV but ended up just pacing around. The house was lonely and quiet, and all I could do was think about Stewart, then Kaela, then my mom, then my dad, then back to Stewart again, getting more and more agitated by the minute.

"Fuck it," I finally said, and left.

I headed down the hill, crossed over to Ralph's, and banged on the door. No one answered, but his crappy old Camaro was parked in the driveway, so I knew he was around. I banged some more. Finally, he appeared.

I hadn't seen Ralph much since the Great Taco Spat almost a month ago. My mother had been out with him only a few times since, and he'd pretty much steered clear of our place. You'd think I'd have been dancing in the street over this turn of events, but oddly enough, I felt kind of bad. I didn't know if I'd put her off Ralph, or if it was because of him—he *was* Ralph, after all—but either way, she seemed more miserable than ever.

"Oh," he mumbled, seeing me. "Hey, Frenchy."

"Hey, Ralph."

He looked fucking awful, which for Ralph is really saying something. His eyes were squinty-baked and bloodshot; his face was covered with a shitty-looking beard, all black and patchy; his mullet was uncombed, with hair sticking out at weird angles; and his clothes looked and smelled like they hadn't been washed for a few weeks. Between Ralph, the car, and the house, the place was like white-trash central.

"Jesus, Ralph, you look like shit."

"Thanks, Frenchy," he said, his voice flat. I wondered if he'd even heard me. "Want to come in?"

"Sure."

I stepped through the door and into the kitchen. The whole house reeked of pot and cigarette smoke, but there was another smell mixed in. A delicious smell.

"Are you cooking or something?"

He went over and opened the oven door, then pulled out a big fucking turkey in a roasting pan and started slowly basting it.

"Yeah, bro. Cooking makes me feel better. And it's almost November. Time for turkey."

He finished basting and closed the oven. I followed him into the living room. It had gone back to being a mess, which made me kind of sad, even though it looked more like it was supposed to. Maybe that's what made me sad.

"So what's up?" He flopped down into his chair. He was dressed in jeans and a T-shirt underneath a ratty old bathrobe. I realized why—it was cold as hell in the house.

"Not much, I guess." I hesitated. "I was wondering if I could get a little weed. You know, just a joint or something."

Ralph raised his eyebrows once and nodded.

"Sure thing, bro," he said, standing up. "I'll roll you a few. Help yourself in the meantime."

He gestured to the bong on the coffee table, then headed down the hall to his room. While he took care of business, I fired up the bong and took a hit. It didn't go far. I hadn't smoked pot for a whole month, and as soon as it hit my lungs, I started hacking and choking. My whole chest felt like it was on fire. I wiped my eyes and tried to get a hold of myself.

"You okay?" Ralph said, drifting back into the room.

"Fine," I croaked, still coughing. I took the two joints he offered and tucked them in my shirt pocket. "Thanks, Ralph. How much?"

"Don't worry about it." He dropped back down in the chair and lit a cigarette. We were quiet for a few minutes. Then he looked up at me.

"I'm sorry about the whole play thing," he said. "You know, calling you queer and all that."

"Thanks, Ralph. I said some shit too."

He nodded. "So how's the play going, anyways?"

"It's getting there. We've got a few more weeks to go. Opening night is the Friday before Thanksgiving."

"Cool, bro. Can't wait to see it."

"Me too."

He nodded and went quiet again, staring down at the floor, lost in his own little whatever. I could feel the bong hit now, rocketing in faster than I would've liked, and I found myself wishing I were somewhere else. Even the double-wide had better vibes than this place. But I couldn't just get up and leave, not after his generosity.

"So," I said, "haven't seen you around much lately."

I didn't realize how rotten it was going to sound until I actually said it. I tried not to grimace.

Ralph sighed. "Yeah. Your mother hasn't really been returning my calls. I don't know what the deal is. Maybe it's over." He sighed again, then looked up at me. Christ, his eyes were all wet. I had this sudden panic that he might start to cry.

"Am I really a loser, Frenchy?" He reached up to wipe his eyes.

"Forget it, Ralph. I was just talking shit," I said. "Besides, we're all losers in one way or another. You can't win."

"I don't know where I went wrong with her," he said, shaking his head. "I thought everything was going real good, and then it all just sort of went away. *You* know her, bro. What's the deal?"

Fucking Ralph.

"I don't know, man," I said, then hesitated. Here it was—my opportunity to be rid of the douche bag forever, floating right there in front of me. All I had to do was reach out and pluck it.

But there he was—miserable, wasted, pathetic. And what had he done to deserve it? What had he ever done to me?

"Women. Go figure," I said at last. I stood up, wavering for a second against the sudden heaviness of my body. "It's been a tough year, Ralph. Maybe you've got to give it some time." I closed my eyes and gritted my teeth. "Just be patient. Don't give up."

He struggled out of his chair, and the next thing I knew he was giving me a hug—a big one with those fucking lanky arms of his. I let him hug me, stinky body and all. If it kept him from bawling, it was worth it.

"You're the best, bro. The fucking best."

"Yeah, thanks," I replied, giving it a silent three count before untangling myself. My whole scalp was prickling now. The pot, the smoke in the air, the smell of roasting turkey—it was all catching up with me. I had to get out.

"Hey, Ralph, I gotta go. But listen, Mom's making a nice dinner tomorrow night. Why don't you come over? I'm sure she'd be happy to see you."

He broke into a big smile and slapped his hands together.

"Thanks, bro," he said, pointing at me. "You're the fucking bomb. The best."

"Yeah, yeah." I turned to leave. He followed me into the kitchen. As I reached the door, a loud ding made us both stop.

"Yeah, baby!" he called out. "Turkey's done! Hold on, Frenchy."

I waited while he took the bird out and set it on the stove-top. It looked like something out of an issue of *Good Housekeeping*, for chrissake, all mahogany brown and steaming. I watched him expertly cut off one of the drumsticks with a carving knife and wrap the end in a paper towel.

"Something for the road." He handed me the leg. "That's serious fucking man food right there."

"Wow. Sure is," I said. "Thanks, Ralph."

He nodded and gave me a cheesy wink. "See you tomorrow."

"Right," I replied, returning the wink.

The cold air cleared my head some as I stepped off the porch and into the twilight. I felt instant relief, in spite of everything I'd said to Ralph.

I thought about saving the drumstick for dinner, but as I left the driveway and headed back up the road to my house, the smell got to me, and I dug in. I have to admit, it tasted pretty goddam good.

CHAPTER FIFTEEN

Stewart came knocking at ten o'clock, tapping out his usual rhythm on my bedroom window just as I was about to turn in.

I usually didn't go to bed until at least midnight—even later on Fridays—but I was pretty beat from the long week. Besides, my mother would be home soon, and I didn't feel like talking to her. I wasn't really high anymore or anything—I just didn't want to get into the whole Stewart thing, not to mention the business with Ralph. It could all wait until tomorrow.

I cranked the window open a few inches and peeked out.

"What's up?" I said.

"Hi, Frenchy," real-Stewart whispered. The hair, the makeup, the clothes—they were all gone. He looked like his old self again, standing there in the dark. His hair was pulled back into its usual ponytail, and he waited with his arms crossed, shivering without a jacket, his sword cane tucked under one arm.

"What's the cane for?"

"Bears."

I laughed. "How many times do I have to tell you—you don't need to worry about any goddam bears."

We actually did have quite a few black bears around. They were pretty shy, though, and unless you had too many bird feeders in your yard or liked to leave trash bags filled with leftovers on your lawn, you hardly ever saw them. But Stewart had this perpetual fear of bears. It was his flatlander upbringing, I guess. That or too much imagination.

"And you don't need to whisper," I added. "Mom's at work."

"Oh," Stewart said, still whispering. "So, can I come in?"

"Meet me around front. I got another idea."

I threw on a heavy sweatshirt, grabbed my wool hat and peacoat, and went out the front door. Stewart was waiting in the driveway, barely visible in the thin light coming through the kitchen window. It was cold—easily below freezing. It wouldn't be many more weeks before the snows would come and cover everything until April.

"Where's your coat?" I asked, putting on my hat.

"What?" he said, starting. "Oh. I forgot. I guess it's pretty cold out."

I tossed him the peacoat. He put it on without argument.

"Come on," I said. I turned onto the road and headed downhill.

"Where are we going?" he said, catching up.

"For a walk. It's a nice night."

All kinds of stars blazed overhead—and even though I was tired, I knew Stewart wanted to talk, and we always talked better on the move. Besides, we hadn't walked together for a while, not since the play started taking over everything.

Sure enough, Stewart got right to the point.

"I wanted to say I was sorry," he said after we'd gone a ways. "I don't know what happened at rehearsal. I guess I sort of snapped. You didn't deserve any of that. I feel awful. Ashamed, actually."

Wow. Two apologies in one day. I was starting to feel pretty special. Well, at least they were real. Sometimes people say they're sorry, but you know they're not sorry at all. But Stewart meant it—I could tell he really *was* ashamed. And even though Ralph's apology hadn't been as eloquent, I knew it was honest too. I'd like to think that's why I forgave them, but I did it because I had to. I've never been able to hold a grudge. Even people I hate, I have trouble staying mad at. It's a real weakness. Nobody likes a pushover.

"Fuck it. No big deal."

"No, it *is* a big deal." His voice sharpened. "I attacked my best friend. That's lame."

"It's been a pretty intense few weeks. Ms. Vale warned us it would be tough."

Stewart snorted. "She called me tonight."

"Why? To make you apologize?"

"No," Stewart snapped. He hesitated. "She just told me to get it together. Said if I didn't, she'd replace me."

"What? With who?"

"Guess."

"Quentin."

"Bastard's been learning my part all along."

I could just see that smug little prick sitting in front of the mirror at home, reciting Stewart's lines.

"No way can he do it as good as you. Besides, if you're out, then I'm out too. She can't lose both of us."

"Thanks, Frenchy."

I leaned over and pushed him. "Don't thank me, dude. Just don't screw up again."

We went a ways farther without talking, walking at a good clip, letting gravity pull us down the hill. In the dim starlight I could make out the tree line bordering the pit stop at the bend below.

"I have to tell you, Stewart, I just don't get it," I finally said. "Onstage, at rehearsals. I mean, where the hell do you go? It's like you're not there anymore."

He didn't say anything at first. "I just . . . ," he started, then hesitated. "I can't . . . ." There it was again—that same desperation, the haunted confusion I'd seen in his eyes at rehearsal. Only now it had crept into his voice. "He's not afraid," he said at last. "It's better this way. I'm safe."

"Safe from what? I don't know what the hell you're talking about anymore. It's weird, Stewart."

"I just need to . . ."

"Need to what? Be somebody else?" I said. "That's fucked up."

"You just don't understand the theater, Sancho." His voice was louder now, defensive.

"Horseshit. That's what that is, Stewart. Artsy horseshit. And stop calling me Sancho. My name's Frenchy, okay?"

"No, it's not, Gerry."

Fucking Stewart. "Yeah, well, you know what I mean."

"Sorry."

"Look, I just want to understand what's going on."

"I've got it figured out. Don't worry."

Don't worry. That's what my father would tell my mother every time they got in a fight, which was almost every day after he'd come back. He'd say to it me too. I'd get home from school and find him in the backyard, sitting in his plastic deck chair, chain smoking, catch him with the tears running down his face before he'd turn away and wave me off. "Don't worry. Don't worry," he'd say over and over. The more I tried to believe those words, the more I grew to hate them.

We crossed the road, then the tree line, and passed into the field. The grass was already crunchy with frost and dead leaves from the maples, and we made a lot of noise until we reached our accustomed spot. I pulled out one of the joints Ralph had made and lit it.

"Come on," I said, holding it out.

"Where'd you get that?"

"Ralph. Where else?"

"Are he and your mom still together?"

"Yeah. I mean, no. I don't fucking know." I gestured with the joint a second time. "Let's just forget about Ralph, forget about Don, forget about the play, and have a Friday night."

I could sense him hesitating in the dark. Finally, he took the joint from me. Maybe he really wanted to; maybe he felt he owed me. Either way, he did it. I could see the red light of the ember flare once, then again.

He started hacking like I'd done back at Ralph's.

"Christ." He thrust the joint away from him.

"Burns a little, don't it," I said, laughing.

We finished quickly, then stayed there in the field, laughing, telling jokes, talking shit, just like we used to.

"So we're still going out tomorrow night?" he asked.

"Hell, yeah," I said. "But I need a costume."

"Already taken care of," he said. "My mom made it last week— same time we put together mine."

"Gee, I wonder what it could be."

"Yeah, well, you've already seen mine. The Sancho suit's a lot simpler—just peasant clothes, basically. In fact, Mom made it out of hemp, just to keep it real."

We both started giggling.

"This will be great," he continued. "We can promote the play everywhere we go. Even act out little scenes, like walking advertisements. I told Ms. Vale about the plan. She thought it was a good one."

I stopped laughing. The whole thing sounded like work. But I didn't say so. He seemed pretty excited about the idea.

"It's going to be our last time trick-or-treating," I said instead.

"Yeah," he whispered.

We turned and looked across the valley. Like it did every night, the sky above the ridge glowed from the wind tower lights. They'd put these honking arrays on top of the towers to keep planes from crashing into them, and there they shone, a wavy line of red flares floating in the sky. It wasn't as bad on clear nights, like this one. But on overcast nights when the clouds were low and thick, the glow enveloped the whole region.

"Look at those fucking things, Frenchy," Stewart said, pointing his cane toward the far ridge.

"Pretty bright."

"They're like eyes. Like some monster's eyeballs. They've turned that beautiful mountain into a twenty-eyed beast."

It was probably the pot, but I could suddenly see what he was talking about.

"Maybe we should go," I said. I didn't want him to start going off again, not to mention I was freezing my ass off. But he didn't listen.

"I have to see those things at night," he went on, "from my window, in my room. They just hover there, watching me. That's why I moved my bed into the other room. I can't sleep with those things watching me. Fucking abominations."

"I can't see them from my house," I said, mostly because I was stupid and stoned and didn't know what the hell else to say. "Too many trees in the way."

"You're lucky, Sancho. You're a lucky man."

He swung his cane, whipping it in an arc, then backed up a dozen yards before turning and running for the trees. By the time we got to the road, he'd slowed down again, and we walked back up the hill in silence. But I kept stealing glances behind me from time to time, and every once in a while I could see some of those eyes, peering through the trees, following us home.

ACT THREE:
CLIMAX

CHAPTER SIXTEEN

My mother and Ralph were in the kitchen fixing dinner when Stewart showed up. He took his time getting out of the car. He had to. He was back in full Don Quixote garb—armor and helmet, wig and makeup, the works—and it was slow going, at least when it came to getting in and out of a Volvo.

It's going to be a long night, I thought, standing on the front steps, watching him try to maneuver.

Mom and Ralph came out and joined me, and the three of us waited as Stewart made his way toward us. Already, my mother was giggling. Ralph just stared with his mouth half-open like an idiot. Stewart was taking his time, walking with his shoulders drooped, and even behind that fake nose, beard, and wild eyebrows, I could see the downcast look on his face.

"Hail, Knight of the Woeful Countenance," I called out. It was one of Don Quixote's names from the musical. I thought it was a pretty clever joke myself, but Stewart didn't even crack a smile. He merely bowed in acknowledgment.

"Oh. My. God," my mother cooed. "Will you look at that!"

"Don Quixote de La Mancha, at your service," Stewart replied, bowing low again, this time with a flourish of the hand. He'd gotten used to talking with that stuff in his mouth—barely a lisp.

My mother burst out laughing at the elaborate display. Ralph smiled and shook his head and muttered "Holy shit!" a few times under his breath.

At the sight of Stewart's morose gaze, my mother sobered up a bit.

"Why so sad, Don?" she asked.

"My lady, I have lost my sword. Where it went, I do not know, but a knight without a sword is no knight at all. Hence, my sorrow."

Definitely going to be a long one, I thought.

"Oh!" my mother exclaimed. She turned and ran into the house, emerging a few seconds later with the antique sword I'd lugged home yesterday. "Would this be the sword you seek?" she asked, stifling a giggle.

At the sight of the weapon, Stewart's eyes lit up. He dropped down on one knee before her and held out his arms.

"Dearest lady!" he cried. "You have found my trusty blade. No longer will I be vulnerable to the Enchanter and his minions."

Still laughing as she played along, my mother ceremoniously laid the sword across Stewart's open palms. Stewart, in turn, took the blade and kissed it, drawing guffaws from Ralph, before returning it to his scabbard. I sighed and shook my head. In the play, the Great Enchanter is Don Quixote's imagined enemy. The old knight's all paranoid and thinks the Enchanter's after him the whole time. Don Quixote's crazy talk never bothered me that much in the play—a lot of it was kind of sweet, actually—

but for some reason, the whole Enchanter business really creeped me out. Aside from rehearsal, I'd never heard Stewart mention him before.

Stewart glanced over at me and stood up.

"Let's see. I have my sword. All I need now is my trusty, loyal servant, Sancho Panza. Has anyone seen the good fellow?"

"Right here, dipshit," I said with a little wave.

Stewart did a double take, then came over and embraced me.

"There you are, old friend!" he exclaimed, patting me on the back. "I hardly recognized you in those strange clothes. What foreign land do they hail from, pray tell?"

"It's called Walmart."

Stewart paused. "Never have I heard of such an odd place. Is it in Africa?"

"Oh, Jesus Christ."

"Well, Sancho," Stewart went on, ignoring me, "fortunately for you, I brought along some extra clothes. If you'll be so kind as to retrieve them from my carriage, you may put them on."

"Do I *have* to?"

"Frenchy!" my mother snapped. "I mean, Sancho—don't be an old fart. It's Halloween, for chrissake."

"Yeah, right, whatever." I headed for the car.

"We'll finish making the salad while you get changed," my mother called out. "Dinner in ten minutes."

"We eagerly await the feast, my lady!" Stewart replied.

My mother giggled again as she and Ralph walked up the front steps, holding hands. Stewart watched them disappear before turning back to me with a smile. I gave him a couple slow claps, and he bowed.

"No, I'm not coming out," I said. "I look like an idiot."

"Come on, sweetie," my mother called from the other side of the bedroom door. "We just want to see you. And these ribs are going to get cold."

Fucking ribs. My mother had been baking a huge pile of baby back ribs—my favorite meal—all afternoon, adding layer after layer of barbecue sauce, so that the whole trailer smelled like pork heaven. I was so hungry now, I could hardly stand it.

I slowly opened the door and walked out. What can I say? I'm a slave to my animal urges.

Sure enough, everyone started laughing as I came into the kitchen.

"Yeah, thanks," I muttered. "Thanks a lot."

In my beige hemp peasant gear, I looked like an extra from one of those old Mexican cowboy movies. You know that guy—the one in the village who gets shot by banditos in the first scene and no one really gives a crap. It was the wide-brimmed floppy hat that did it. That and the stuffing Stewart's mother had sewn into the stomach of the shirt, making me look even fatter than usual. I didn't bother with the beard. I hadn't shaved since yesterday morning, so I already had enough black stubble to pass for a grubby servant.

"Oh, don't you look cute," my mother said, coming over and pinching my cheek.

"Sancho!" Stewart cried, taking my hand. "It's so good to finally see you. I've been lost without you, old friend."

"Yeah, yeah." I turned to Ralph. "Don't say a fucking word."

"No way, bro," he said, holding up his hands. "You look pretty sweet."

My mother made Stewart and me stand together against the wall and took a million goddam pictures. It wasn't that bad, actually—we really did look like Sancho and Don stepping right out of the movie.

After the photo shoot, we dug into dinner. The quiet was okay at first—everyone was just eating—but after a while it started to get uncomfortable. I guess none of us really knew what to say. Ralph, for once in his life, was keeping his mouth shut no matter what. You could tell he was terrified of blowing it and wasn't going to take any chances by saying something stupid. Mom, for her part, kept giving him little glances between bites, with this weird sort of curious look on her face, as if she was wondering when he was going to say something stupid and why he hadn't already. Having Ralph around was like having a pet chimp in your house—funny and cute for a while, but you never knew when he was suddenly going to take a big crap right in the middle of your floor.

Mom didn't seem too thrilled that morning when I first told her I'd invited Ralph over for dinner, but her mood improved almost right away, especially when I mentioned him saying how much he'd missed her, so I figured she was secretly pleased. Still, she seemed a little uncertain at the dinner table. Maybe she was having second thoughts. I couldn't blame her. I was feeling pretty uncertain too—half pissed at myself for not cutting the douche bag out when I had a chance, half proud of not being a selfish asshole for once in my life.

Stewart was the only one at the table who seemed oblivious to any awkwardness. He just looked around and smiled from time to time and picked a little at his food without really eating much.

"Oh, God!" my mother cried. The rest of us jumped a little in our chairs. Even Stewart.

"Stewart, I'm so sorry. I forgot you were a vegetarian. I should have made you something else."

Sure enough, Stewart hadn't touched his ribs. But he wasn't a vegetarian. Not anymore. He had been one for most of junior year but fell off the wagon last spring. The whole Bolger family ate meat, actually, but only the organic stuff, and only once in a while.

"*Don Quixote* is no vegetarian, my lady," Stewart said with a stern gaze.

"Yeah, and neither is Stewart. So don't worry about it, Mom."

"As warriors, we knights are, by nature, carnivorous," Stewart continued, ignoring me. "However, while on a quest, it is my custom to avoid an excess of food and drink, essentially to fast, if you will. One must purify the body to purify the soul."

"Oh," my mother said, hesitating. "I see."

"But make no mistake, my lady," Stewart added. "This feast you have prepared and the company of your table in this fine castle far exceeds my worthiness. I do humbly say, if I were not already pledged to the beautiful Dulcinea and you were not already under the protection of this most noble gentleman, I would surely undertake to be your knight."

"Oh," my mother said. "Well, that sounds nice."

"He just doesn't want to get barbecue sauce on his beard," I said.

"Oh, stop it, Frenchy," my mother said. She smiled across the table at Stewart. "Thank you, Don, for those kind words. It's nice to hear the voice of a *gentleman* for a change." She cast a quick glance first at me, then at Ralph, who squirmed a little in his seat.

"No thanks are needed," Stewart said. "As a knight, it is my duty to honor all fair creatures of virtue such as yourself. There is nothing in this world more worth cherishing than the essences of purity, goodness, and beauty one finds in a lady, nothing except perhaps the love that such an essence brings. I can tell you that the love I bear for my sweet Dulcinea gives me enough strength to fight a hundred battles, to slay a thousand giants. Surely your own knight feels the same way about you."

My mother and Ralph swapped shy smiles. Mom gave a quick, nervous laugh. Both of them were blushing. Trying not to gag, I pretended not to notice the exchange. Instead I reached across the table for Stewart's ribs. *No point letting them go to waste,* I thought.

"You know something, Don, you're one funny bastard," Ralph said, reaching over to give Stewart an affectionate slap on the back. "All that Dungeons and Dragons talk. That's crazy shit, bro."

It was the first time he'd spoken since we'd sat down for supper, and my mother and I glanced at each other quickly, wondering if the chimp were about to crap. But Ralph went back to gnawing on a rib. Stewart just shook his head a little and gave a sad smile.

"Crazy?" he said. He paused dramatically. I could tell he was getting ready to really start slinging it. Sure enough, out it came.

"Some say I, Don Quixote, am mad. But I ask you—when life itself seems lunatic, who knows where madness lies? Perhaps to be too practical is madness. To surrender dreams—this may be madness. To seek treasure where there is only trash. Too much sanity may be madness. And maddest of all, to see life as it is and not as it should be."

We were all quiet for a moment when he finished. Ralph and my mother were both staring at Stewart with their mouths slightly open. I just snorted and shook my head. I'd heard that speech about ten times already in rehearsals last week.

"Wow, Stewart," my mother whispered. "That was beautiful."

"It's just a line from the play, Mom," I said. "That's all it is. Besides, you can see life as it should be all you want, but that's not going to stop life as it is from kicking you right in the balls."

"I don't know," Ralph spoke up. He was shaking his head and had this funny look on his face. I imagined a deep-thought alert (ah-*ooh*-ga!) going off in his pea-sized brain. "What Don says there is kinda true, if you think about it. I mean, you gotta dream, bro."

Stewart nodded his thanks. My mother gave a wistful sort of sigh.

"Reminds me of your father, Frenchy," she said. "He used to say the whole world was crazy. Said that's why he liked being a soldier. War was the only thing that made sense to him."

I snorted again. "There's nothing crazier than war, Mom. It's just one big clusterfuck."

"Not if you're a soldier," she said. "You have your mission. You have the enemy. The battle lines are drawn. That's what he used to say, anyway."

"Yeah, well he didn't say that when he got back."

Her eyes filled with tears. "No," she whispered. "I guess not."

I looked away, toward Stewart. He just sat there with a faint smile on his lips, not eating, his hands pressed together as if he were praying, his eyes far away.

Chapter Seventeen

"We're not taking any candy," Stewart said as we set out. It was the only time he broke character all night.

"But it's Halloween. Probably my last time trick-or-treating. I got to get *something*."

"You want candy, I'll buy you some. Tonight is just about promoting the play."

"Fine," I groused. "But pull over a minute." We were approaching the pit stop.

"For what purpose, Sancho?" he asked, falling back into his Don Quixote voice.

"Maybe you can pull this shit off straight, but I can't. I'll need some enhancement if we're going to go around performing for the whole goddam town all night."

Stewart sighed and shook his head. "All this talk of 'need,' Sancho. I'm disappointed in you, old friend."

"Look, do you want me to do this with you or not?"

Without a word, he slowed down the Volvo and pulled into the field. I started to open the door, then hesitated.

"You joining me?"

"Always the peasant, dear Sancho," he said. "No, thank you. Your crude form of intoxication has no appeal to me."

I laughed. "Oh, come on, Stewart. You just smoked up with me last night."

"Whatever this Stewart fellow you continue to carry on about did or did not do last night, or any other night, is of no interest to me. Now, if you will please hurry up, Sancho, I'd like to get on with our quest."

"Fine." I slammed the door behind me.

It was a bit warmer than last night. The clear sky was gone. A breeze was picking up, and the clouds were moving in, low and thick. I fired up the joint, took a few quick puffs, then put it out. For a minute I just stood there, watching the sky glow over the valley from the wind tower lights.

Glancing down at my outfit, I felt a strange sort of giddiness. I could feel one of those moments coming upon me. You know the kind, where you look around and wonder how you got to this spot, and you think about the person you're with and the things that happened to bring you both here, and none of it seems real.

Before I knew it, I was humming, then singing. My voice sounded strange, like someone else's.

I'm Sancho! Yes, I'm Sancho!
I'll follow my master till the end.
I'll tell all the world proudly
I'm his squire! I'm his—

The horn beeped twice and the engine started. Don was tired of waiting. I got back in the car.

"Ready, Your Grace," I said, and we continued on our way.

I wasn't sure how the night was going to go when we started. As we headed up the walkway of the first house, an elderly couple met us on the front porch. They'd seen us coming and had decided to launch a preemptive strike.

"How old are you boys?" the old man asked.

I was too busy staring at his long, rubbery earlobes to speak. Fortunately, I had Stewart.

"My good sir," he said, "we know no age. I am the illustrious Don Quixote de La Mancha, and this rotund little fellow by my side is my slow but ever-faithful manservant, Sancho Panza!"

I shot him a dark look as we both bowed.

"You boys are too old for trick-or-treating!" the old woman barked, glaring at us through a huge pair of glasses. "Go on, shoo!"

"Oh, fair one—we have no need of your confectionary delights. As you can see, my dear servant is nearly too plump to carry my baggage as it is."

"I'm going to kick your ass when this is over," I whispered to him. He ignored me and kept going.

"We only wish to entreat you to come to Gilliam High School on November twentieth for the opening night of our play. Refreshments *will* be served in the lobby at intermission."

"Something wrong with that boy," the old man muttered. He kept saying it as Stewart stepped up and knelt before his wife.

Stewart produced a rose from somewhere inside his costume. "A blossom for a blossom."

She took the offered flower, brought it to her face, and gave a tentative sniff.

"It's the real thing," she said, turning to her husband, who just continued to mutter.

"And now," Stewart continued, "we'd like to regale you with a brief snippet of what you will enjoy if you make it to any one of our shows."

We launched into an early scene where Quixote attacks a windmill with bewildered enthusiasm, mistaking it for an evil giant. It's one of the most familiar scenes, not to mention one of the most dramatic, with lots of physical comedy. The old woman's mouth turned up into a smile as we performed, and even the old man stopped scowling for a minute. We ended with a couple verses from the title song, then took a long bow.

A round of applause and cheering broke out behind us. We turned to see a group of kids watching us wide-eyed in their cute little costumes. They cheered even louder than the parents standing behind them did.

We took a second low bow. Stewart and I looked at each other with shit-eating grins as the kids ran up to check out our costumes and ask us about the play. It was my first taste of real acting, and I could feel the love that had been growing ever since we started rehearsals take hold on a whole new level. Stewart, of course, was on the money, but I held my own. You might even say I was just as good.

I have to admit, I was a bit surprised. Until our last stop, the night turned out to be a blast. We went from place to place, hitting houses in the village, then outside of town.

"That was awesome, Stewart," I said as we started home. "I mean, we fucking rocked it."

"It was a most successful evening indeed, old friend."

I thought back to the lines he'd recited at dinner about playing it too safe, being too practical, the problem with too much sanity. Stewart had fallen into the role, had been driving me crazy the last couple weeks with his obsession, but if it weren't for him becoming Don Quixote, I never would have become Sancho and we never would have made all those people so happy tonight. And remembering the look on my mother's face, that look of hope, and how he'd cast a spell over them, even that douche bag Ralph—I couldn't help but think that maybe Stewart becoming Don wasn't such a bad thing. I hadn't seen her look that happy since the day my father came back from the Middle East. Maybe Stewart was right. Maybe I needed to start relaxing more, start dreaming more, and not worry so much.

I was about to tell Stewart when I noticed he'd turned off the main road.

"Where are you going?" I asked. "I thought you said we were done." I was pretty exhausted and looking forward to heading home and crawling into bed.

"One more stop, old friend." He stared straight ahead at the road as it twisted and turned its way up a steep hill.

I looked around, trying to figure out where we were, but with all the trees it was hard to say. Stewart had grown very quiet in the meantime. When I asked him again where we were going, he smiled.

The road leveled off. Soon I could see a gate ahead, a chain-link fence stretching away on both sides. Then we were out of the trees, and I suddenly realized where we were.

I hadn't been up to the wind towers in the year since they'd become operational. In fact, the only time I'd been here was when work at the site was getting started. Then it was nothing but a bunch of cement trucks and bulldozers buzzing around a vast, blasted-rock-strewn clearing, with cranes unloading huge piles of material from a steady stream of trucks.

Not anymore. It's one thing seeing the towers from afar, sprouting from the ridge in a lazy line. Even though the mountain and the surrounding distances give a sense of proportion, it's another thing entirely to see one up close, to see the massive network of steel soaring into the sky, the sixty-foot blades of the turbine stretching out. I had to lean forward and practically press my forehead against the windshield just to see the top of the nearest tower.

"Holy shit, Stewart," I whispered as we came to a stop. I turned to him. "What the hell are we doing here?"

Stewart didn't answer. He turned off the headlights and, after the usual struggle, got out of the car. I stayed where I was, listening to my heart pound, while he went around the back and fetched something from the trunk. A moment later my door opened, and there he was, a set of bolt cutters in his hands.

"Onward to glory we go, Sancho."

"You mean there?" I cried, pointing to the towers. "Are you out of your fucking mind?"

"Come, old friend, our quest awaits."

"What quest?"

"The quest for knowledge, of course."

He turned and strode off toward the gate. For a second I thought about just staying put, but finally I couldn't take it and jumped out.

"This is a bad idea," I said, catching up to him at the gate. I tried to ignore the signs hanging from the fence. It was too dark to read them, but I could guess what they said.

"I need to see it, Sancho," Stewart replied, grunting as he cut through the huge padlock on the gate. "I need to see the Great Enchanter's work up close with my own two eyes."

He pushed through the open gate, and I followed him, glancing around me as we made our way toward the nearest tower.

I could see pretty well under the tower lights. Not that there was much to see—aside from the row of towers stretching across the treeless ridgeline, the clearing was mostly empty. Just some broken boulders here and there, except along the edges, where the ground was still ripped up, strewn with the remnants of tree stumps and bulldozed piles of torn earth. A few dark spots littered the ground—bird carcasses, all feathers and bone, victims of the turning blades. The lighting was strange. The twenty towers' shadows cast bizarre patterns, fragmenting the bloodred glare. Strangest of all was the noise—there was enough of a breeze to get the turbines spinning at a steady pace, setting up a sound that rose and fell between a rumble and a groan. Not the place you want to be on a Halloween night when you've been smoking pot. I felt like I was in hell.

We stopped at the base of the first tower. Stewart wanted to keep going, but I refused. The unrelenting sound, not to mention the fact that we were trespassing, had turned me into one giant exposed nerve. I started to worry that someone was going to come along. Police, security guards, power company ninjas rappelling down from the towers, ready to kill us and attach our bodies to the spinning blades above.

"Quest completed," I hollered. "Can we go now?"

Stewart just looked around, turning slowly in a circle, spreading out his arms.

"Look at this place, Sancho," he shouted back. "Behold the Enchanter's wasteland. The heart of evil!"

"Yeah, so let's go."

He shook his head and kept turning. Spotting a pile of beer cans nearby, I went over to check it out, happy for the distraction. A bunch of rocks had been put in a circle, a few burned ends of logs still within the ring.

"Well, someone's been partying up here," I called over to Stewart. I kicked one of the cans. "Probably the Pokers. This is their kind of place."

Stewart wasn't listening. He was now crawling around one of the legs, inspecting the base. I watched him for a while as he felt along the steel, tapping and knocking. Finally, I'd had enough.

"Okay, that's it," I shouted. "I'm going back to the car!"

He looked over at me, then picked himself up, turning back to gaze into the ruby light. The wind had picked up, and the roar along with it, all twenty turbines now ripping at a steady pace. Stewart raised his fist and shouted something, but with all the noise I couldn't hear what he was saying.

Then he drew his sword.

I started running toward him just as he swung at the nearest footing with all his strength.

The scatter of sparks from metal striking metal, the piercing ring that cut right through the roaring, the sight of the sword shattering, Stewart's wounded cry—it all became one sensation. The next thing I knew, I was at his side as he lay there on the ground, moaning with his eyes closed.

"Stewart! Come on, get up!"

He didn't answer. He didn't even open his eyes. He just kept moaning.

"Jesus Christ, Stewart!" I was starting to get afraid now. I slapped his face lightly until he finally opened his eyes. They looked dark, hollow in the red light.

"Stewart!" I hollered again. "Stewart, are you okay?"

He moved his mouth a little, but no words came out. A faint smile appeared on his lips. I jumped up and paced back and forth a few times. I wanted to get the hell out of there before anything else happened.

"All right, buddy, let's go." I helped him to his feet, led him back to the Volvo, and put him in the passenger's seat.

"I'll drive," I said. He nodded before closing his eyes again. It wasn't until we reached the village that he finally opened his eyes and leaned forward.

"Welcome back," I said. He looked down at his hands.

"Still vibrating, are they?" I asked.

He gave a little smile and sank back into the seat, though he didn't really seem to relax until we were well up on the Heights and nearing home.

"Care to tell me what the hell happened back there?"

"Got a little carried away, that's all."

"Yeah, just a little."

So much for life as it should be and all that Don Quixote bullshit from dinner.

I thought of Kaela's number, sitting on my desk back at the house. I'd forgotten all about calling her after changing into my costume. She was probably out there right now, sitting around a fire, having a beer, talking to somebody who wasn't me.

"Pull over, Sancho," he said as we approached my house. I didn't slow down.

"Screw that. I'm bringing you home."

"No need. I am quite recovered."

I ignored him and kept driving all the way to Shangri La.

I turned off the engine in front of the darkened house, and we sat there for a moment, tired and empty in the silence. Finally we both got out. He was still a little unsteady on his feet, but he could make it on his own. I was glad—I'd had to help my old man into bed more than a few times last spring on those nights when he'd been boozing. It was a major pain in the ass.

Stewart patted me on the shoulder as I walked up onto the deck with him.

"Thank you, old friend." He paused before the door.

The crescent moon had risen enough to cast a thin light over us. The night was cold—no crickets, no birds. The silence had followed us from the car. I didn't know what to say to the small shadow of a person standing beside me in the dim. I looked out across the valley to the row of red lights on the ridge. They looked smaller, too.

Gazing at the tower lights, I realized I'd forgotten to grab the remnants of his sword. I wondered what else we'd left on that mountaintop.

"Call me tomorrow, Stewart. We need to talk."

He looked back down at his hands and nodded before going inside. Shaken by the transformation, I watched him disappear. He'd given me this spectacular night, only to turn around and destroy it, as if it were too good for me to keep. It seemed to be the way of things these days with Stewart.

"Farewell, Your Grace," I whispered, then stumbled home to bed.

CHAPTER EIGHTEEN

The next day was a Sunday, cold and wet and gray. I kept waiting for Stewart to call, but he never did. I even thought about going to Shangri La to see how he was holding up, but in the end I chickened out. I figured it wouldn't hurt to give him some time to get his shit together. I was pretty exhausted myself—it had been an intense night on the heels of an intense couple weeks, not to mention that two days of smoking after a month of abstinence had left me feeling a bit fuzzy. It had been so long since I'd gone more than a week without getting baked, I wondered if I'd been this way all along and just never noticed. Either way, I didn't like it much now. I even almost threw away what was left of the second joint Ralph had given me. Almost.

All through the day, the weirdness of the previous night kept coming back to me. It seemed foggy, like a dream—being there under the towers, watching Stewart lose it, watching his sword shatter in the red light. It made me feel better to think of it that way. Nothing but a dream, like the ones that come in the night, the kind you shrug off before falling back asleep because you're just so tired. Of course, what you wake up to can be far worse. My father had taught me that. His last lesson.

But this was different. Stewart wasn't like Dad. It was just a blip. I'd simply underestimated the stress Stewart was up against, the feeling—at least in his mind—that he was carrying the weight of the production on his shoulders.

That's what I told myself, anyway. But deep down in my gut, as I looked out the bedroom window at the empty plastic chair in the backyard and watched the rain turn to snow, I couldn't help but wonder whether this whole thing was bigger than that, bigger than the play, bigger than I could handle.

I waved a hand in front of my face, the way Stewart always did. "Put it away, put it away," I whispered. I could hear his voice in my head. *No fear, Sancho. No fear.*

Then Monday morning came along. Hearing a vehicle pull in, I grabbed my backpack and headed out the door, only to see Mrs. Bolger in the driveway, her SUV idling. As I came over, she didn't smile the way she usually did.

She rolled down the window.

"Frenchy, hi," she said, managing a slight smile. "Stewart's not feeling too well today. He's going to stay home."

"Oh," I said. "Well, that's okay. I can walk to school."

"Nonsense! Stewart insisted I give you a ride. Hop in."

I went around to the passenger side and got in, and we headed off. We didn't say much on the way down Suffolk Heights. It was pretty awkward, actually, just the two of us in the car. We'd never spent any real time alone.

"So I hope he's okay," I offered as we crossed the river and headed toward the village. "What's he got? Cold or something?"

She hesitated. "Nothing like that. He's just tired, that's all. Poor thing hardly got out of bed yesterday. It's the play—the production is running him ragged."

"It's a lot of work," I agreed. "And he has the biggest role of anyone."

She nodded. "But we're so pleased he's doing it. That you both are. It's just so cool. Stewart says you're quite good."

"Not as good as him."

"Well, it's certainly become his new passion. You know Stewart—whatever he does, it's all or nothing."

"Yeah, you could say that."

She nodded again, her mouth tightening into a little frown. "He was furious with me for keeping him home. Didn't want to miss rehearsal. But . . . I insisted."

"It won't be a big deal for him to miss one day," I said. "We can work around it."

"Good."

We didn't say much else until we reached the school.

"Well," she said as we turned into the parking lot, "tell Ms. Vale she'll have him back tomorrow, rested and ready to go."

"I will."

We pulled up in front of the school. I thanked her for the ride and was about to get out when she stopped me.

"Frenchy, you don't think this whole theater business is too much for Stewart to handle, do you?"

She had this weird expression on her face, all worried and intense. With her long hair pulled back in a ponytail, she suddenly looked like Stewart in a way I'd never noticed. I shifted a little in my seat. We were moving beyond awkward now into something else entirely. I knew she was looking for me to say the right thing;

I just couldn't tell what it was she wanted to hear. I didn't even know the right answer myself.

"I don't think so," I said at last. I hesitated. "I mean, do you?"

"I don't know. He's so focused. It's been difficult." She took a deep breath. "He's just going through a phase." She looked over at me and smiled. "Everyone does at some point, don't they?"

"I've certainly had my share."

As soon as the words left my mouth I regretted it. Her smile vanished, her eyes filled with tears, and there it was—the look.

"Oh, Frenchy, you poor thing," she said. "Of course you have."

I opened the door and grabbed my backpack.

"Yeah, but it's okay. I'm good."

She nodded. "I'm sorry," she said. She could tell I was embarrassed. "I'm just a little tired this morning."

"No problem," I said. "And don't worry about Stewart. Three weeks from now, this'll all be over. In the meantime, he's got me to look out for him."

"I know he does. Thank you, Frenchy."

"Yeah, well, thanks again for the ride." I shut the door and took off. My skull felt like it was on fire, like I'd just come from a pit stop. I wished I had.

"Want another?" Bryant said, pushing the candy dish a few inches my way.

"No thanks."

We'd been at it for ten minutes or so. Nothing too serious— just the normal chitchat, a little update on how things were going, that sort of thing. "Checking in," he liked to call it.

He leaned back in his chair—slowly, quietly—and gave a little smile, and that's when I knew we were heading for deeper waters.

He always made that move when it was time to get serious. By now, I also knew it was up to me to go first. Hence the pause, the inviting smile. Another little trick from the old shrink handbook, I figured. No big deal. I could play along.

"So, did you miss me?" I asked.

At our last session, Bryant had suggested we start meeting every other week. "You seem to be making progress," he'd said. I didn't really know how the hell he could tell something like that based on a few hours of conversation, but I didn't argue.

"Sure did. You're quite entertaining, you know."

"Yeah, thanks. I get that a lot."

"You'll be getting it a lot more, I'm sure, after the play. Ms. Vale says you're very talented."

"Oh yeah?" I said. "So what else did she say?"

Bryant laughed. "Not too much else. Just that you're a hard worker. That the other kids really seem to like you. You know, that kind of stuff."

"Oh. That's cool, I guess. What about Stewart?" I started to reach once more for the candy dish, then hesitated and grabbed the baseball sitting next to it instead.

"What *about* Stewart?"

"Well, what did she say about him?" The ball's leather felt soft in my hand, the stitches worn. I guessed it had seen some serious play.

"What makes you think we talked about him?" he asked.

"Never mind," I said, and tossed him the ball. He caught it with one hand.

I could see his gaze sharpen. Just a little.

"Do *you* want to talk about Stewart?"

Ah, good one, Bryant. Very clever.

"We can," I said. "If you want. I mean, I don't feel a need to or anything."

He tossed the ball back. "No. But he is an important person in your life. You mention him quite a bit."

My thumb traced the curve of the ball's stitching, an endless loop. "Well, we're in the play together. We spend a lot of time together."

"Would you say your friendship is a good one?"

I looked up at him. "Sure. Why wouldn't it be?"

"No reason. It's good to have a close friend, Gerry, especially in tough times. And this whole development with the play is great too. You've seemed a lot happier in our last few conversations compared to the beginning of the year."

"Yeah, well," I said, putting the ball back on the desk, "there've been a lot of changes."

"Like what? I mean, besides the play."

"Just stuff," I said. "I've gotten to know this girl a little. She's pretty cool."

Bryant nodded. I thought for a second he was going to let me get by with that, but then he came right at me.

"How about the smoking? How's that going?"

I glanced up at him, then shook my head and looked away.

Bryant held up a hand. "Don't worry, I'm not going to get you in trouble or anything like that. Not in this room. It's just part of the conversation. And it's something we haven't really talked about yet. Maybe now's the time."

"Yeah, but it's not really that important, is it?"

"That depends," he said. "It can be pretty important."

"Okay. Well, the good news is that I stopped. When the play started, I stopped. For the most part."

"And what does that mean?"

"Well, I had a little this weekend. You know, Halloween and everything."

He smiled. "Halloween, huh? It didn't have anything to do with Friday? With what happened at rehearsal?"

I frowned. "Who told you anything happened at rehearsal?"

He didn't say anything. Just gave me his goddam Yoda smile.

"I'm not a druggie."

"I never suggested you were."

"I mean, it's not like any time something bad happens to me, I have to turn around and get high. It's not like I was walking around baked all the time or anything. In fact, it wasn't even my idea most of the time. Most of the time, I couldn't have cared less. It gets kind of boring after a while."

"So whose idea was it, then?"

I didn't say anything. I just folded my arms and frowned.

"Fair enough," he said. "Let's try this instead—if it wasn't your idea, if getting high was boring, then why did you do it?"

"I don't know. Something to do. I mean, I was doing it way before everything happened with my father."

He hesitated. "Listen, Gerry, people do drugs, alcohol, all that stuff for a whole bunch of reasons. Sometimes it's to have fun, sometimes it's because they're bored, sometimes it's to fit in, that sort of thing. And in terms of the outcome, it can vary too. Sometimes it's a problem from the very start. Sometimes it's never a problem. And sometimes it starts off okay, only to become a problem later on. As a counselor, I get especially concerned if a person's using while going through a rough patch, through something major."

"You mean like a death, right?" I snapped. "Yeah, I get it."

"I'm sure you do. So you probably know that when you're going through a difficult spell, you're more vulnerable. Your defenses are down. Drugs and alcohol—they're kind of like medicine. They make you feel better. You know, keep the demons at bay. It's really as simple as that. There's even a term for it: self-medicating."

"Hey, if it works, right?"

He raised his eyebrows. "Well, that's the problem, Gerry. It doesn't. Not in the long run. All you're left with is a nasty little chemical dependency problem on top of everything else. Makes everything more complicated. Very tricky."

"So it's a good thing I stopped, then." I sat back in my chair with a grin.

"Yeah, I'd say so. A smart move."

"Well, it was Stewart's idea for us to quit, really. He's on this whole purity kick."

"Because of the play?"

"Something like that." I looked up at him.

"Speaking of Stewart," he said, "I wanted to ask you about him. How's he been lately?"

I kind of froze up. I tried not to, but I started thinking about the Friday afternoon freakout, about Saturday night at the towers. And then that look on Mrs. Bolger's face this morning, that look of fear.

Bryant, of course, noticed. When I didn't answer, he tried again.

"So this thing happened on Friday, right? Stewart lost control. You fought."

"You make it sound so dramatic."

"How did it make you feel?" he asked, ignoring me.

"How did it make me feel? Wow. What a penetrating question. Where'd you learn that one—*Therapy for Dummies?*"

He just laughed, the bastard. "You're stalling now. Come on. Did it make you angry?"

"No."

"Worried?"

"Not really," I said. "We'd been busting our asses all week. We were all a bit punchy."

"Well," he said with a shrug, "there's punchy, and then there's punchy."

"Everyone has bad days. Besides, why are we even talking about him? I'm the one who's fucked up, right?"

Bryant didn't say anything. He just leaned back in that stupid chair of his—slowly, quietly. I don't know how much time passed, but it felt far too long.

"He's going through a phase, that's all," I said at last. Mrs. Bolger's line suddenly sounded pretty good. "A lot of pressure with the play and everything. It's just a few more weeks."

"Did you know he's failing all his classes?"

I looked up. Bryant wasn't smiling anymore.

"Why are you telling me this?" I said. "I mean, you're not supposed to go around talking about other students' grades like this, are you? Isn't it, like, a confidentiality breach or something?"

Bryant shrugged. "Normally, I wouldn't. But you're Stewart's best friend. And you're a pretty smart guy, even if you do try to hide it. I figured I'd ask if you knew what was going on."

"Why don't you just ask him?"

"I probably will. But I wanted to see what you thought first."

"Okay. Well, here's what I think—there's nothing wrong with Stewart. He just thinks about things differently. He always has. That's what I like about him. But he knows what he's about. And if other people have a problem with that, then that's too fucking bad for them."

I was looking down at my feet, but I could feel him staring at me.

"You're a very loyal friend, Gerry," he finally said.

"Yeah, thanks."

He glanced at his watch. "See you in two weeks?"

"Fine."

He gave me one last smile. "We can meet next week instead, if you want. You can come here anytime."

"That's okay," I said, standing up. "I'm good."

⠃⠃ CHAPTER NINETEEN ⠃⠃

At rehearsal that afternoon, people were still weirded out by Friday's events. When Stewart didn't appear, they got even more nervous.

It made me realize just how much he was the heart of the production, and not because he was the lead role. We tried blocking out the last few scenes, focusing on some places where Don Quixote—or Cervantes—wasn't as prominent, but the performances were lifeless. The timing was off, none of us could get our lines straight, attention wandered. Without Don Quixote, without Stewart, the show had no soul.

I was relieved when Ms. Vale called it quits early. I wanted to get back and check on Stewart.

"Okay," Ms. Vale said, gathering us all onstage. "Every production has a bad day or two. We just happened to have ours back to back. That's good—now that we've got them out of the way, we can really focus. We've got less than three weeks of rehearsal left. Not much room for mistakes. When Stewart comes back tomorrow, we'll finish blocking, squeeze in another stumble-through or two, then start working scenes. That'll take us all the way to the end of next week, leaving a week for dress rehearsal. Then it's showtime. Any questions?"

I raised my hand. "Yeah, what does 'working scenes' mean?"

When we first started, questions like that usually drew snarky eye rolls or sighs, but no one made a peep. Maybe they'd gotten used to my ignorance. Or maybe they were just too freaked out by the schedule to care.

"When we block out scenes," Ms. Vale explained, "we're not going for perfection. But then we go back and work through the scenes that were problematic. You know, to give them a bit of polish. So we basically work the scene until it's just right."

"Oh, and one more thing, folks," she said. "It looks like we're going to have to have not one but two Hell Saturdays, so mark your calendars."

We all looked at one another and groaned.

I turned to Kaela. "Hell Saturday?"

"We go from eight in the morning until six. A full day of rehearsal."

"No moaning, people," Ms. Vale snapped. Everyone quieted down. She looked each of us in the eye and smiled. "I know it's a lot to ask, but keep centered on the performance. I said when we started that I thought this would be the greatest show Gilliam has ever produced, and now I'm sure of it. So go home, relax, and come back ready to work. *Off-book.*"

We quietly dispersed, all of us feeling the weight of what was ahead. Ms. Vale pulled me aside on my way out.

"You sure Stewart will be back tomorrow?" she asked with only the slightest hint of desperation in her voice. It was weird to see her so on edge. I didn't like it at all.

"Yeah. I talked to his mother this morning."

She nodded quickly. "Good. We can't have another day like this."

"It's Monday," I said. "Nothing good ever happens on a Monday."

She smiled. "You okay? How was the weekend?"

"It was all right. Stewart and I went out and drummed up some publicity."

"He told me his plan," she said, laughing. "I'm sure you were wonderful. That was a great idea."

"It was."

"I called Stewart Friday night. We had a little chat."

I nodded. "He told me."

"He sounded tired. Keep an eye out for him, will you, Frenchy? Just like Sancho would."

"Yeah, okay."

I hurried out of the auditorium. As if trying to be Sancho in rehearsal wasn't hard enough, now I was stuck with the role twenty-four hours a day.

"Frenchy?"

I felt a hand on my shoulder and jumped. It was Kaela. She looked amused.

"Sorry. I didn't see you."

"You in a hurry?"

"I just want to get home."

"Well, let me give you a ride. I mean, Stewart's not here, right?"

I nodded. We walked out to her car together in silence. I kept trying to think of something to say. I'd never had trouble talking to her before, but now that it seemed there was something between us, it was different. All awkward and wonderful and scary all at once.

"So this is becoming quite a habit," I said as we got into the car, then grimaced. Fucking cheesy.

She just laughed. "I missed you on Halloween."

I grimaced again. "I forgot that I already had plans to go out with Stewart. It's kind of a tradition."

"Yeah, I heard all about your little escapade."

"You did?" My heart started pounding.

"Well, yeah. Lots of people were talking about you performing *La Mancha* in your costumes."

"Oh." I sank back against the seat in relief.

"I mean, it's cool," she said, misreading the look on my face. "I wish I'd seen it."

I mustered a smile. "It was fun. Good practice, actually," I said. "I'm sorry about the party. I should have called you."

"That's okay. Next time."

"Definitely."

We left school and the awkward silence behind and headed for the Heights, chatting the whole way. I cracked a few jokes and got her laughing pretty hard. She had a nice laugh. Loud and rugged and full, with a little snort at the end that was kind of goofy and cute.

Pretty soon we were back at my house.

"So," she said, drawing out the word and pausing, making my heart beat hard all over again. "Should I come in? I don't have to be anywhere for a while."

"Oh," I said. I must have sounded surprised because she shrank a little bit.

Of course, I *was* surprised. I was shocked, in fact, because I'm an idiot. I'd been so focused on getting home and running up to Shangri La that the possibility of something like this happening hadn't even occurred to me, and now I didn't know what to do. I mean, all day I'd been thinking about Stewart, one worry piling on another with every new conversation, from Mrs. Bolger to Mr.

Bryant to Ms. Vale. And now this girl was inviting herself into my house and all I wanted to do was ditch my friend and say yes. Life has a cruel sense of humor sometimes.

"Well, yeah . . . that would be great." Then I hesitated. "Normally, that would be awesome, actually."

She winced a little and so did I; we both knew what I was going to say.

"But I can't today. I've got some stuff I have to do. Sorry. Really, sorry."

"It's Stewart, isn't it?"

I sighed. "I want to check on him, see how he's doing. Ms. Vale's really worried, I think."

She gave a smile and nodded. "You should go."

"I mean, any other time. Really."

She laughed. "It's okay. Tell Stewart we missed him today."

She reached over and squeezed my hand, and I panicked all over again. Was I supposed to kiss her or what? I didn't have a clue.

So I did the gentlemanly thing. I yelped some sort of goodbye, jumped out of the car like a pussy, and ran for the house without looking back. Look, I'm no Don. Just a sad little Sancho.

It was getting gloomy in the woods. Yesterday's storm had finally started to move out, leaving a narrow band of open sky on the horizon through which the sun was quickly sinking, casting an eerie glow against the trees under a roof of purple clouds. The temperature was dropping and the air was getting crisp, but the ground was still soaked from the day of rain, so my steps were silent on the leaves.

By the time I'd made it up to Shangri La, Stewart was gone. Mrs. Bolger met me at the door with her usual grin through the window.

"Frenchy, hi," she said, finally opening the door. Whatever angst she'd had this morning seemed to have disappeared.

"Hello, Mrs. Bolger." I stepped inside. "Just wanted to stop by and check on Stewart."

Mr. Bolger was sitting on a stool at the counter, reading the *Boston Globe*, which is what he could usually be found doing when he wasn't in his shop. He lowered the paper when I came in and gave me a nod.

"Stewart's outside," he said. "Wanted to go practice his lines, since he missed rehearsal."

"Outside?"

Mr. Bolger shrugged. "Why not? Good to get some fresh air. He's been cooped up in his room for almost two days straight."

He went back to reading the paper. Mrs. Bolger's smile faded. There it was, that same look from this morning.

"Try the path," she suggested.

So I headed out, all rattled by a day of bizarre turns. Forget the weird ride to school and the crappy rehearsal—Kaela's invitation was gnawing at me more than anything, and the farther into the woods I got, the more I felt like an idiot for turning her down. Then there was Bryant with all his bullshit talk about self-medicating, like I was some pathetic basket case who couldn't handle it.

I could see Stewart up ahead now through the maples, perched on the smoking rock, doing what looked like some weird sort of dance. Slowing down, I pulled my coat tight around me and drew closer. Pretty soon I was close enough to see that Stewart was back in costume—everything but the makeup. And I realized he wasn't dancing at all.

He was fighting. Cane sword in hand, he alternated thrusts and slashes, pausing in between, taking time to murmur words I couldn't make out.

So I crept closer, coming in behind him, quietly, to listen.

At first I thought he was muttering lines from the play. Mr. Bolger had said he was rehearsing. But as I drew near, I realized they weren't lines at all. Not from *La Mancha*, at least.

"Shut up. Shut the fuck up." He whipped the sword before him. "I don't care. I don't care what you say. You can't hurt me. You'll never hurt me."

And then he laughed. Laughed so goddam loud, his voice seemed to ring through the empty trees. The noise shook me from my spell, and I shivered and looked around. I felt like there were others with us, or should be. Others in the audience. But I was the only one.

"See that?" He thrust again with a grunt. "See how I defy thee? See how I stab at thee?"

I started to feel sick. I hadn't eaten much at lunch, but my stomach was turning, and I could feel my pulse throbbing in my ears. I wanted to leave, run away, back to the house. He hadn't seen me yet. But even as I turned to go, I stopped. I couldn't leave him there alone.

"Stewart?" I called out.

He whirled, swinging the blade around as he turned. I flinched, worried he might throw it at me.

But he didn't. He just squinted and leaned forward, as if searching through a thick fog.

"Sancho?" he cried at last. "Sancho, get up here, quickly. Quickly, quickly!"

His voice was so urgent, I scrambled up onto the rock without even thinking.

"What's the matter?" I asked as he grabbed me by the shoulders before clutching me in a quick embrace.

"Oh, thank God you made it. It's safe here, Sancho. He can't get us here."

"Who can't get us?" I kept trying to figure out what he was up to. For a moment I thought it might be some kind of game or some bullshit acting exercise. He was always reading those goddam Web sites; who knew what he'd picked up? Maybe, for all his talk of purity, he'd spent the day doing bong hits in his room. Or worse. But seeing the terror on his face, I realized it was none of those things.

"The Enchanter!" he cried, his eyes widening as a drop of spit flew from his mouth. "Who else would it be? He's after me. After both of us, goddam it! Don't you dare deny it, Sancho, or I'll have you flogged!"

There it was, the Enchanter again, Quixote's imagined enemy. And Stewart seemed to have made him his own, made Quixote's delusions his own. I had my hands on Stewart, gripping the edges of his armor, but he was slipping away from me. I could see it in his eyes—that glassy, distant look, pulled farther and farther away by some force deep inside him.

It was too much. I had to look away. Glancing down, I noticed a dark crack running the width of the stone between us. Was it new or had it always been there? I suddenly couldn't remember. I looked back up to see his eyes darting back and forth, searching in fear.

"So where's the Enchanter, Stewart? Help me see him."

"You can't fucking see him. That's what makes him so good! All you can see are his minions."

"Where?"

"There! There, there, there!" he shouted, thrusting his sword toward the woods in the direction he'd been sparring, before turning away.

I looked out into the trees, trying to figure out what the hell he was talking about, but all I could see were bare maples and beeches clustered along the slope running down toward my house. That sick sort of feeling started up again in my stomach. Then I shifted, my eye caught something, and I felt even sicker.

It was the farthest row of trees, the ones against the horizon. Something was wrong with them. They were too straight. Then I realized they weren't actually trees.

"The wind towers?" I looked over at him.

He gave the slightest nod. He was trembling now.

The cold had drawn the moisture from the earth, forming a band of mist that drifted down the slope and circled the rock we were standing on. I tried to say something, but my head was spinning. I could hardly think. All I knew was that something was wrong with Stewart. Not just off, not just funny or annoying, but really, really wrong. Worst of all, I began to realize that, deep down, I'd known it for a while. I took the sword from his hand, spotted the empty cane scabbard at my feet, and sheathed the blade.

"Stewart, they're just wind towers. That's all."

He stopped shaking. That look came back into his eyes. He grabbed me.

"No, they're not. They're with him. They all laugh at me. Just like he does. All day, they just laugh at me and call me names. I can hear them. When the wind blows, I can hear them mocking me and my parents, all of us. The whole town. Like a bunch of overlords. Like a bunch of fucking corporate pigs, turning and laughing."

"Stop it, Stewart." I tried to ease his grip on my peacoat.

"And we're just a bunch of peasants to them. Just a bunch of fucking rubes, toiling under their shadow. They want to make all of us their slaves."

"Stop it, Stewart."

"No!" He pushed me. "I won't be a peasant, Sancho. I won't be like you. I am Don Quixote!"

"No, you're not!" I grabbed him by his cloak and shook him. "You're not fucking Don Quixote or Cervantes or anybody else but yourself, so get a fucking grip!"

He froze, his eyes widening in surprise. He felt so thin beneath his cloak, beneath the armor, like of a bunch of sticks all ready to break. I let go of him. He sank down onto the rock and burst into a string of sobs so horrible I had to look away.

"Oh shit. Oh shit. Oh shit." I turned in a circle, looking around the woods, half searching for someone to help, half afraid someone was actually there to see us.

I bent down beside Stewart and patted him on the back.

"It's okay, Stewart. It's going to be okay."

It only made him cry harder. I'd never seen another guy bawl before. Not since I was a kid. I mean, I'd seen my father with tears on his face plenty of times. But this was on a whole different level. Pure pain.

"You have to help me, Frenchy," he whispered. "Please."

I took a little box from my pocket, the one I'd grabbed before leaving the house, and pulled out the leftover joint from Halloween night. I lit it up and took a long, steady hit.

I held it out to Stewart. Still heaving from the sobs, he glanced over at it, then reached out and accepted it with trembling fingers.

We finished the joint, then sat there on the rock for a long time without saying a word, watching our breath form clouds of steam as the night air settled in, feeling it nip at our ears and noses. It was so quiet in the woods. The songbirds were long gone, and not even a crow or squirrel disturbed the silence. Stewart seemed to have settled down, settled into himself. It was strange to see him so at peace after all that agitation. It was the pot, I guessed, which had calmed him. Fucking Bryant.

"You know what day it is, don't you," he said at last.

"Yeah. It's Monday."

"No, no. What day it is. What *day*."

"November second?"

"That's right. That's right, Frenchy. All Souls' Day. The day we pray for the departed dead. We should pray for your father."

I turned away. "I'm not much the praying type, Stewart. Neither was Dad."

"Not one prayer?"

"No."

"Well, I'll say one for him, then. He deserves it. He was a noble warrior, after all. A fellow knight."

I sensed the wave coming in before it hit and managed to close my eyes against the tears. Then I bit the inside of my cheek. The pain distracted me. I held on until the wave passed. Finally I could speak.

"Yeah. We should go. It's almost dark."

I helped Stewart to his feet, then turned and jumped down off the rock. He wouldn't come at first. He just stood there for a moment. I could see him holding back, hesitating. He wouldn't look at me.

"It's okay," I said. "Come on."

He finally stepped down off the rock and we headed for Shangri La. I walked behind him. There was just enough light to follow the path. Pretty soon, I could make out the kitchen lights through the trees.

"Maybe you should quit," I said as we neared the house.

"Quit what?" He stopped.

"Quit the play. Quit being Don. I'll quit too."

He turned to face me. It was dark enough now that I couldn't really see his face.

"Impossible."

"Why?"

"We *are* the play, Frenchy. If we quit, it's over. We can't do that to everyone. Besides, maybe you can drop Sancho, but I can't quit being Don."

"Yeah, but why?"

"I just can't, okay?" he hollered.

We were both quiet for a minute.

"Listen," I said, "I know it seems hard, but if you just explain—"

"Explain what, Frenchy?"

I hesitated. "You know."

He grabbed the sleeve of my coat. "You can't say anything, Frenchy. Not a fucking word. I mean it."

"Yeah, but Stewart—"

"I'm okay. I've just got to sort it out. Don't worry, I'll sort it out."

You're not okay, I thought. But after getting him calmed down, I didn't want to say anything. I started to walk past him, but he stopped me.

"Promise me, Frenchy. I want you to swear on your father's soul that you won't betray us."

I hesitated again. "I promise," I said at last, "on one condition—when the play's over, you talk to somebody."

"Fine." He started to let go of me, but it was my turn to grab him.

"No. You *promise* me, Stewart. I mean it. You promise you'll get help."

"Yeah, I promise."

We continued on in silence to the house. I couldn't tell if I felt better or worse. Maybe better. But as I followed him onto the deck, I saw him lean toward the house, at his right, away from the ridge across the valley, and cover his left ear. I didn't follow him inside. I stayed behind to watch the distant towers, watch their red lights come to life, one by one, winking all in a row.

ACT FOUR:
FALLING ACTION

ᴄ CHAPTER TWENTY ᴍ

The next morning Stewart picked me up, dressed in full Don Quixote garb. He didn't smile or even look at me when I got in the car.

"You've got to be fucking kidding me."

"Good morning, Sancho," he said. His voice was much clearer now, in spite of the prosthetics. All that practice, I guess.

"Halloween's over, Stewart," I said as we coasted down the hill.

He didn't answer.

"Why are you still dressed like him? I thought you were going to sort it out."

"I am. I will," he said, waving a hand in front of his face.

"Yeah, it really looks like it."

"Just remember what you promised, Frenchy."

I reached up and punched the roof of the Volvo. "Yeah. You too, asshole."

By lunchtime, half the school was talking about Stewart. He'd only made it through three periods before getting sent to the office. Nobody had seen him since. Standing in line with my tray,

I heard all kinds of rumors. He was being sent home. He'd been expelled. Mr. Ruggles had torn off the wig and half of Stewart's hair in a fit of rage. Ms. Vale had threatened to quit. Mr. and Mrs. Bolger were suing the school.

So you can imagine how surprised I was to see him walk into the cafeteria toward the end of lunch. The prosthetics were gone, but everything else—the wig, the cloak, the armor, even his cane—remained.

The whole cafeteria came to a halt as Stewart strode in. He stood there in the doorway for a moment, peering around at all the gawkers frozen over their trays. Then, without a word, he bowed, sweeping his cloak around to drape the floor before him. The whole place erupted, breaking into a mix of laughter and applause. Everyone loved it.

Everyone except a scowling Mr. Ruggles, who ushered Stewart over to where Eddie Edward and I sat at a nearby table.

"Thought you were getting sent home," I said as Stewart pulled up a seat next to me.

He shrugged. "We reached an agreement." He laid his cane on the table.

"You shouldn't bring that to school."

"No one knows."

"So what happened, anyway?"

"I was in AP Calc, just minding my own business. Mr. Goodwin didn't like the costume. Said it was a distraction. I told him his stupid class was a distraction from my life."

"Christ, Stewart."

"Whatever. I apologized. All part of the arrangement."

"Yeah? What arrangement?"

"Oh, you should have seen it, Sancho. Me and Ruggles, your pal Bryant, and Goodwin. They wanted to bring in my parents too, but I forbade it. It didn't matter anyway. Ms. Vale came. She told them it was Method acting, that it was all part of my preparation. And they agreed. Can you believe it? They made me take off the nose and beard and shit, but that's okay. I don't need that stuff. Until the play's over, this is it. It's all Don."

I shook my head. Method acting. For someone struggling with reality, he seemed to know exactly what he was doing. He had all of them—all of us—wrapped right around his finger.

He blinked a few times, then whispered, "All Don," again to himself.

For the hundredth time, my thoughts went back to yesterday on the rock. He'd crossed over to a dark place and pulled me with him, and all I wanted was to get us both back in one piece. I just had to wonder how much he really wanted to come with me.

"What are you trying to prove?"

His face tensed, and he blinked once more before putting his head down on the table. For the rest of lunch, he just stayed there like that.

And that became the pattern for the rest of the week—a weird stretch of anxiety wrapped in a layer of calm. Stewart spoke less and less every day. He still picked me up, still took me home, but I could feel him pulling away, sinking more and more into himself. Or rather, Don Quixote, whose costume he still wore. I thought about getting another bag of weed from Ralph to see if Stewart would come around that way, but all I could think about was Bryant's little lecture about self-medicating. It was stuck in my head now—the bastard had ruined it for me. For good, probably. Besides, Stewart had called it at the very beginning: He didn't need pot anymore—he had Don. What the hell did I have?

I guess I had Don too. I was always by his side. Even when he stopped talking to me, I was there with him until the moment he dropped me off and headed home each night. I watched every move he made, analyzing every little eye twitch, every little whisper, looking for some sign that it was all about to break for good.

It didn't help that he showed up exhausted every morning, his eyes all droopy and dark. I asked him why he was so tired.

"Not sleeping much." He took a slug of coffee from the huge travel mug that had become a morning fixture.

"Yeah? Why not?"

"Working."

"What do you mean, 'working'? You mean, like schoolwork?" I guessed he was still failing his classes.

He shook his head and yawned. "Sorting it out. Taking care of it. Taking care of business. Just like we talked about."

"Yeah, how?"

"You'll see, you'll see. Don't worry, Sancho. I feel much better now. Much clearer."

"Yeah, you look it," I muttered, glancing at the dark circles under his eyes.

The only time he came alive was in rehearsals. As soon as he hit the stage, the sullen, withdrawn Stewart disappeared, replaced by the charming Cervantes or, more often, the passionate Don Quixote. It was all there—the commanding dialogue, the fluid moves, the striking voice. Good thing, too. We all felt the need to get back on track, and Stewart's focus brought us all around.

The relief on Ms. Vale's face about ten minutes into rehearsal the day Stewart returned said it all. By Wednesday the production was humming along with even more energy than before, helped along by the fact that the end was now in sight. And the part we'd dreaded most—going off-book—turned out to be not so bad, forcing us to be more disciplined.

Even as I fretted about Stewart, even as I held on to a promise I worried I had no business keeping, I was enjoying the play more than ever. It had become comfortable now, my own little escape. We all shared in one another's competency and talent, helped the few who still struggled a little with a line or verse or element of blocking. The set started to take shape as the tech crew became a more regular feature of our rehearsals. Of course, that meant I got to spend more time with Kaela. In fact, when I wasn't directly involved in a scene, I was pretty much by her side. Since Stewart basically sat by himself now on a stool in the shadows and didn't talk to anybody, I was free to do what I wanted and—for the first time, really—be my own man.

That's what I tried to tell myself, anyway. But the truth is, I couldn't stop being Sancho. Even in the middle of cracking a joke, I found myself glancing toward the wings to check on Stewart.

And then there was Kaela.

"Come on," she said at the end of Friday's rehearsal. "The techs are all going out for pizza and then over to my house. Your fanboys are calling for you."

"I don't know. Once I start eating pizza, I have a hard time stopping. It's not good for anyone. Especially for Sancho Junior here." I slapped my gut.

She reached down and patted my belly. "I think he's cute," she said with a grin.

I looked over to where Stewart sat in the wings. His head was down, his arms were folded, and he was swaying a little. Even from here, I could hear him humming "The Impossible Dream."

I winced. "Tonight's not good."

She frowned. "Yeah, that's what you said yesterday, and the day before." She followed my gaze over to Stewart. Before the play, she'd always looked at him with adoration. Now there was just resentment in her eyes.

"I know. What can I say? I'm a loser."

"Well, a lovable loser, anyway," she said, grinning. She wrapped her arm around mine and started dragging me toward the edge of the stage as everyone gathered their things. "All right, mister, you're coming whether you like it or not."

I took a deep breath of her perfume, felt the warmth of her body as she pressed against me, and let myself be pulled. A burst of laughter from Stewart made us both stop. I looked to where he sat, shaking his head, still gazing at the floor. A few other kids stopped to look, but not many. It wasn't the first time this week he'd done that.

I untangled my arm from hers and stepped back. "Look, it's not you."

"Well, of course it's not, sweetie," she said. "I mean, come on." She struck a sexy pose and gestured to herself. We both laughed. She glanced back over at Stewart. Her smile faded. "No, I get it."

We both looked down at our feet for a moment as the crowd shuffled around us.

"So what's going on with him, anyway? He's been acting weird all week. I mean, even for Stewart. He just sits there. And that whispering."

"I don't know," I said. "He's probably just practicing his lines."

"Like he really needs to. Anyway, people are starting to talk—wondering if it's starting to get to him. Opening night's only a couple weeks away."

I shrugged. "We're all under a lot of stress."

She looked back at me, her eyes softening. "Look, I just want to hang out."

"Me too," I said, taking her hand. "Don't worry. Once this is over, I'm all yours." I tried to hold back a grimace. Christ, I sounded like Stewart.

She glanced back over at Stewart and let go of my hand. "You just better hope I don't get tired of waiting," she said, then walked away.

Hell Saturday was heaven for Stewart. He got to be Don for almost an entire day. You could see the difference in him—he smiled when he picked me up that morning and talked to the others during breaks between scenes. Once or twice he even dropped character, something he hardly ever did now. For the first time in over a week, I actually felt relaxed at rehearsal. In fact, I felt so good, I made the mistake of asking him on the way home if he wanted to hang out that night.

"I can't," he said, his smile disappearing.

"Um, okay. Why not?"

"I just can't."

"Give me a fucking break."

"Have to work," he said, blinking a few times in agitation.

"You keep saying that. What are you working on, anyway?"

"You know," he said. "I told you I'd sort it all out. That's what I'm doing. I'm right in the middle of something. Something big. Something that will make this all right."

"You're bullshitting me."

"No, I'm not," he snapped. "How about a little trust?"

We didn't say much after that. I just looked out my window. It had snowed quite a bit last night. We'd had a few dustings already, but it was always gone by late morning. Not today. In the headlights, I could still see patches of white glowing between the trees and along the stone walls.

"Sorry," he said as we pulled into my driveway. He kept the car idling.

"Well, how about tomorrow? I'll come up."

He sighed and shook his head. "Parents want to go to Burlington," he whispered.

We both looked straight ahead for a while. It had started to snow again, and the flakes were falling fast against the windshield.

"Listen, Stewart," I finally said. "I know you're scared by what's happening. I'm scared too. But spending all this time alone isn't going to help. When Dad died, I didn't lock myself away in my room every weekend. And that was because of you. Because you wouldn't let me."

"You just don't know," he murmured, closing his eyes. I could feel him pulling away again, going off into that little place he'd been carving out for who knew how long.

"Let's watch a movie or something. Whatever you want."

He didn't open his eyes. He just leaned forward until his head was resting on the steering wheel. For a minute I thought he'd fallen asleep, but then I saw him open his eyes.

"Going to Burlington."

"Yeah, okay," I said.

I got out of the car to a sudden squall, the snow coming so hard and fast it stung my eyes all the way to the house.

I was outside shoveling the driveway the next morning when the Bolgers' SUV went by. Stewart wasn't in it.

Fuck him, anyway, I thought, watching it disappear around the bend.

"What's wrong?" my mother said at lunchtime, watching me poke at the leftover Chinese takeout she'd brought home last night for dinner. "You've been down all morning."

"Nothing."

"Is it the play?"

"Something like that."

"Don't be nervous, honey. You'll be great. You've just got to really get into the role. You know, like Stewart. I bet he's not scared at all."

"Yeah," I said. "No fear."

She paused. "I'm so proud of you for doing this. It takes a lot of guts to do what you're doing. To put yourself out there like that. Your father would be so proud of you."

I snorted. "Yeah, I can just see him in the audience. The look on his face."

She smiled. "People can surprise you, Frenchy. Your father always admired competency. Didn't matter what it was—if you could do something well, you were okay in his book. And if you were brave enough to do the tough stuff, even better."

I dropped my fork and pushed the plate aside.

"Do you ever think about how things could have been different?" I asked.

She looked away. I traced her gaze to the picture of my father on the wall.

"Every day." I could hear the rawness in her voice.

"What did we do wrong?"

"Nothing. Everything. I don't know. I could tell he was hurting. I just thought he could handle it. Ever since we were teenagers, he was the toughest guy I knew. I thought nothing could take him down. I never guessed it would be himself."

I finally looked up. Her face had settled into that old sadness.

"I just feel like we ignored him," I said. "Abandoned him. Because we were afraid. Or because it was easier."

"It wasn't like we didn't try. We took him to the VA hospital. He didn't want to go, but I made him."

"Yeah, they were a real help. Tossing him enough pills to put down an elephant and basically telling him to suck it up. So much for the government. They abandoned him just as much as we did."

Tears began to well up in her eyes. Shit.

"Nothing was easy about that time, Frenchy. Don't you remember?" She wiped her eyes. "What's easy is second-guessing yourself. But it doesn't change a goddam thing."

"I guess it doesn't."

She came over and put her arms around me. "I just wish you hadn't gotten there first," she whispered. "I could've kept you away, Frenchy. You should never have had to see him like that."

There was a long pause. I could feel her awkwardness building.

"Do you want to go visit him?" she said at last.

I shook my head. We'd only been to the cemetery once since the burial. Last August, on his birthday. I'm sure I don't have to tell you how much it totally sucked.

"Me neither." She got up and walked over to the window. "Not with the snow. Everything's covered."

She turned back to me. "But you've got to get out of the house, Frenchy," she said, trying to smile. "You're driving me crazy, moping around here. Why don't you go see Stewart?"

I thought about his brush-off from yesterday. How he'd lied to me.

"Yeah," I said, standing up. "Yeah, maybe I will."

Stewart's car was in the driveway next to his father's Audi. I paused. Mr. Bolger always kept his car in the garage. In fact, he hardly ever drove it unless he really had to. Then I saw bright lights flashing in the garage door windows, which puzzled me even more. Maybe Mrs. Bolger and Stewart had gone to Burlington alone. But why was Mr. Bolger working in the garage and not in his shop?

I went to the side door and looked in, wincing against the torchlight.

It was Stewart, leaning over a fountain of sparks, a heavy apron over his Quixote costume, the locks of his wig sticking out from beneath the welder's mask. He was hunched over a rectangular metal frame, like a box with no sides. Seeing me, he killed the torch and lifted the mask. I could see the anger on his face.

"Get out!" he shouted. "Out! Out! Out!"

I was so startled, I ducked out of the doorway and walked back to the gravel drive. A second later he came out, slamming the door behind him. He still had his apron on.

"What are you doing here?"

"Me? What am I doing here? What the fuck are *you* doing here? That's the real question, Stewart. Aren't you supposed to be in Burlington?"

He frowned. "I changed my mind," he said. "I needed time."

"For what? To work on your precious project? What the hell is that in there, anyway?"

He paused. "You told me to take care of it, so that's what I'm doing." He glanced at the ground and poked a stone with his toe. "Welding relaxes me," he said at last.

"Oh, great. I'm glad somebody around here is relaxed, because it sure as shit isn't me."

"I told you not to worry." He paused again, his eyes narrowing. "It's not like I'm going to kill myself or anything."

For the first time since we'd met, I actually hated him. "You're a real first-class asshole."

He shook his head. He knew he'd crossed the line. I could see the familiar panic return to his eyes.

"Who told you to come here and spy on me, anyway?" His voice was shaking now. "I thought I could trust you, Sancho, but you're with them, aren't you? You've joined them."

"Them?" I shouted. "Who is 'them,' anyway? You mean *them?*" I pointed at the towers on the distant ridge. "You mean those big pieces of metal that can't talk, can't think, and have never done anything to you? Listen to yourself, Stewart. Do you have any idea how you sound? This is just like the other day. It's crazy, Stewart. Fucking crazy."

His face turned red. "I'm not crazy!" he screamed. "Your dad, he was the psycho! Not me! You understand?"

I could hear myself utter this weird noise—part growl, part scream. I wanted to smash his face in, and if he'd been closer to me, I just might have done it. But that rage had to go somewhere, and the next thing I knew, my boot was driving into the side of his Volvo with all the force I had.

Ka-thunk!

For a second I just stared down at the huge dent in the panel of his back passenger-side door. I glanced over to see him standing there, his arms hanging at his sides, a look of shock on his face.

Without a word, I stormed off, walking, then running down the driveway, not stopping until I got home. I got back to find my mother had just left for her shift. A lucky break. But I needed to get away. Besides Shangri La, this was the last place I wanted to be. I picked up the phone and dialed the number I still carried in my pocket.

"What's up, Frenchy baby?" Kaela said.

"Still want to get that pizza?" I asked, trying to control the shaking in my voice.

"Oh, so *now* you want some face time with the stage manager."

"Something like that."

She could tell something was up. "I'll be right there," she said.

She pulled into the driveway about twenty minutes later. I jumped into the passenger side.

"Thanks, Kaela."

She didn't say anything. She just grabbed me and pulled me toward her, and the next thing I knew, we were kissing. Her lips were so soft; everything about her was soft. I could feel myself letting go as a wave of giddiness washed over me. It felt so strange after the fucked-up day I'd had.

"Let's go," she whispered, patting my cheek when it was over.

She backed up and was about to take off when she suddenly looked up into the rearview mirror.

"Oh," she said. "Stewart."

I turned around to see Stewart running down the road, waving his hands for us to stop, his cloak flowing behind him.

"Just go."

She hesitated. "Really?"

"Yeah," I said. "Please, Kaela."

She nodded and we took off. I watched Stewart continue to run past my house before drifting to a stop as we sped away. Then I turned around, forcing myself to look ahead and ignore the shrinking figure in the side-view mirror.

I was getting ready to call Kaela the next morning to see if she could bring me to school when, to my shock, Stewart pulled in at his usual time. I hesitated at the door, watching him through the window as the Volvo steamed in the morning sun. Finally I grabbed my bag and left the house. Coming around the front to the passenger's side, I could see a crease on the back door. It looked even bigger in the light of morning.

Stewart was still in costume, still tired, but he managed a big smile as I got in, as if yesterday had never happened.

"Morning, old friend," he said.

"Yeah, it's morning."

"And a beautiful one at that."

I glanced over at him as we started off down the Heights.

"You're awful chipper."

"I feel better today, Sancho. Progress has been made. All is coming together. You'll see. You'll be quite pleased, I'm sure."

"You call yesterday progress?"

His smile faded. "I wasn't myself when you came over. I said things I shouldn't have. You forgive me, don't you? You have to. You don't have it in you to stay angry."

He had me there. Or thought he did, at least.

"I just don't know how much more of this I can take, Stewart."

He nodded a little. I could see his knuckles whiten along the rim of the steering wheel. "I know the feeling."

"Sorry about your car, by the way."

"All good armor has some dents," he replied with a smile. We rounded the corner and passed the pit stop. Beyond the naked maples, the towers gleamed in the distance.

"Those fuckers," he said, pointing toward the ridge, "are going to come down."

He gave me a sideways glance, but this time I didn't feel like laughing.

Chapter Twenty-One

Stewart's good mood carried through the rest of the day. In fact, as the week went on, Stewart seemed to grow more relaxed, less withdrawn. One morning he even showed up without his costume.

"Where's Quixote?" I asked, doing a slight double take as I hopped in the car.

He shrugged. "Didn't feel like it, I guess. Takes forever to put on."

"I hardly recognized you for a second." I leaned over and gave him a light punch on the shoulder. He looked up in the rearview mirror with an intense stare and traced his fingers along his face.

"I feel naked."

"Well, you look better." I hesitated. "You feel better? You pulling out of this?"

He did his little wave, as if brushing off a fly. The next day the costume was back, though he did call me Frenchy a few times.

I figured he was coming out of it, the phase was phasing out. I wondered if the top-secret project he was working on was doing the trick. Whatever the reason, I felt a general sense of relief. I got over the nasty things he'd said on Sunday. Even the smoking rock episode started to seem like a long time ago, seem somehow less real, like just another scene from the play, and I started to let my guard down so that by the end of the week, I was hardly paying attention.

Of course, I had other distractions. I kept thinking about the kiss. A few more had followed since, but that first one had been a doozy. I'd be sitting in class when the memory of it would spring up, and I'd find myself trying not to laugh, trying to figure out how I'd suddenly gotten so lucky. I'd flirted with girls, even had a few girlfriends, but mostly lame junior-high stuff. Things had been pretty dry these last couple years. Then again, like most things in my life, I hadn't been working too hard at it. Hanging out with Stewart, getting baked and doing stupid shit—I'd thought it was enough. It was just plain sad that it had taken so long to find out it wasn't. Idiot.

Things started out well enough that Friday. It was a clear, sunny morning. Stewart picked me up as usual. We joked around a bit on the way to school and talked about the afternoon practice schedule. With opening night a week away, we were wrapping up work scenes and getting ready for next week's dress rehearsals.

Then came lunch. Then came the Pokers.

Not knowing what to make of Stewart's getup—or of the popularity we'd both started enjoying as word about the upcoming performance spread—they'd been dormant for quite a while. Besides, Mr. Ruggles kept a watchful eye on them at lunch—he liked them even less than we did—and now that we were stuck late in rehearsals every day, we never ran into them after school, either.

But the last few days had brought some name-calling. Weirded out by the costume and whispers about some of Stewart's more eccentric behaviors, they'd shifted focus—now it was *Little Donny Whack Job*, *Fuck Freak*, the old classic *Psycho*, stuff like that.

"At least they're not calling you a homo anymore," I offered. "Maybe they're evolving."

He didn't laugh. In fact, the new names seemed to bother him even more than the old ones. It wasn't hard to guess why.

We'd almost made it through lunch when Mr. Ruggles got called out of the cafeteria. Stewart and I were returning our trays. Out of nowhere, Scott slipped between us and stepped on Stewart's cloak.

There was a loud ripping sound as the cloak tore along one side. Even worse, the force caught Stewart by the throat, yanking him backward so that he lost his balance and fell with a crash of armor, broken dishes, and scattered silverware. Everything stopped in the cafeteria as kids turned to gawk, then laugh.

Shaking off my efforts to help, Stewart struggled to his feet before the gathered Pokers.

"Monsters!" he shouted, his face red and trembling.

"What's the matter, Sir Whacks-a-Lot?" sneered one of the Pokers, a sophomore everyone called Pimples.

"Oh, thou heart of flint and bowels of cork!" Stewart shook his fist at them. "Now shall I chastise thee!"

I groaned. More lines from the play. The Pokers, meanwhile, began yukking it up, laughing among themselves in hilarious disbelief. Other students were starting to whisper to one another and giggle, too.

"Come on, Stewart." I took him by the arm. "Fuck 'em."

"No!" he shouted, shrugging me off again. He picked up his torn cloak. "Look at what they did, Sancho. I cannot let this insult stand."

The Pokers laughed even louder. Taking on the implied challenge, a few even started toward us with nasty looks in their eyes when a voice stopped them in their tracks.

"What's going on here?" Mr. Ruggles roared. The cafeteria went quiet again.

It was a rhetorical question, really. Ruggles was sharp enough to guess right away what had happened.

"Get your butts in my office," he snapped to the Pokers, who shot us one last glare before slinking out.

He glanced back to Stewart and me. Stewart was still red and shaking. Ruggles looked us over and shook his head.

"Clean this mess up." He turned and followed the Pokers out.

The bell rang just as we got down on our knees and started gathering all the pieces back onto the tray. Kids were trying to step around us; Stewart was still rattled. The whole thing just plain sucked.

"I'll take care of it," I said when we finished, removing the tray from his shaking hands. He nodded his thanks, eyes still down at the floor. "See you after school?" I asked, but he just turned and left.

Practice started out fine. We finished working the last few scenes, took a break, then spent the last hour getting fitted for our costumes. Since Stewart and I already had ours, there wasn't much for us to do. We could've just gone home, but Stewart wanted to get his cloak stitched back up by one of the mothers who'd volunteered to help with the costuming. Fine by me—it gave me a chance to hang out with Kaela and help her get one of the last set pieces painted.

"Hey, when are you going to get us some real brushes?" I said, looking at the smattering of bristles stuck to the plywood with fresh paint.

"When I get a real painter."

"I was hired for my good looks and sweet pipes. You're the one with the mad skills, sweetheart." I reached over and dabbed her cheek with the brush.

She reached up and wiped at the smear of paint. "You bastard!"

Whap! The width of her brush caught me broadside. I could feel the paint running the length of my face. We both stared at each other for a second in shock before she burst out laughing.

"Definitely an improvement," she said.

"I'm sure. Whatever. It's just good to hear you laugh for a change. You've been all business this week."

"Yeah, well, dress rehearsal's coming up. Somebody's got to make sure this place is ready when you finally put on your pretty little costumes and play make-believe. But we're in good shape. Things are falling into place. I mean, look around."

We were all in a good mood, going about our business— sorting through clothes and props, applying finishing touches to the set, laughing, joking, singing sometimes, just trying to relax a little. Tomorrow was our second Hell Saturday, and we all wanted to savor the last few moments of downtime before the real crunch began.

Some of the techs started talking about going out after for dinner, and they invited me and Stewart along. In spite of the scene at lunch, he'd been doing better these last few days, and I figured I could get him to go. He owed me.

I searched around but couldn't spot him. In fact, it had been a few minutes since anyone had seen him.

I was just about to go check the lobby when Stacey McGovern's voice—loud, agitated—broke through the general murmur, silencing cast and crew one by one until everyone was quiet. She marched out from the wings, looking seriously pissed off, with Stewart in pursuit, muttering words I couldn't hear.

"Oh, my God!" she yelled, stopping in the middle of the stage, then whirling around to face Stewart, who dropped down on his knees before her. "How many times do I have to tell you to leave me alone?"

For a second I thought it was an act, the variation of a scene. The moment had this dramatic charge, the kind I'd seen only when Stewart was fully immersed in the role and Stacey was at her fiercest best.

"My lady knows better in her heart," he said, murmuring a line from the play.

"Stop staying that! We're not rehearsing."

"But, Dulcinea, I do protest—"

"Shut up!" She stamped her foot. "Shut up with that crap! God, I'm so sick of hearing it. For the last time, it's not happening, Stewart. I don't even like you, you freak!"

Stewart flinched. Stacey turned and walked away from him in a huff. Kids were whispering now to one another, trying to figure out what to make of the scene. Even Ms. Vale seemed bewildered at the outburst. Stewart glanced from side to side at the assembled crowd in dismay, as if noticing them for the first time. I could see the fear, the confusion on his face. There was a long pause as everyone tried to figure out what to do.

"You better get over there," Kaela said.

"Yeah, I think you're right." I headed for Stewart. All I could think about was the cafeteria scene, how much it had rattled him. That, or I'd been fooling myself all week that things were better. Either way, it was time to get him out. Exit, stage right.

Unfortunately, Quentin got there first.

"Are you okay?" he said, sidling up to Stacey, who stood nearby with her arms crossed, glaring at Stewart.

Stacey muttered something in response. At first I wondered if she'd staged this entire humiliation to put Stewart in his place, but she seemed as mortified as anyone. Fortunately, it looked like the scene was pretty much over now. People were breaking up, going back to whatever they'd been doing before, though some still whispered.

"Hope you're happy," Quentin spat, looking down at Stewart before putting his arm around Stacey's shoulder.

"Unhand her!" Stewart shouted, leaping to his feet. "How dare you defile her with your sordid touch!"

"Come on, Stewart," I hissed, tugging at his cloak.

"What was that you said?" Quentin replied, raising his voice to draw attention. Sensing another scene, everyone grew quiet again, turning back to the center of the stage.

"I know who you are," Stewart growled. "I know what you do. You're with *him*, aren't you?"

I looked over to see Ms. Vale approaching with a frown. I grabbed Stewart's arm to pull him away, but he shook me off like before.

"Oh boy, here we go," Quentin said, gesturing toward Stewart as he glanced around at the crowd. Catching sight of Ms. Vale, he turned to face her. "Come on, Ms. Vale. Are you listening to this?"

"That's enough, Quentin," Ms. Vale said, narrowing her eyes.

But Quentin wouldn't quit. "I'm sorry, but this is ridiculous. I mean, have you seen him rocking on his little stool in the wings these last few weeks, muttering under his breath? He won't leave poor Stacey alone. And that costume—he's turning this entire production into a joke. You should hear what everyone in school is saying."

Stewart shrank all over again, even worse than before.

"Quentin, this isn't the time to—"

"I can do it, Ms. Vale! I know the part as well as he does. You know I do. It's only a matter of time before he loses it and takes us all down with him."

He turned to me. So did everyone else.

"You know what I'm talking about, don't you? You must know better than anyone," he said. "Come on, Frenchy. We could do it together. There's still time."

I hesitated for a second, standing there in the middle of the stage, in the middle of the cast and crew, with all eyes on me, with Stewart beside me watching too, shaken and pale. The next thing I knew, the words were just coming out of my mouth.

"Fuck you, Quentin," I said. "If he goes, I go."

Quentin laughed. "Yeah, right."

"Try me."

"You're telling me you'd really quit? After all this work? I don't think so."

"Doesn't matter what you think, Quentin," I said, "because Stewart and me are staying right where we are. Stewart's the best thing about this play and everyone knows it. So get over yourself and leave him alone."

"Leave him alone?" he sneered. "Or what? Is he going to start crying or something?"

Throwing his cane down, Stewart launched himself at Quentin with a howl. In an instant, the two were on the ground, going at it. A cry rose up from the cast and crew. I couldn't tell if the other kids were excited or horrified at the prospect of a real fight, but I wasn't going to find out. As soon as Stewart rolled on top, I grabbed him with both hands and lifted him up so fast he practically landed on his feet.

"Did you see that?" Quentin yelled, jumping up and hopping around as he pointed at Stewart. "Did you see how he attacked me?"

He was greeted with silence and uneasy looks, but no one seemed too sympathetic.

"That's it, Ms. Vale," Quentin continued. "He's got to go. Now!"

"Oh, knock it off, Quentin," Ms. Vale muttered. She turned to me. "Get him out of here," she said, gesturing to Stewart. She seemed generally disgusted with all of us.

Stewart grabbed his cane, and I half dragged him off the stage and up the aisle toward the exit.

"Okay, everybody," Ms. Vale hollered as we left the auditorium, "back to work!"

"Jesus Christ," I said as we turned into the lobby. "What the hell is up with you today?"

"He's one of them," Stewart said. "His father works for the power company. He helped raise those monsters."

"I don't think so, Stewart. In fact, I'm pretty sure his father owns that gas station north of town."

We headed out into the parking lot. All we had to do was get to the car and go home. And that's exactly what would've happened if it hadn't been for the beat-up Honda filled with Pokers waiting three spaces away from Stewart's Volvo.

⠀⣧ CHAPTER TWENTY-TWO ⣧⠄

There were six of them, all squeezed into Pimples's shitbox like a bunch of clowns at the circus. One by one they popped out as we approached Stewart's car. I couldn't remember there being that many at lunch, but since Pokers all tend to look the same, it's easy to confuse their numbers.

"There's the faggots!" Scott crowed as they gathered into a pack.

So much for evolution.

The Pokers were out for blood. I could tell by their quivering half 'staches. They'd spent an hour in detention, and the days of mere intimidation were over. I wanted to run for it, hide some-place where they would never find us—I figured the library was a safe bet—but we were too far away from the main building.

I glanced around the parking lot, looking for a teacher, any adult who might be able to save us, but the place was empty. It was Friday, and just about everyone had bugged out early. A few girls were gathered on the other side of the parking lot, but that was it. They watched us, babbling into their cell phones at the same time. Probably summoning their friends to watch the slaughter.

Then I saw her—Kaela was in the window of the lobby entrance. She had her cell phone to her ear and was watching too. Even from here I could see the worry on her face.

Great, I thought, *now I get to have my ass kicked* and *be humiliated*.

"What's up, dudes?" I said, turning back to the Pokers, trying to sound as sketched out as possible in the hope that it might convince them we were all joined together in the brotherhood of misfits and losers.

"Thanks to your whack-job friend here, we're stuck in detention for a whole week—that's what's up, drama queen," Pimples snarled.

"Come on, guys," I said. "Don't blame us for that. What can I say? Ruggles is an asshole."

I hated to throw Ruggles under the bus, but if it meant getting out of this in one piece, I could live with it.

Stewart, meanwhile, hadn't said a word. In fact, he hadn't even moved. He just stood there with his head down, mumbling under his breath.

"Guys, we got to get out of here," I said. "Stewart just got in a fight with Quentin Bernard, and we got kicked out of practice. Shitty afternoon."

I tried to make us sound all tough, but the Pokers weren't buying it.

"Doesn't look like he's been in a fight," Scott said, walking up to us. The others followed. "Then again, Quentin's almost as big a pussy as you two are, so it's not surprising. We'll have to finish the job for him."

Before I could reply, Scott reached out and shoved Stewart. I started to my right to catch him, but to my surprise, Stewart didn't fall. He stumbled back a few steps, then recovered.

Scott stepped up to shove him again, but this time Stewart was ready. He grabbed both of Scott's outstretched arms and flipped him right over onto the pavement. It was like something out of a kung fu movie. While Scott rolled moaning on the ground, Stewart and I both looked at each other in shock.

"Good one, Your Grace."

Stewart grinned. Then all hell broke loose.

I don't remember a lot of what happened next. I remember seeing Stewart take down a Poker with some kind of karate kick, then trip another with his cane. I remember kicking Pimples in the nads, dropping him on the spot. Not too sporting, I know, but with three-to-one odds, I didn't give a shit. At one point, I even saw that Kaela had joined the fray, jumping on a Poker's back and pummeling him with a flurry of punches worthy of a pro hockey player. Then I got creamed in the nose and there was blood running down my face and Kaela was running over screaming something and somebody tackled me and another started punching me and wouldn't stop. . . .

And then I heard the ring of steel and *everything* stopped. I took a deep breath and closed my eyes. I knew that sound.

I sat up to see Stewart and Scott, face to face. Only now it was Scott who was shaking, stepping back as Stewart pressed forward, the tip of his sword against Scott's chest.

The Pokers looked one another in shock. We *all* looked at one another in shock. Everyone but Scott. He just gasped and turned green, like he was about to puke. He backed farther and farther away, finally bumping against the front of Stewart's car, then leaning back until he was lying completely on the hood. Stewart raised his sword tip until it was right under Scott's chin.

I got up and stumbled over.

"Come on, Stewart. Put it away."

"'Tis a scabrous villain," Stewart whispered. He must have taken a blow—his face was red and swollen along one side.

"You're fucking crazy!" Scott shouted.

I came up close to Stewart until I was right in his ear.

"It's not worth it. Think about the play. You can never finish if you do this. You can never be Don again."

At that point, I'm not sure it would've mattered. He had the look of real murder in his eye. Four years of frustration all focused into the razor-sharp tip of a blade. Just one little push, and it would all come pouring out.

The rapid blips of a siren made us all stop and turn, even Stewart. Chief Sullivan—head of the town's three-man police department—pulled up, his tires grinding over the thin layer of parking lot gravel as he slammed on the brakes. A pair of state police cruisers pulled up behind him.

"Drop the weapon!" Sullivan yelled, jumping out with his side-arm pointed right at Stewart. Stewart looked over at me in panic.

"Christ, just do it!" I hissed.

He dropped the sword. I couldn't help but wince hearing it clatter against the concrete.

The rest was like a scene from one of those cop shows. They made us all lie flat on the ground. One by one, we were handcuffed and hauled to our feet and stuck in cruisers. A few of the staties smirked when they saw me—they knew who I was, of course, because of Mom. One of them even winked at me as he put me in Sullivan's cruiser, which helped because I stopped being so scared. I figured he wouldn't have done that if we were truly fucked.

Stewart wasn't so comforted. He was shaking, breathing hard, and trying not to cry as we sat together in the backseat, watching the rest of the Pokers get rounded up while a pair of troopers rummaged through Scott's car. One of them got out, holding up a big bag of weed. I wondered what else they'd find in there.

Kaela stood off to the side, pale and shivering against the cold, talking to Chief Sullivan. She kept looking over at me, and whenever she did, I just smiled and nodded.

It was Kaela who had saved us, phoning the police as soon as she saw the Pokers get out of the car. That and shit luck, since Sullivan and the troopers happened to be just down the street getting coffee when the call came in.

"Want me to call your mom?" Kaela asked, coming up to us while Sullivan crossed the parking lot to talk to the other girls.

"Don't bother. If she doesn't already know, she will soon enough."

"Are you hurt?"

"Nah." Actually, my head throbbed like a sonofabitch and my chin was all scraped up, but what was I going to say? I already had her sympathy. Might as well make her think I was at least somewhat tough. Actually, sitting there in the backseat of a cop car—bruised, handcuffed, defiant—I'd probably never looked more attractive to a girl in my life. She reached in and touched my shoulder.

"You were pretty hot stuff back there," she quipped.

"You weren't so bad yourself. Never seen a girl who could hit like that."

She smiled, then left with a worried look of good-bye.

Ten minutes later, we were off, Stewart and me in the back of the chief's car, the Pokers stuffed into two state cruisers. I thought we'd go right to the station, but a minute later we passed it and headed out of town.

"Where are we going?" I asked.

"St. Johnsbury. Thought it'd be better to handle this at the state police barracks."

"Oh shit," I said. Stewart started moaning.

"Just take it easy, Frenchy," Sullivan said. "We'll sort it all out."

The next three hours were almost as bad as getting beat on by the Pokers. At least that was over quick.

First we all got separated and questioned. I had to tell the story, like, three different times before they finally brought Stewart and me back together. Next came the parents—the Bolgers, swooping in to embrace Stewart and fuss over his bruise, followed by my mother, who just looked pissed. Not that I expected any love—I'd embarrassed her in front of her colleagues. In fact, she looked like she wanted to hit me even more than the Pokers had. I wished she would've. I would've felt better about the whole thing.

After they left, Principal Masure came in, her eyes full of quiet rage. She launched into a ten-minute lecture: How could we do such a thing? Circumstances didn't matter—we had a responsibility not to stoop to violence. She had half a mind to cancel the whole production. A weapon had been involved. On school property! Lawyers would be calling. Her hands could very well be tied. Were we out of our minds?

That's when Stewart started laughing, which—as I'm sure you can imagine—really helped our case.

Masure's face grew red, her cheeks began to quiver, and her eyes literally bulged. I imagined steam shooting out of her ears like in those old cartoons.

"He always does this when he's upset," I jumped in, praying she hadn't yet heard about Stewart's tussle with Quentin. "Stress does funny things to people. We're both really sorry. Please don't let everyone else's hard work go down the drain because of one incident."

My pleading seemed to work. Both Masure and Stewart composed themselves, and the lecture continued: We'd see who was sorry. A decision would be forthcoming. In the meantime, we (and here she turned to Stewart) could be assured that suspensions would be handed out. Several days of them, in fact.

In the end, it could have been a lot worse. Our story matched that of the witnesses, so no charges were pressed—the whole thing was deemed self-defense. Stewart's cane sword got confiscated, though. A look of pain crossed his face at the news, but he didn't say a word. He was smart enough to know he was getting off easy. The Pokers weren't going to be charged with assault, either. But they had bigger problems—Scott, Pimples, and a couple others had gotten cited for possession and were headed for the state's diversion program, not to mention the threat of future arrest if they bothered either of us again.

I thought we were out of the woods, but before we were allowed to rejoin our parents in the lobby, Jason Barr, one of the detectives, came in carrying a big yellow envelope with something clunky inside.

"I need to ask you about this," he said.

He opened the envelope and scattered its contents onto the table. It was the hilt of Stewart's antique sword, along with several scraps of blade.

"You know who this belongs to?" He turned toward Stewart.

Stewart nodded.

"And you know where we found it?"

Stewart closed his eyes and nodded again.

"We were just fooling around, Detective," I said. "We'd heard there was a party up there, but when we got to the top, nobody was around. The gate was already open."

I don't know if Barr believed me—he didn't even seem to be listening—but I got the impression it didn't really matter.

"Just stay away from there. The power company's lawyers have threatened to take action the next time anyone trespasses. They're a pretty skittish bunch. The last thing they want is some idiot doing something stupid up there, getting hurt, and suing them. So stay away."

"We will," I assured him. Stewart just looked down at the hilt in silence.

"Don't even go up that road."

"We won't."

"Good, because next time there's a problem, you can guess who I'll be visiting first."

He gathered the pieces back into the envelope and left.

"I wonder if they're going to install a surveillance system up there," Stewart said as we left the barracks. It was dark now, past dinnertime. We paused to look at the wind tower lights, a small row in the distance. Even from this far away, they rose above the horizon, lighting up a good portion of the northern sky.

"Who gives a shit. We're not going up there anyway. Right?"

"Barr's with them. He's working for them."

"Jesus Christ, Stewart, he's a detective. He works for the state."

"It's all the same."

Fucking Stewart. "You just don't know when to quit."

My mother still had to finish her shift, so I followed Stewart out to the Bolgers' car. They were going to take us both to a nice restaurant to celebrate our narrow escape from the law. They were all feeling pretty good about themselves, as if we'd somehow managed to stick it to the Man.

Then I noticed Kaela across the lot by her car. She'd been waiting for us to be released.

"Thanks for the invite, Mr. and Mrs. Bolger, but I think I'm going to go."

"Come, Sancho," Stewart said. "We must rejoice together in our triumph."

"Our triumph, huh? No thanks, Stewart. I'm good."

Stewart followed my gaze over to where Kaela waited. His eyes narrowed.

"Fine," he said at last. "Rest up. Tomorrow's an important day."

I turned and walked away. As I crossed the lot, it hit me all at once—the sound of Stewart's drawn sword ringing in my ear, the sight of its point against Scott's throat, the image of what could have been with one little push. By the time I got to Kaela's car I was shaking. In fact, I shook the whole way home as the images kept flashing over and over again in my mind, an endless loop.

"Hey, listen," Kaela said as we pulled into the driveway. "It's early. Why don't I come in and we can watch some TV or something?"

I reached down, grabbed onto the edge of my seat, and squeezed, hoping it might steady my grip.

"I don't know. Mom's going to be home soon."

"So what? I can meet her."

"I don't know," I repeated. I felt like I was down in some deep hole, like Kaela was talking to me from way up on the surface, her voice thin and distant.

"It's just TV."

When I didn't answer, she shook her head. "I feel like *we're* in a play, Frenchy. You and me. And we keep rehearsing the same scene over and over."

"I know the feeling."

She turned and stared out the windshield. "See you tomorrow."

I let go of the seat and dragged myself out of the car and to the door, still shaking. For a second I looked at my hand under the porch light, hovering over the handle, trembling. Listening to her back out and drive away, I realized just how right she was. I was caught in a goddam cycle. And I had to do something to break out.

So I went inside, looked up the number in the book, picked up the phone, and dialed.

"Hi, Ms. Vale, it's me, Frenchy," I said after she answered. Then I took a deep breath and said the hardest thing I've ever had to say. "I'm really sorry, Ms. Vale, but I have to quit the play."

◄▌ CHAPTER TWENTY-THREE ▐►

There was a long pause on the other end of the line. I tried to imagine the expression on her face. Disappointment? Anger? Disgust?

"May I ask why?" she said. Her voice was oddly calm.

I closed my eyes. There it was again—that naked blade, quivering in the air. I tried to speak, but my voice stuck in my throat.

"Look, Frenchy," she said at last, "I know what happened after practice. Trust me, I spent the last hour on the phone with Mrs. Masure. It was a lively conversation, as I'm sure you can imagine."

"Did she want to cancel the show?"

She snorted. "Well, let's just say we came to an eventual understanding. Stewart will be suspended, but I managed to persuade her to postpone it until after the show. I told her how hard we'd all worked. What an amazing job everyone was doing. You and Stewart especially."

"And now I'm going to screw it all up."

She paused again. "It will be very hard to proceed at this point if you drop out."

"I just don't think I can do it, Ms. Vale. And Stewart . . ." I hesitated, trying to think of how to tell her, how to let her know without breaking my promise. "Stewart hasn't been himself lately. Maybe it's better for everyone."

I could hear her sigh. I was suddenly glad I'd decided to call instead of doing it in person. I knew it was a chickenshit thing to do, but there was no way I could face her.

"Frenchy," she said at last, "this is a very normal reaction. I've seen it many times, even with seasoned actors. And this is a totally new experience for you. I can only imagine how nervous you must be. Both of you. Everyone has different ways of coping. You have yours." She paused. "Stewart has his."

I stifled a groan. She had no idea. A pang of guilt washed over me.

"It's times like this that you have to dig deep, Frenchy. Push that panic away. Both of you have had a horrible day. The last couple weeks have been tough on everyone. It wouldn't be the theater without a little drama, right?"

She chuckled. Not me. I felt sick.

"Listen, I want you to take tomorrow off."

"It's Hell Saturday."

I could hear her shift into damage-control mode. "We can work around it. Your part's in pretty good shape, anyway. Just take some time to collect yourself. Have you told Stewart any of this?"

"No."

"You need to tell him. The two of you are in this together, after all."

"Yeah, you could say that."

"All right, then. As for tomorrow, we'll just tell everyone you're under the weather. In the meantime, rest up this weekend, collect yourself, and I'll check in Sunday night."

"Fine."

"And Frenchy," she said, "we really do need you. As much as Quixote needs Sancho, this play needs your steadiness, your strength. Stewart may be the bright star, but you're our anchor."

"Yeah, thanks," I said and hung up. I hoped to hell she was just blowing smoke up my ass. If I was the anchor of this production, we were all screwed.

I waited until the next morning to call Stewart. I didn't tell him about quitting. I stuck to Ms. Vale's story. But Stewart doesn't miss much. He knew something was up.

"Is this about yesterday?" he said.

"No. I'm sick."

"You don't sound sick."

"Christ, Stewart, you almost killed Scott, not to mention nearly getting us shot by Chief Sullivan."

"You're afraid, aren't you, Sancho? Afraid of the stage. No fear, old friend. No fear. No fear."

"This isn't about me, Stewart," I snapped. "You know it's not."

He hesitated. "Sancho, we've come so far," he finally said. "We can't stop now. All the way, all the way, all the way to the top. I need you, Sancho."

"No, Stewart. You don't need me; you just need Don. It's pretty obvious."

"Don't be jealous. Surely you know Don is nothing without Sancho."

This was going nowhere.

"Look, I'm not coming to practice today. I might not come back at all. I warned you, Stewart, and you went too far. I can't do it anymore."

I heard him swear, then hang up.

A few hours later, I went for a walk. Ms. Vale had told me to collect myself, and walking always did it for me. It had gotten colder again, and what was left of last week's snow had stuck around as a brittle crust. I didn't mind. It felt good to bundle up in my coat, to pull inside my shell against the cold and breathe the sharp air. I tried to convince myself how good it was to be on my own, to get away from the production, but I couldn't help thinking about everyone back at the school, singing, joking around, polishing each scene until it took on a life of its own.

Not that I had to worry about being alone. I hadn't gone too far when a beat-up Camaro sidled up beside me.

"Where you going?" Ralph called out, rolling down his window. He had on a blaze-orange hunting hat and a red flannel jacket.

Ever since Halloween, Ralph had come sniffing back around. Sometimes he'd just show up on our doorstep, and my mother would make him wait outside in the cold while she paced around the trailer a few times, complaining, before finally letting him in like some stray mutt she felt sorry for. As for me, I continued to rag on him for a while, but he never fought back, and so I'd let up some. I don't know; I guess I'd gotten used to the dope.

I shrugged. "Just walking."

"Well, hop in. I'm heading up to the state forest for a little peace and quiet and maybe shoot a deer. It's opening day, bro!" He let out a loud hoot and took a drag off a skinny little spliff he'd rolled.

"I'm good, Ralph. Thanks anyway." I'd never gone hunting with anyone but my father, and even that I just did to get him off my back. Besides, I'd rather be thrown into a pit of Pokers than go within a hundred yards of Ralph with a loaded rifle in his hands.

"Suit yourself. But tell you what, when I get back tonight, your mom and me are going bowling. Come with us, Frenchy. Live a little. Just like your friend Dan Quixote says, right?"

"It's Don, you douche bag."

"Whatever, bro. Just come with us."

"Yeah, maybe." I actually had a weakness for bowling. Bowling and ribs. I glanced into the backseat where his rifle lay. All of a sudden, I shivered. It wasn't from the cold. "Just be careful with that thing, Ralph. Knowing you, you'll shoot your nads off or something."

He leaned out the window and winked. "It ain't loaded. In fact, I think I only got one cartridge on me. Don't matter. Can't shoot for shit."

"Then what the hell are you going out for?"

He shrugged. "I just like to be out in the woods. Hunting always clears my head." He looked at the joint in his hand for a second, then looked up at me. "You want a poke?"

Fucking Ralph. "No thanks, man."

He flicked it over the roof of the car and into the snowbank. Then he got all serious looking and shook his head. "I got some thinking to do, Frenchy. Some real thinking."

"Yeah, well, don't hurt yourself, Ralph."

He laughed, then I laughed, then he took off down the road.

I'd almost reached the pit stop when another familiar car approached, this time from the other direction. And though usually I was happy to see Kaela's car, this wasn't a usual day.

She drove into the pull-off and got out, waiting for me with her hands thrust deep in her pockets, a funky hat pulled down over her head.

"Aren't you supposed to be at practice?" I called out to her.

"I was going to ask you the same question," she replied with a shy smile.

"Funny," I said, coming up to her. "I'm sick. Didn't you know? Seriously, you should be at practice. Big day and all."

"I'm on a mission," she replied, "to see how you're feeling."

I pushed past her and she followed me into the field, hurrying to catch up, taking my arm in hers the way she always did. Our boots punched through the thin crust in lockstep.

"Brushing me off again, eh?" she said. "It's okay, I'm getting used to it."

I stopped and turned to face her. "Sorry about last night."

"Me too." She looked down. "I just want to know where I stand."

"You're out standing in the field," I said.

She rolled her eyes and laughed. "That was bad."

"Sorry. Best I could do on short notice." I took her hand. "Kaela, you stand wherever you want."

She pulled her hand away. "Wherever I want, huh? I'll have to think about that." For a second we just stood there, quiet, then kept walking.

"Ms. Vale sent you, I'm guessing. To try to talk me out of quitting."

She frowned. "So it's true? I didn't actually believe her."

"I've been a quitter my whole life. Why stop now?" She didn't laugh at that one. "Come on, Kaela. I got no business being a part of this play. I was an idiot for letting Stewart talk me into it in the first place."

"That's a load of crap," she said, shaking her head. "You don't really want to quit. You love this play too much. I see it every day in rehearsal. You can't fool me, Frenchy."

"I don't want to fool anybody," I murmured. "That's how I got into this mess to begin with."

She hesitated. "Stewart told a few of the actors that you were scared. You know, stage fright."

I paused for a second and shook my head, then started walking faster than ever.

"Yeah, that's right," I said at last. "Terrified."

"You're a shitty liar, Frenchy."

"How do you know?"

"You've got a tell. Every time you lie, you rub your belly. That's how I know."

I stopped and looked down at my gut. "Damn you, Sancho Junior! Betrayed again." This time, she laughed. "How the hell are you so smart, anyway?"

I looked out over the field. The clouds were low and thick, hiding the towers from sight.

"My father may have taught me how to swing a hammer, but my mother taught me how to play poker."

She pulled me around. I tried to look away, but she held my gaze.

"Frenchy, what the hell is going on?"

I closed my eyes and tried to figure out what to do. I felt more tired than I'd ever felt before. I'd made Stewart a promise, but where had it gotten me? Where had it gotten him? And Kaela was smart, smarter than me. She could tell me what to do. She could help me through this. I couldn't rely on Stewart, that was for sure.

She saw me struggling. "It's Stewart, isn't it?"

I nodded. And then I told her. Told her everything. The confusion, the paranoia, the delusions, the voices. The more I said, the better I felt. But it was like I was pushing all the darkness onto her—she kept looking more and more upset. Her eyes began to well with tears.

"Poor Stewart," she said when I'd finished.

"He's just so afraid."

She shook her head. "I had no idea it was that bad. I mean, Stewart's always been different. And lately, with the play . . . I just thought it was the role. Everyone does."

"It's so hard, Kaela. Sometimes he's his old self. And I thought he was getting better. He seemed less afraid this past week. He said he was taking care of it. And then yesterday happened. He could have killed that asshole Scott."

"But he didn't. He listened to you."

"Yeah, well maybe next time he won't."

She looked up at me. "So that's why you're quitting?"

"I don't fucking know. I just don't feel like I can deal with this anymore. I'm tired of playing along, Kaela, of feeling so goddam powerless. I just want to *do* something."

I brought my hands to my face. I had to cover my eyes—I knew what was coming.

"I didn't do shit when Dad came back." My voice sounded strangled, like someone else's. "He was just so different, this freaked-out stranger who hardly spoke to us. I didn't know how to deal with him and I was scared, so I just tried to pretend that everything would be okay. And it ended up with him in the ground. Now it's happening all over again. It's a fucking nightmare, Kaela. I just can't escape it."

I dropped to a crouch, balancing on my heels with my hands on my head, and stared down at the ground. I could see stalks of grass where our boots had punched through the crust, matted and broken in the snow, still holding on to a touch of their summer green. I reached down and tore up a handful of the frozen stuff, feeling the fibers bite into my hand. I grabbed another handful, yanking so hard I lost my balance and fell back onto my ass.

Kaela came up and crouched down behind me, wrapping her arms around my neck. I closed my eyes, feeling the coldness of the snow under me, the warmth of her above. When I opened my eyes, everything was blurry. I reached up and wiped the wetness from my face with one hand.

"Goddam it." I tore the handful of grass in half and threw it on the ground.

"It's okay."

We were quiet for a minute. Finally, she stood up, then helped pull me to my feet.

"I understand what you're feeling, Frenchy. But will quitting the play make things better? If the whole production falls apart— forget everyone else—will it help Stewart get through this?"

"Maybe."

"Okay, maybe," she replied. "But tearing him away from it now might make things worse. He needs to say good-bye to Quixote. Maybe the performance will give him a chance to do that."

"I don't know if he'll ever be able to let go. Now or later."

"It's only another week, Frenchy. And he promised to get help when it's over. He's your buddy—you've got to trust him."

I shook my head. She gave me a little push.

"You're a loyal friend. It's one of the things I love about you. And maybe that's all Stewart needs right now. Maybe that's all you need to be."

"Maybe that's all I can be."

She nodded and wrapped her arms around me again. This time, she held on for a good long while before breaking away.

"I better get back," she said. "What do you want me to tell Ms. Vale?"

I thought about her going back to the auditorium, back to the bustling brightness of the stage with its cast and crew, with Stewart in the middle of them all, turning in confusion, like an old man looking for something lost. Don without his Sancho.

"Tell her I'll see her Monday."

When the knock came Sunday evening, I was expecting Stewart. I figured he'd been champing at the bit all weekend to know what I'd decided to do. But when I turned on the porch light and opened the door, I was surprised to see Mr. Bolger standing there instead.

"Frenchy," he said, giving me that slight nod he often gave me.

"Mr. Bolger. What's up?"

He was fidgeting around on the step. It was weird to see him nervous, since he hardly ever seemed anything at all. It made *me* feel nervous, and I got a sick feeling in my gut.

"Is Stewart okay?"

He nodded. "It's been a tough weekend for him. Apparently practice didn't go well yesterday. Obviously, being attacked by those thugs and then apprehended by the police the day before didn't help matters. He was in a real state last night."

"Yeah? Like how?"

He just shook his head. "Stewart," he finally said. "Who can figure him out?" He offered a meager smile. I didn't smile back.

"Anyway, he told us you might quit the play." He wasn't smiling anymore.

"I thought about it," I said.

His mouth tightened. He nodded a little. I'd seen him get that look with his son plenty of times. Especially when Stewart wasn't following the party line.

"So you're here to talk me out of it?"

"Something like that."

"You can come in if you like. It's cold."

He waved off the invitation. I could see where Stewart had picked up the gesture. Then he cut right to it.

"It's vital, Frenchy, that you see this to the end. Surely you know dropping out now would be a severe blow to the production."

"I know, Mr. Bolger, but the thing is—"

He held up his hands to cut me off. He had a speech to give.

"I understand you're scared right now. There's a lot of pressure. On both of you. Lord knows Stewart's been feeling it lately. And I'm sure last Friday's fight shook you up as much as it did him. So I wanted to offer you something. A little encouragement, you might say."

He pulled something from his pocket and handed it to me. I looked down at the roll of cash in my hand. I don't know how much it was, but it was wrapped in a fifty.

A look must have crossed my face because he lifted his hands again.

"Now listen. This isn't a bribe or anything like that. Think of it as an incentive. I'm sure you and your mother could use it," he added, wincing as he said it.

I ignored the insult and instead weighed the roll in my hand, marveling at the heft of it, fighting off the urge to lift it to my nose and smell it. Damn, it was heavy. Heavy as a cell phone, a new computer, maybe as heavy as a decent used car. He was watching me. I looked up and could swear I saw the slightest smile cross his face.

That was all I needed. I savored the weight of the cash one last time, then tossed the wad back.

"Keep your money, Mr. Bolger. I already decided to go back. But thanks anyway."

His shoulders settled, and he took a deep breath.

"Okay, then. Good." He hesitated. "Stewart really thinks highly of you. He depends on you, in a fashion." The words seemed to cause him physical pain. I almost felt bad for the guy.

"He's never had many close friends," he continued. "And since moving up here . . ." He took another deep breath. "Lucinda and I are grateful."

I looked over his shoulder at the Audi idling in the driveway. I don't know which of us felt more awkward.

"Anyway, just a week to go," I offered. "You must be excited to see him."

"I have to admit, I wasn't in favor of him joining the production. I worried it would be a distraction. Stewart's applying to some big schools. Harvard, Yale. But it's turned out for the best, I think. Being the lead will look great on his applications. We're even putting together a video portfolio. The arts are important when you're going for the Ivy League. Between that and his new project, he should have all the bases covered."

"Yeah, what's that all about, anyway?"

Mr. Bolger snorted. "Some pretty serious metalwork. A sculpture of some kind. Beyond that, your guess is as good as mine. Top secret. He's taken over my garage, though he's been working on a good chunk of it off-site. Almost as devoted to it as he is to the play. Of course, from what he says, the two are connected. The Quixote Project, he calls it."

I thought back to the metal frame I'd seen Stewart working on in his father's garage and tried to think of what the hell it could all mean. Whatever it was, I didn't like the sound of it.

"You're not worried it's another distraction?"

He shrugged. "His schoolwork has slipped. We've gotten the warnings from school. But second-quarter grades won't come out until after the new year. He can turn it around, I'm sure. Besides, by then the applications will already be in."

"Sounds like you've got it all figured out."

He looked up sharply and opened his mouth as if to speak, then just nodded and turned to go. As he walked down the steps, I took a deep breath. My legs wobbled at the thought of that wad sunk in the right pocket of his trousers. And to think I'd held it in my hands. Fucking Frenchy.

At the bottom, he stopped and looked back. I had a fleeting hope he might ask if I wanted to keep it anyway for being such a great guy.

No such luck.

"Stewart doesn't know I came here tonight."

"Don't worry, Mr. Bolger. I know how to keep a secret."

We didn't say anything else. I watched him get back into his car, then I turned off the light and shut the door.

⅏ CHAPTER TWENTY-FOUR ⅏

Stewart was quiet the next morning when he picked me up for school. He gave a smile when I got in, though, and I could see the relief in his eyes that I'd changed my mind. A few strands of gray hair from his wig had come loose and were hanging down over his face. Between that and the vestiges of Friday's bruises, he looked more bedraggled than ever. It was two weeks now since he'd started wearing that goddam costume to school. Of course, at this point it had become normal looking. In fact, I had trouble picturing him without it.

We didn't say much at lunchtime. We just sat eating while people glanced our way and whispered about the fight. The whole school had heard about it by now, or at least some version of it— the story seemed to change by the hour. By lunchtime, Stewart and I had singlehandedly wiped the Pokers out and taken on half the state police before finally succumbing to tear gas and stun grenades. Some even whispered that Stewart had put Scott in the hospital.

The Pokers weren't in school to get their side of the story out there. They were gone for the week. Unlike Stewart, they weren't getting a delay on their suspensions. I almost thought it was unfair. Almost.

I should've enjoyed it more, but I was distracted. And not just by Stewart.

It had come upon me in the middle of the night. Stage fright—the same kind of fear that had visited me after the audition, when I realized I might actually get cast, only this was ten times worse. Stewart's talk of it to the other cast members on Saturday must have jinxed me. Of course, everyone telling me how nervous I must be didn't help.

It came in the form of a nightmare. There I was, onstage with Stewart and Stacey and Quentin and everyone else in front of a packed audience. Everything was going smoothly until it came to me. I opened my mouth to say my first line, but nothing came out. I tried again. Same thing. The others were looking at me now, pissed. The crowd started murmuring. But no matter how loud I screamed, it was no good—nothing but silence, a total vacuum. It was as if someone had pointed a remote at me and pressed the mute button.

Which was exactly what had happened. The crowd's muttering and laughing stopped, and when I finally got the courage to turn and look, the audience had disappeared except for one figure in the shadows. Then the house lights came on, and there he was—my father—standing with the big black TV clicker in his hand pointed right at me.

I'd actually forgotten about the dream until right in the middle of second period, when it all came rushing back. The next thing I knew, I was thinking about the play, about screwing up. Screwing up big. Why wouldn't I? After all, I was me.

I wanted to tell Stewart, but I didn't. Not because I was scared of admitting it, but because I didn't want to give him the satisfaction of having been right about me.

"So," he said, right before the bell rang, "I got to spend an hour in Bryant's office this morning."

"Really? What for?"

"Just a friendly chat. A little bit of this, a little bit of that." He glanced over at me with this nasty sort of look. "Actually, it was quite the inquisition. Under that mellow shell, he's cunning."

"So did you talk to him?" I tried to hide my excitement. I couldn't help it. I just felt this huge sense of relief. "Did you tell him?"

"Of course not." He frowned. "I just want to know—why did you put him up to it? I thought we had an agreement."

I shook my head. "I didn't tell him shit, Stewart."

He stared at me for a moment, then nodded. "I believe you. It was probably Mrs. Masure, the bitch. I'll find out. Not that it matters. I didn't tell him anything anyway."

"Yeah, well, maybe you should."

He blinked and looked away.

"Fuck it." I looked down at my watch as the bell rang. "Now I've got to go see Bryant."

Stewart laughed. "Quite a pair, aren't we?"

"So this is it, huh?" Bryant said. "Coming down to the wire."

"Something like that." I leaned back in the chair and looked up at the ceiling.

"Nervous?"

"A little, maybe." I proceeded to tell him about my nightmare.

He raised his eyebrows. "That's some dream. You'll probably have a few more stress dreams before this is all over." He paused. "Do you dream about your father often?"

"So, I hear you had Stewart in this morning," I replied.

He hesitated, then laughed. He knew I was dodging. "Yeah, finally got to spend some quality time together. We had quite a conversation. Told you about it, did he?"

I snorted. "He said you really grilled him."

Bryant shrugged. "I did my job. Asked him a few questions, chatted about the play, about school. Same sort of stuff we talked about at your first visit."

"How'd he do?"

"Fine. He seems tired, a bit flat maybe. But he said all the things I would expect to hear."

"So he seemed okay to you, then?"

"I'm not sure what you mean." His look sharpened. "You know him better than anyone. What do you think?"

"You asked me that last time." I stared down at my feet. The sole was starting to detach from the tip of my right sneaker. Cheap-ass Payless shoes.

"And you said everything was fine."

"I'll just be glad when the play's finally over."

"I understand you two had a pretty tough day last Friday. Some trouble in the cafeteria, a scuffle in rehearsal, then that whole business in the parking lot afterward."

"So that's why you called him in."

Bryant smiled. "You never answered my question before."

"Which one?"

"About your father. Do you dream about him a lot?"

"Never. Well, except for last night."

"Never?" he said. He didn't say it in a nasty way, really, but I felt my hackles rise. "It must have been hard seeing him there, then."

"I don't know. He was pretty far away. I didn't really get a good look at him."

"What do you miss most about him?"

"I don't know."

"Okay. Let's try this—what do you remember most?"

Fucking Bryant.

"I don't know," I said, louder now. "In fact, you want to know the truth? Sometimes I can't even remember what he looks like. I close my eyes and try to see him, but I can't. Not the real him. It's ridiculous. It's only been a few months, and I have to look at a photograph to remember my own fucking father. I mean, how pathetic is that?"

My voice was shaking, my eyes were watering, so I shut the hell up. I'd already gotten choked up on Saturday. And now, twice in three days. So lame. Bryant waited, letting me regroup before speaking.

"That's pretty normal, Gerry. You shouldn't feel upset. You shouldn't worry about it, either. It'll start coming back. When you're ready, it'll come back."

"I don't even know if I want it to. Those last few months—everything got spoiled. But that's the way it always is, right? Anything you have that's good, something will come along and just fuck it up."

"It certainly seems that way sometimes."

"Seems? Screw 'seems.' It *will*, trust me."

"Maybe. Yet we keep on trying. Why do you think that is?"

"'Cause we're all stupid. Or crazy."

Bryant got a laugh out of that one.

"I don't think you really believe all that," he said. "I can tell the true cynics—you're not one of them."

"Really? So, what am I, then? What's the diagnosis, Gerry?"

"Oh, that's easy," he said. "You're a worrier. You worry about everything. Even the things you can't control. Especially the things you can't control."

"Well, if I could control them, then I wouldn't need to worry. Right?"

"That's one view. On the other hand, if you can't control them, then what's the point?"

"Yeah, well, that *sounds* good in theory, but it doesn't mean squat in real life," I muttered. He nodded a few times. "So," I said. I wanted to change the subject. "Guess you deal with a lot of screwed-up kids, huh?"

Bryant didn't answer. He just gave me that Zen smile of his.

"Depression?" I asked. "You see depression a lot?"

"Yes. Too much of it."

"Tough to treat, I bet."

"It can be. Sometimes it's just a matter of time and a lot of talking. The person's just going through a phase. Like you said before, right?"

I laughed. "Yeah, that happens. But what about when it's really bad? What do you do then? Drugs, right? Antidepressants, that sort of thing?"

"Sometimes."

"What about other things?" I asked. "Really crazy things? Like, I don't know, hearing voices, imagining things that aren't real?"

"Well, those are pretty serious symptoms, indicating some degree of psychosis. Those cases wouldn't be handled by this office."

He hesitated, then fixed me with a smile. I held my breath, afraid of what was coming.

"Are you hearing voices, Gerry?"

I shook my head. "God, no."

He paused again. "Did your father?"

"No. I don't think so. I mean, I think he heard things, but they weren't make-believe. They were real. Or at least, they had been. He just couldn't stop remembering."

"I knew your father," he said. "We went to high school together, actually. Right here in Gilliam. Not too well—he was a couple years behind me—but I used to see him around. A pretty quiet guy. Friendly. All hot to join the army."

"Yeah. Served six years. Then stayed on after in the National Guard."

"He became a mechanic in town after he left the army, right?"

"Well, he tried to repair things. Not very good at it, though. Least, that's what they tell me. I don't think he was that into it. He just wanted to be a soldier."

Bryant shrugged. "He fixed my car four years ago. It still works."

"You're one of the lucky ones, I guess."

He gave a little laugh, then looked back at me. "He was a decent man, Gerry."

"Yeah, I suppose he was."

He looked at his watch. "So, good luck this weekend. Break a leg, right?"

I laughed. "Thanks," I said, getting up. "So you coming or what?"

"Don't worry," he replied. "I'll be there."

CHAPTER TWENTY-FIVE

Stewart sang. I watched him from the wings, Kaela and I together, with the house lights down and most of the stage lights dimmed as well, with only the blues and reds and greens still shining, so that the stage took on the look of a moonlit night, just like it would tomorrow night during the real thing. He and Stacey moved slowly, almost dancing around each other in a hypnotic circle—Don, singing his love to Aldonza, breaking through her resistance bit by bit; Aldonza, already broken by life, trying not to give in to any kind of hope as the wacky old knight sang "The Impossible Dream."

No, Stacey hadn't changed her mind about Stewart, not even after a week of dress rehearsals, but it was what the scene called for. So every afternoon she came through, because even though she didn't love him, she loved the performance. I don't even know if, deep down, Stewart actually loved her, but it was always real enough for him in its own way.

Funny how the scene I'd first hated most had ended up becoming my favorite. Maybe it was because it was one of the rare sections of the play where I got a break. Onstage—especially now in dress rehearsals, with parents and teachers stopping by to get a sneak preview—I was usually so worried I'd forget a line or miss a cue that it was hard to relax.

"He sounds so good," Kaela whispered.

"Better than ever."

It was true. No matter how much Stewart had pulled back from the cast, from school, even from me, his voice was always pure and present—especially during this scene. All the stress, all the suffering that hovered in his eyes like a dark cloud seemed to clear out as soon as Franco began playing from his spot at the base of the stage. Maybe that was why I loved the scene so much.

"It's hard to believe someone in so much pain can create something so beautiful," she murmured.

I watched him weave in his armor. "He's just wounded. A wounded soldier."

We looked at each other for a moment, then she put her arms around my waist and laid her head against my chest. I brought my hand up and felt the softness of her hair. The lights, the music, the feeling of her against me—it was a perfect moment. I thought how funny it was that the sound of Stewart singing helped bring me to a place where I forgot all about him. I didn't want to let go of her. But everything ends.

Stewart and Stacey finished the song and we made our way through the rest of the afternoon without too many problems. It was our last dress rehearsal, and as the final notes of Franco's piano faded, Ms. Vale called us all onto the stage.

"Very good," she said. She was quiet, calm, a big change from the fiery woman who had driven us for weeks. "Not perfect. But as you all know, a flawless dress rehearsal is bad luck."

She continued her pep talk, telling us how proud she was, how inspired she was by our talent and devotion. She said all the right things, and we responded, sharing smiles and good feelings, as if we knew this would be our last chance to be together this way before it was all over. It was so quiet in the auditorium, so peaceful in a way I'd never felt before, and I realized it was really going to happen. We were going to pull it off.

"So when this is all over," I said, "we're going to celebrate, right?"

We'd just pulled into my driveway after a quiet ride home. After the dress rehearsal, I was in a good mood for a change. I thought maybe I could coax one out of Stewart too. Like he always used to do for me.

"It's not over yet." He leaned back and rubbed his eyes. "Besides, tomorrow *is* the celebration. And Saturday night, and Sunday afternoon. Each performance is its own creation, its own reward. What comes after is nothing. Try to remember that, will you?"

"Oh, come on, Stewart. 'What comes after is nothing?' What about a new start? We could all use one."

He stared out over the steering wheel. "Good-bye, Sancho."

"Yeah, right. Whatever."

And that was it. I got out and watched him take off in the Volvo.

"Put it away, put it away." I waved a hand in front of my face. Doing that made me feel better because it made me laugh, because it was so silly and weird, and because it made me laugh at him, and that's what I suddenly needed to do.

I went inside and made a sandwich. Like the laughing, it made me feel better, so I made another one. Then I heard a knock at the door.

"Yeah?" I said, opening the door to a vaguely familiar man. It wasn't until he smiled that it really hit me. "Holy shit."

It was Ralph. Sort of.

"Hey, bro. Mind if I come in?"

The mullet was gone, along with the patchy facial hair and cheesy mustache. Even the skinny-legged jeans were gone, replaced by a pair of chinos. Tacky, I guess, but an improvement. I think he'd even brushed his teeth.

"Jesus, Ralph, I didn't even recognize you."

He flashed a smile. "Can I come in?" he repeated.

"Sorry," I said, stepping aside to let him in. "Mom should be home pretty soon."

"Yeah, I just talked to her. She invited me to join you guys for supper."

"Wait till she sees you."

"Yeah, I told her I had a surprise for her. That's why she let me come over."

"So what the hell, Ralph? You go on one of those makeover shows or something?"

"Aw, fuck no," he said. "Just felt like it. Trying to make some changes, that's all."

"Changes, huh?"

He sat down at the kitchen table. "Yeah. I've been thinking about things ever since that day you called me a loser."

"Ralph, I told you I was sorry about that."

"Well, it's not like I didn't really know it, Frenchy. But it wasn't that. Not completely. It was that nutty friend of yours. All his talk a few weeks ago at dinner, all that crazy shit about how to treat a lady, and trying to make the best of things. Being a gentleman.

Your mother liked it, I could see that. So I was out in the woods last weekend, after I seen you, waiting in my stand, freezing my ass off, and in the middle of it all, I decided."

He paused, his lips tight, as if he were holding back a grin. I knew he was trying to be all dramatic, waiting for me to ask, so I played along.

"Decided what?"

"I'm going back to school."

"What school?"

"Jesus Christ, culinary school. Remember?"

"Oh yeah. That's cool."

"Damn right. I'm going to start back in next semester. Want to have my own little restaurant someday."

"That's great, Ralph," I said. I meant it too. "But I don't know if Stewart's the best guy to take advice from."

"It's not a matter of advice, Frenchy. It's inspiration. That's what counts, right? Making something good of something bad."

"Yeah, I guess."

"I just got stuck. When my mother died, I didn't know what to do with myself. So I didn't do jack, and look what happened. Well, not anymore, mister. That shit's in the past." He was all eager and excited, like a little puppy.

"Well, take it one step at a time, Ralph. Baby steps, right?"

"Fuck that. Life's too short, bro."

"I suppose you're right." Fucking Ralph, the philosopher.

"Can't wait for your mother to get home. Got a question to ask her."

At that, my blood went cold.

"Yeah? What kind of question?"

"About tomorrow night. Your big opener." He shot me a worried look. "She's not going with anyone, is she?"

"No," I said, smiling. "I think she was planning on going it alone."

"Not anymore," he said with a flick of his eyebrows. "I got tickets."

He pulled a couple out of his shirt pocket and waved them in the air like they were tickets to the goddam Super Bowl or something. I breathed a sigh of relief.

"Sounds like you got it all figured out," I said.

"Sure as shit, bro."

Fucking Ralph. I started laughing. I just couldn't help it. After everything Stewart had put me through, after all the madness, it was good to see that he'd at least helped somebody, that his Don had led one person out of the darkness. That it was Ralph, of all people, was the funniest part. And who knew—if a douche bag like Ralph could get his act together and find happiness, maybe there was hope for us all. Even for an idiot like me.

"Hey, Ralph," I said, seeing the flash of my mother's headlights in the window. "Got a makeover suggestion for you."

"Yeah? What's that?"

"Stop calling me bro."

The muffled buzz of the audience on the other side of the curtain came to me alone. Kaela was tending to some last-minute costume fixes, checking on lighting, making sure set pieces were ready to go. She probably had the most work of all of us these last few minutes before the show. Other kids were hustling back and forth, smiling, pale, nervous, whispering. Everyone was doing something.

Not me. I just stood there, listening to the sound of a packed house settling into their seats and into their expectations. I could feel the energy. I knew I should try to tap it, draw from it, but the power suddenly seemed to be going in the opposite direction. A force too big. It was sucking the life out of me, and I couldn't reverse the flow. What the hell was I doing here? Where was I? Who was I? The whole thing was like a bad dream. Fucking Stewart.

"Hey," he whispered in my ear.

I glanced over my shoulder. Stewart was in his Cervantes garb—fine medieval clothes, hair tied back, fake mustache and goatee, minus the armor and prosthetics the Quixote costume called for. It was always strange to see him as Cervantes. Not quite Stewart, not quite Don, but someone in between.

"It's funny seeing you in that costume."

He made a little face. "Yeah, I don't like it much."

"Why not?"

"It's not really me."

I snorted, then turned back to the curtain.

"Hey, you okay? You don't look so good."

I did my best to nod and smile.

"I'm nervous too," he whispered. "Listen, Sancho . . . Frenchy, I just want to say thank you. I told you before I couldn't have done this without you. You stuck with me to the end."

"Almost to the end, anyway," I said. "As far as I could go."

His smile faded. "Well, we're here, aren't we?"

"We are."

"Then that's all that matters. This is the beginning of the journey's end. It'll all be over soon enough."

"Knock it off."

"It's okay. Screw everything, let's just have fun tonight. And don't worry—Don will keep us safe. He hasn't let me down yet."

This time I smiled for real. When I looked down, he was holding out a little box.

"Go ahead, open it."

"Christ, Stewart. No more gifts."

"One last one. A little something to remember this adventure."

I opened the box. Inside was a watch. Silver, heavy, expensive. I looked at the face, with its luminescent hands. It was set—five minutes to curtain.

"Check out the back." He was all excited, the way he always got when he gave me something.

I flipped the watch over. It was a bit dark backstage, but I managed to catch enough light to read the letters etched into the silver.

Sancho and Don.

"Thanks, Stewart." I started to put it on.

He stopped me. "Sorry, can't wear it now."

"That's right." I slipped it back into the box. "No watches in the Middle Ages."

"Not that so much," he said. "Peasants don't wear watches. Not like this one, anyway."

I looked at him and shook my head. "Blow me."

We both started laughing. Then he threw his arms around me and hugged me tight.

"No fear, old friend."

"No fear, Your Grace."

There's not much to say about the play. First it wasn't, then it was, and there I stood, onstage, under the lights with Stewart and all my new friends, and it wasn't that much different than it had been all week. The house lights were off, the stage lights bright upon us, so that the audience was nothing more than shadows. Our first lines came and went, and from there on out the musical just became itself—it wasn't the movie version, the Broadway version, it wasn't anyone's version but ours, and not even ours, since it seemed to take on a life of its own. I was aware of the audience only when they gasped or clapped or—best of all—laughed.

Of course, I got most of the laughs.

But it was Stewart's night. As if there were any doubt it would be otherwise. And he deserved every second of glory he got. Even I was in awe. After all the days, weeks, of rehearsal, after hearing him sing those goddam songs over and over again until I was singing them in my sleep, I still found myself pausing to catch my breath. He'd never been Don Quixote more than he was that night; the transformation was complete. With each scene, with each number, the silence grew more silent, the applause afterward grew louder. Then came the curtain call, and though everyone was already standing, when Stewart and I came out last to take our bow together—Stewart insisted—the place went wild.

Then it was over, and the curtain was closing, and Kaela was jumping into my arms and kissing me, and even Stewart was laughing and hugging people, and everyone felt great. After that I lost track of Stewart. In fact, the whole rest of the night was a blur as kids, teachers, and parents—hell, even Mrs. Masure—kept coming over to congratulate me and tell us how much we'd rocked.

I was so tired and happy, I felt like I was floating as I rode home in the car with Mom and Ralph. Both of them kept going on about the show until I finally had to tell them to shut up.

"Fine," my mother said. "But I'm going back tomorrow night."

"You are?" Ralph said, turning to her in amazement.

"Don't worry, Ralph, you don't have to go."

Ralph paused, then shrugged. "Why the hell not?"

ACT FIVE:
DÉNOUEMENT

CHAPTER TWENTY-SIX

I bowed to thunderous applause. I bowed again, Stewart and I together, as the curtain closed for the final time. There was no jumping or laughing or kissing today—not like Friday night, or even Saturday—just smiles and a few handshakes, maybe a hug or two.

Not that it hadn't gone well. It had gone well. All the shows had. But it was Sunday afternoon, and we were spent. Happy, but totally spent after a blurry three days.

"You're all exhausted," Ms. Vale acknowledged, calling us to the center of the stage even as the applause died down and the voices rose with the house lights on the other side of the curtain. "That's the way it should be. But it's not over yet. So go out there and get your accolades, then say your good-byes and get ready to work."

There were a few groans, but Ms. Vale just laughed.

"Suck it up, people. It should only take an hour or two to break everything down if we all work together. Then it's pizza time—all you can eat. Principal Masure's treat."

At that, everyone cheered. Everyone except Stewart, who stood off to the side, eyes cast downward, quiet.

We all dispersed to greet the well-wishers. I didn't have anyone waiting for me—I'd actually managed to talk my mom into staying home—so I tagged along with Stewart as he met his parents at the bottom of the stage. They'd been to all three shows.

"Another good one, Stewart," Mr. Bolger said. He looked over at me and gave a nod. "You too, Frenchy. Very impressive. All weekend."

"Thanks, Mr. Bolger."

"So it's finally over," he went on. "I have to say, thank God. Now we can all rest. What're you going to do with all *your* free time, Frenchy?"

"Sleep." I looked over at Stewart. "Actually, I hadn't really thought about it. Maybe I'll start doing my homework."

"Not a bad plan," Mr. Bolger said, frowning in Stewart's direction. "Right, Stewart?"

Stewart didn't reply.

"Oh, that's right," Mr. Bolger said. "He's still got the Quixote Project to contend with. For all I know, this might never end."

I stirred uneasily and glanced over at Stewart, who continued to look sullen.

"Frenchy," Mrs. Bolger said, "would you like to join us for dinner? We thought we'd go out and celebrate your newfound fame."

I laughed. "Thanks, Mrs. Bolger, but Ms. Vale wants us to stay and take down the set and clean up. We're going to have a cast party afterward, I think."

She turned to Stewart. "You didn't mention that, sweetie. That's okay. Stay and have fun with your friends. We'll take you out tomorrow. How's that?"

Stewart didn't say anything. In fact, he wouldn't look at either of his parents. He just kept his eyes down, his mouth tight. Then he lifted a hand and waved it a few times in their direction, as if he were shooing away a fly. Mr. Bolger's face darkened as he and his wife exchanged looks.

I'd seen Stewart be a prick to his parents plenty of times, but this was in a class by itself.

"I'll see you later," I said, trying my best to smile. I jumped up onto the stage and headed over to where Kaela was directing a few of the techs.

For the next half hour, I worked my ass off, helping Kaela mostly, as we started breaking down set pieces, putting away costumes and props, cleaning the stage as best we could. Everyone was laughing and joking now, relief and exhaustion and success all mixing together to make everyone punchy. From time to time, I'd glance over to where Stewart stood alone in the middle of the stage, still in his costume, holding a push broom but not really doing much with it. The bright stage lights had been turned off, dulling the space. It wasn't La Mancha anymore, that's for sure.

The kids noticed Stewart, but most seemed to make a conscious effort to ignore him. A few teased him, shouting over to make himself useful. He just shook his head and stared down at the stage. I wanted to be annoyed. I mean, this was our moment of triumph— the school goofballs turned stars. We should be basking in the glow of success. But seeing him swaying there, so lost, I couldn't feel anything but anxious. All week, I'd wondered what this moment would be like for him, how the reality would hit him. It was over. Done. There was no more reason for him to be Quixote anymore. Not to everyone else, at least. He could no longer hide.

As the minutes passed, he seemed to grow agitated. Pretty soon I could hear him muttering to himself. I couldn't tell what he was saying, but his voice was angry, the way it sounded our last time together at the smoking rock. I started over to check on him.

"Hey, Frenchy," Kaela called. "Could you give me a hand with this?"

She and two of the techs were struggling to lift one of the platforms. I glanced back at Stewart, who still stood there muttering, then went to help Kaela.

Just as I got there, a racket broke out from across the stage. Everyone turned to look. Not me, not right away. I just closed my eyes and listened to the smashing and the yelling and the swearing ringing out in the silence as everyone stopped what they were doing.

When I finally opened my eyes, there was Stewart, going after one of the set pieces. It was the windmill, a backdrop piece Kaela and one of her friends had built for fun to set in the distance during a few of the early scenes. It was only about five feet tall but beautifully detailed, one of the highlights of the entire set.

Not anymore.

Stewart had started with his broom, then switched to a nearby two-by-four when the broom handle snapped. Not much was left of the windmill, but he kept whaling on the broken pieces anyway while everyone gazed with stunned looks, Kaela especially, as all her hard work collapsed into rubble.

Ms. Vale walked up to Stewart, shaking her head. I thought she'd be pissed, but she looked more tired and sad than anything.

"Stewart!" Ms. Vale hollered. Stewart stiffened at her call. Then his shoulders sagged. He dropped the makeshift club.

"That's enough," she said, her voice quiet. "Go home."

He blinked and shook his head a little. "But—"

"You need to leave. Now."

He turned and started to go, his eyes watering. At the edge of the stage he stopped and glanced back at me with this desperate look on his face. For a second we just stared at each other. I couldn't tell if he wanted me to go with him or if he wanted me to stay away. He just looked lost. Then he jumped off the stage and ran out of the auditorium.

"I should go with him," I said as Kaela took my arm.

"Forget about him," she said, looking over at the remains of her windmill. Then she turned back to me. "Maybe he needs to be by himself right now."

"I guess," I whispered. I wasn't so sure, but looking around at everyone going back to work, finishing the cleanup, and getting ready to really celebrate, I told myself that she was right.

"You knew this wasn't going to be easy," she said afterward, catching me staring at the auditorium exit as we gathered up what was left of the windmill.

"For me or him?"

"You know, Frenchy, sometimes you need to take care of yourself," she said as Mrs. Masure came in with a stack of pizza boxes. "You can worry tomorrow. For tonight, savor this. You deserve it."

"Yeah, thanks to him," I said, then went back to picking up the pieces.

"Howdy, beautiful," I said, getting into Kaela's car the next morning.

"Shut up," she said, breaking into a grin as we pulled out.

"Thanks for the ride."

"I was tempted to let you walk. You could use the exercise, chubby."

"Hey," I snapped. "I resemble that remark."

She laughed. "I suppose you'll need one tomorrow too."

"Yeah. He's out both days."

Stewart's suspension was in effect, for these next two days at least. After tomorrow, we had the rest of the week off for Thanksgiving. I wondered if he'd have to serve more days when we got back or if Mrs. Masure would let him go with just the two.

"Too bad," she said. "He's the man of the hour after this weekend. Guess all the glory's going to have to fall on your shoulders instead."

"Yeah, right."

"Are you kidding? I had, like, thirty texts last night about you two. Girls are talking."

"*Girls*, did you say?"

"Don't even think about it."

"Don't worry, thinking's never been my strong suit. Besides, I'm still too tired. I crashed as soon as I got home last night, and I still barely managed to drag my ass out of bed this morning."

"I'm just saying—be prepared."

Kaela was right. As soon as I walked into the building, people were all over me, and most of them *were* girls. Kaela was right next to me the whole time until the bell, not saying much but definitely staking out her territory. The scene was so alien to me, I had no idea what to do or say. The whole thing freaked me out, to tell you the truth.

The rest of the day went pretty much the same way. People kept saying how impressed they were, how surprised they were.

Surprised! I loved that one. It's amazing how you can flatter and insult someone at the same time. Not that I blamed them. I guess I was kind of surprised myself. My favorite was when a group of kids told me outright they'd thought I was going to bomb. A few even said they'd gone to the show *hoping* I would bomb. They seemed to think Stewart and I had had this big plan to blow the whole thing as a joke. It made me feel good to disappoint someone in a positive way for a change.

As great and bewildering as it all was, the whole time I kept wishing Stewart were with me. He'd have known what to say. He'd have absorbed all the attention for me like a shield, soaking it up, making the most of it. Me, I could barely keep track of what was going on. I told myself it wouldn't last. Pretty soon, I would go back to being old Frenchy again. This was just another part I had to play. Then again, so was old Frenchy.

The house felt weird when I got home from school. Partly because it was early—I was used to getting back in the dark—and partly from the quiet. After all the craziness at school, the double-wide felt bigger than usual, empty. I felt kind of empty too. Like you do the day after Christmas.

There was a note from my mother on the refrigerator. She was pulling a double shift tonight to make up for the one she'd missed over the weekend because of the play. As I read her note, it suddenly occurred to me that maybe I should get a job, start making some money. Mr. Bolger had asked me what I was going to do with all my free time. A job was probably a good place to start. But I had other things to worry about first.

I tried calling Stewart at his house. His mother answered.

"Frenchy, hi," she cooed. "Stewart's not here right now."

"Oh. Do you know where he is?"

"Well, he was in his father's shop, but I think I saw him drive out about an hour ago. I'll tell him you called."

"That's okay, I'll just try him on his cell."

"He doesn't have it with him," she said, hesitating. "He stopped using it, actually."

"Really?"

"He says they're not safe. Trust me, we went through it all last week. He was quite convincing."

"Okay," I said. "How's he doing, anyway?"

She paused. "It's been a rough day. He's so spent from the performances. It's good he's taking a few days off. He needs the time to recover."

Taking a few days off. She made it sound like he was on vacation. I wondered if she even knew he was suspended.

"Well, tell him I'd like to see him later."

It was around nine o'clock that night when I got my wish. I was still tired as hell and was just about ready to turn the TV off and go to bed early when I heard a heavy pounding at the front door. I flipped on the porch light to see Stewart standing there on the steps in full costume, arms folded, his head down, the replacement prop sword hanging from his belt. He banged again, hard, steady, and I suddenly couldn't help thinking I should have wished for something else.

Chapter Twenty-Seven

"There you are, Sancho!" He burst past me into the house. The temperature had dropped, and he was shivering in his armor.

I plopped down at the kitchen table and kicked out a chair for him, but he ignored it. "Where have you been? I've been waiting all night for you to call me."

"Well, wait no longer. Get up! Get up! Get dressed, for God's sake." He was all wound up, pacing the floor, fidgeting with his wig. "And stop this Stewart foolishness. You don't know when to quit. None of you. None of you do."

I stood up, coming around to look him in the face. He had all the makeup on, the prosthetics, but I could see his eyes well enough. There it was—the same look he'd had at the smoking rock. His eyes were wide, liquid.

I put my hands on his shoulders. "Don Quixote's gone, Stewart. It's over."

He stepped away from me and waved a hand in front of his face. "We have to go."

"Go? Go where? It's late."

"Adventure awaits, Sancho. Pack your things. I've got it all planned out."

"Got what planned out, Stewart?"

"We ride west. West, west, west. There's trouble in the land, no doubt about it. We must find it, face it, defeat it."

"Yeah, and be back in time for breakfast, right?" I shook my head and looked down at my thumb. The cut had long since healed, but a nasty scar remained.

"Breakfast? Surely you jest. There is no going back, Sancho. That's the best part, don't you see? We get to get away from him. From him and them. They'll never bother us again," he said. His face fell. "I've had it with them. There's no beating them."

I started to reach for him again, then stopped and brought my hands up to my head instead, pulling back my hair.

"Why are you doing this to me, Stewart? Why can't you just let go?"

He grabbed my peacoat off the back of the kitchen chair and tossed it to me. I tossed it back.

"No, Stewart," I said. "We're not going anywhere. You promised me that you'd do something about this. You said you were taking care of it."

"Put it on, Sancho. Your beautiful coat. Put it on. It'll protect you."

He lifted the coat toward me, as if to try to put it on me. I pushed him away.

"You said you were taking care of it. You promised."

"It'll keep you safe from the cold. It's so cold. So goddam cold out there, you have no idea."

As he lifted the coat a second time, I snatched it from his hands and threw it across the room. I stepped toward him, my finger in his face.

"You promised me, Stewart! You fucking promised!"

He backed away, his eyes wide, until he hit the counter, knocking over a glass in the process. It rolled off the edge, hit the floor, and shattered. We both jumped at the sound. I looked down at the shards scattered across the linoleum, gleaming under the kitchen light, and shook my head again.

"You promised."

"I tried," he wailed. "It didn't work. I spent hours, but I didn't dare do more."

More what? There it was again—that sick feeling in my belly. I was supposed to do something, say something to make it right. I had to be a good Sancho. But the play was over, and I didn't want to be Sancho anymore.

I could hear the TV in the living room, the sound of the canned sitcom laugh track rising and falling in distant waves. I hated that sound like I hated those shows. They had complications but they were trivial, with easy resolutions and happy endings. Nothing like real life. Nothing like this.

Stewart had given up on the coat and started pacing again.

"Listen," I said. "It's not too late. I can call Mr. Bryant right now. He's a really smart guy. He'll know what to do. He can help us." I started for the phone.

Stewart drew his sword with a flourish. I jumped back and felt something sharp bite into my heel.

"Ow! Fuck!" I leaned against the refrigerator and lifted my foot. A half-inch shard of glass was embedded in the skin. I yanked it out with a yelp. Immediately the blood started to run. I looked up at Stewart, but it seemed he hadn't even noticed.

"Enough!" he boomed. Swaying a little, he brought down his sword and leaned upon it like a cane. "Any more of this disobedience,

Sancho, and I shall have to beat you. You know I don't want to do that, so please be a good fellow and stop with all this nonsense."

As he spoke, one of his eyebrows began to detach. He reached up and pressed it back, but it continued to flop.

"Drat!" he yelled. He strode by me and headed to the bathroom. I followed, hopping on one foot, trying not to get blood on the hallway carpet.

"Come on, Stewart. Just stop it. This isn't funny anymore."

He leaned over the sink, bringing his face right to the mirror, and began fiddling with the eyebrow. He glanced over at me.

"What are you waiting for?" he asked. "Where are your things?"

"Stewart, stop."

"Oh, and pack some food. We'll no doubt need refreshment before the night is out."

"Stewart, you have to stop this. You have to come back."

"Come back?" he demanded. "Come back where?"

"To reality, Stewart."

"Reality?" He finally got the eyebrow to stick, then turned toward me. "I know reality when I see it. I define reality. Everything else is just shadows and dreams, shadows and dreams. The world you live in—that's the illusion, my dear Sancho. You know nothing of reality, you stupid peasant. You know nothing of it."

This time I grabbed him. Grabbed him by his armor and started shaking.

"No, Stewart! No more of this bullshit!"

His eyes widened, the loose eyebrow fell off, his armor rattled, but I kept right on hollering.

"You think I don't know reality? You want to see reality, Stewart? You want to see it?"

I pushed him up against the sink, then whirled around and snatched the floral painting off the wall.

There it was, a large, uneven circle, pale brown under the fluorescent light, hovering on the wall like an evil nebula.

"Know what that is? *That's* reality, Stewart!" I shouted, grabbing him and pointing at the stain. "That's the only fucking thing that's real!"

He started trembling and blinking like crazy, then sank to the floor and closed his eyes. I dropped down across from him.

"I'm sorry, Sancho," he whimpered. "I can't stop it. I'm sorry."

"Why him?" I watched the blood seep from my heel and pool beneath my foot. Already it had begun to spread across the floor. I wanted to reach for the towel above me on the rack, but I was too tired even to move. "Why Quixote? Just because he's crazy doesn't mean you have to be."

He shook his head. "Not because he's crazy," he cried. "Because he's not afraid of them!" He grew quiet. "You know. You were there. Every day for weeks you were there. You saw how he charged them, how brave he was. I need that strength to make it through, to protect me from them."

"You mean the towers, don't you?" I said. "Those fucking turbines." I could see the tears start to trickle from the corners of his eyes.

We were quiet for a long time.

"How long?" I said at last. "How long has this been going on?"

"Last year. Before your father came back, I started hearing them, talking to me, laughing. It was just in my dreams, at first. Then it wasn't."

"Shit, Stewart. You need help. This is serious."

He opened his eyes and looked at me. "I don't want that kind of help. I don't want them inside my head. I can't fit anyone else in there. Besides, I've got Don. Quixote will keep me safe."

"He won't, Stewart. He's making it worse. Ever since you started down that road, you've fallen farther away."

He shook his head. "I have to keep going."

"Well," I said, looking up at the stain, "I can't follow you."

He struggled to his feet. "I need you, Sancho. I can't do it alone." He reached out a hand to help me up. I didn't take it.

"You don't have to do anything alone," I said. "You just have to let me help you, let other people help you. Otherwise, it's never going to go away. You'll never escape them."

He shook his head. "Never," he whispered.

Then he was gone, and I was alone. Just me and the stain.

CHAPTER TWENTY-EIGHT

After he left, I picked up the phone and called Kaela.

"He can't give it up," I said. "He's too scared."

"I'm so sorry, Frenchy," she said. She paused. "What next?"

"I don't know. It's all falling apart. I have to tell them. His parents. Mr. Bryant. Somebody will know what to do."

"It's okay," she said. "Stewart didn't keep his promise. You don't have to keep yours. Not anymore."

"I already broke it when I told you."

"Girlfriends don't count."

"Girlfriend, huh? Wow. Not used to hearing that."

"I'm not surprised. Just be quiet before I change my mind," she said. "And Frenchy, let me know if you need me. For whatever."

"Thanks, Kaela."

"I care about him too," she said, then hung up the phone.

Stewart's car wasn't in the driveway as I came upon Shangri La the next morning, though I could see his tracks in the dusting of snow that had fallen in the night. It was just as well—I hadn't come to see him.

I climbed the steps and rapped on the door a few times. My heart seemed to pound harder with every knock. I'd been up since five thinking about what to say, but it didn't matter now.

Mrs. Bolger opened the door without her usual little game.

"Hello, Frenchy."

"Hello, Mrs. Bolger." My voice was shaking. I wondered if she could tell. "Is Mr. Bolger home?"

"Yes, he's home," she said, looking confused. "But Stewart's not here, I'm afraid."

"Yeah, I see that. Do you know where he is?"

"He said he had some things to take care of. To be honest, I thought he was going to pick you up for school. Do you need a ride?"

"No thanks. I actually came to talk to you and Mr. Bolger. Can I come in?"

She managed a faint smile, then stood aside.

The Bolgers' house always smelled good in the morning. Fresh coffee, fresh patchouli, fresh fruit, fresh bread. There was Mr. Bolger at the counter with the *Globe*. Just like it was any other day. His eyebrows crinkled at the sight of me.

"What's this?" he asked. He was especially warm and fuzzy in the morning.

I stood there for a moment, trying to catch my breath. Finally, I let it out.

"There's something wrong with Stewart. Really wrong. He's sick. He needs help."

They looked at each other for a moment. Mrs. Bolger turned away toward the stove. Mr. Bolger glanced back down at his paper. At first I thought they were just going to pretend I wasn't there, but finally Mr. Bolger spoke up.

"Sit down, Frenchy," he said. "Cup of coffee?"

"Okay." I took a seat at the table. Mrs. Bolger poured a cup and brought it over. The Bolgers drank their coffee black. Guess they thought everyone else did too.

"So what makes you think Stewart's sick? Has he complained about anything?"

"I don't mean sick that way. I mean, you know, mentally." I hesitated. "He won't stop being Don Quixote. He says he hears voices. It's the wind towers. He thinks they're after him."

Mr. Bolger shook his head. "Those goddam towers." He looked over at me. "The problem with Stewart is that he's exhausted. He's been working himself to the bone these last few weeks. Between the play and this project he's trying to finish up, it's a wonder he's still on his feet."

"Yeah, but—"

"Listen," he said. "I know Stewart's been off his game lately, but don't worry. He'll straighten out. You know how he is."

"It's just a phase," Mrs. Bolger murmured.

I shook my head. "No. No, it's not. He came by last night. You should've heard him talk. It wasn't Stewart. And it wasn't the first time."

"Stewart's got a good imagination," Mr. Bolger said.

"He always has," Mrs. Bolger added. She gave a sad little smile.

"The world just can't accept creativity," Mr. Bolger went on. "Anyone who's different, anyone with a spark—forget it. They're going to be misunderstood. Stewart's right—that's what Don Quixote's all about. It's probably why he was so good at the role."

"This is different, Mr. Bolger." I tried not to let frustration creep into my voice. "It has nothing to do with creativity. He's not in touch with reality."

I glanced across the table at Mrs. Bolger, wrapping and unwrapping a dishcloth around her hands, her mouth tight with fear. I knew the feeling. Hearing both of them, I started to get that sick sensation in my stomach all over again, just like last night. They exchanged a dark look.

"You know," I said at last. I turned back to Mr. Bolger. "Both of you know. You've heard him, too, haven't you? Haven't you!"

Mr. Bolger leveled his gaze at me. "My son is not crazy," he said. Mrs. Bolger brought the dishcloth up to her face and choked back a sob.

"Look, can't he just talk to someone? The school psychologist is really good."

"Stewart already talked to him," Mrs. Bolger said.

"Yeah, but maybe Mr. Bryant could try again."

"Try what again?" Mr. Bolger snapped. "I don't want Stewart getting falsely diagnosed by some two-bit guidance counselor, not with college applications going out. You know the stakes, Frenchy. I won't jeopardize his future. Maybe once the acceptances come in and Stewart's settled on where he's going, we can look into getting him some counseling. In the meantime, his mother and I can help him through this. All of us can."

Fucking Bolgers. I couldn't believe what I was hearing. They were supposed to be all progressive and forward thinking. Forget that, they were supposed to be *adults*. They were supposed to be parents. They were supposed to eat up my fears and rush to Stewart's aid and make everything all right.

I shook my head. "*I* get counseling, Mr. Bolger. Trust me, Stewart doesn't need a counselor. This is bigger than that. Bigger than any of us." My voice was shaking even more now. I tried not to let it, but I couldn't help it.

Mr. Bolger's look softened. He sighed and got up from his stool, then came over and put his hands on my shoulders. "You've had a rough year, Frenchy. After everything that happened with your father, I can understand why you might be worried. I appreciate the concern. We both do."

"Yeah, but you're not going to do anything about it."

He sighed again. Mrs. Bolger just looked away, her eyes filled with tears.

"Listen," he said. "We're going to Burlington today. When we get back tonight, we'll sit down with Stewart and have a long talk and figure out how best to handle this."

More talk. More bullshit. My father had a saying: *There's talking, and then there's doing.* It suddenly seemed pretty clear to me there would be no doing. Not by them, at least. Not when it needed doing.

"Okay then." I got up from the table and headed for the door.

"Can I give you a ride to school?" Mrs. Bolger asked.

I looked down at my new watch. I was already late, but I didn't give a shit. I couldn't stand the idea of spending another minute with either of them.

"No thanks," I said. "I'm good."

With the cut on my heel slowing me down, it took over a half hour to walk to school, and that was after someone stopped and gave me a ride the last mile to town. It was fine by me—I was so wound up leaving Shangri La, I needed to burn some energy. But I also hoped I'd meet Stewart along the way. Every time I heard a car up ahead, I quickened my pace, anxious to flag him down, but he never showed.

Second period was drawing to a close by the time I walked into school. I headed straight for Bryant's office without bothering to sign in and knocked on the door.

"What's wrong, Gerry?" he asked, searching my face as I stepped through the doorway.

"I need to see you. Right now."

He nodded. "Hang on."

He told the student in his office to sit tight, then brought me down the hall to an empty conference room.

"Go ahead," he said, closing the door behind him.

It all came out in a gush. Bryant didn't say much; he just let me talk. After the Bolgers, it felt good to talk to someone who actually listened.

"How long did you say this has been going on? I mean, the voices in particular."

"It's been bad for a few weeks, I think. But he said it really started a year ago."

He frowned. "Oh dear."

"I didn't know, Mr. Bryant," I whispered.

"I believe you."

"When the play started, I knew something was wrong, but I didn't—" My voice caught in my throat. I didn't want to say it. "He promised me he'd deal with it."

"It's okay." He said it in that Bryant way that made me feel like it was true.

I nodded. "What's wrong with him?"

"Some form of psychosis," he said. His face was set, all business. "But from the symptoms you're describing—the auditory hallucinations, persecutory and referential delusions, disorganized thinking, that sort of thing—schizophrenia, most likely."

I dropped into a chair, leaned on the table, and put my head in my hands. A hot flash hit me, the kind you feel before you get sick. I didn't know why at first. I mean, I already knew Stewart was crazy. Then I realized. Now it had a name.

Bryant sat down and waited.

"It's been so hard," I said. "He seemed better for a while. Some days good, some days bad. Yesterday—really bad."

"People don't go to bed normal and wake up psychotic, Gerry. It's a gradual process. Symptoms can come and go, depending on all kinds of factors. Like a major stress, for example."

I glanced over at him. "So maybe it was the play after all."

"It could have accelerated things. Of course, smoking lots of pot doesn't help."

I looked down at my feet.

"Listen, Gerry, this is the age when schizophrenia typically starts to show itself. Play or no play, pot or no pot, it doesn't necessarily matter. If the towers weren't around, something else would have become the focus of his paranoid delusions. These things just happen. It's nobody's fault."

"So what are we going to do?"

Then he did the last thing I expected he'd do. He made a sad sort of face and shook his head.

"It's a tough one. The Bolgers didn't sound too receptive to your plea. Is Stewart eighteen yet?"

"No. His birthday's next month."

"He's still a minor, then. Which means the Bolgers have the final say in terms of whether or not Stewart can be treated."

"But you can call them. Maybe they'll listen to you."

"I'll absolutely call them," he said. "But I can't promise they'll change their minds. You have to understand that."

I nodded. "Fine. But you have to do it now. They said they were leaving for the day. You can still catch them if you call now."

"All right." He put a hand on my shoulder. "In the meantime, go to class. Try not to worry."

"Yeah, right."

I checked in at the office and headed to class. It was the day before Thanksgiving vacation, which meant nobody was doing squat. At first I thought it would be good—it would give me a chance to relax a little—but it ended up being the opposite. The minutes dragged by, one by one by one, and pretty soon all I could think about was Stewart—where he was and whether Bryant had caught up with the Bolgers and if they'd changed their minds and so on and so forth, round and round. Along the way, kids kept coming up to me, wanting to talk about the play. People were still buzzing about it. Yesterday the attention had been bewildering; today it was just annoying. A few times I thought about walking out, but I held off and just focused on being patient.

When the final bell rang, I rushed out of class. Bryant was waiting for me. He just frowned when I came up to him.

"You're kidding," I said.

"They pretty much told me the same things they told you. Only not as nicely, I'm guessing."

"But I have to do *something*. There has to be something I can do to help, to stop this."

"It's up to Stewart now. He has to decide he wants help."

"But he *won't*. He can't leave Don Quixote. Believe me, I tried to get him to come back, but he's too afraid."

Bryant nodded a few times but didn't say anything.

"Can't we just force him? Take him to a hospital or something?"

"You can't involuntarily commit someone unless they pose a danger to themselves or to other people. Is Stewart a threat? Are you willing to make the case? If there's anything you haven't told me yet, I need to know now."

He looked me dead in the eye and waited.

"What do you want me to tell you?"

"Just the truth."

"I don't know what the truth is."

I thought about the parking lot, about Stewart pinning Scott against the hood of his car with his sword, about Stewart wrestling Quentin to the stage moments earlier. But he'd been frustrated, provoked, bullied. Anyone could have reacted that way under those kinds of circumstances. Kids fought all the time. Even friends. The more I thought about it, the less sure I felt. And now, in order to help him, I had to label him a threat, make accusations. Who knew where that would lead. I imagined him being hunted, captured like an animal.

I finally shook my head. "I don't think he'd hurt anyone. Not really."

"What about himself?"

"I don't know. I don't think so. He's never said he would."

"Okay, then I think we have our answer."

"It just doesn't seem right. Somebody should *do* something."

"Gerry, I know it sounds strange, but as long as they're not hurting themselves or anyone else, people in our society have a right to be crazy. That's the way the system works."

I forced myself to look in his eyes. "Try telling that to my father."

He sighed. "Want my advice? Find Stewart and keep talking to him. The *real* him."

"I will."

"And I'll try calling the Bolgers again tomorrow. It might take a while for them to come to grips with this. People often struggle with denial in matters like these. Parents especially."

"Yeah. I know all about it," I said, and turned to go.

He stopped me.

"You're okay, Gerry. I just want you to know. That guy I saw onstage the other night, the one I'm seeing now, isn't the same one who showed up in my office at the beginning of September. No matter what happens, remember that."

I tried to smile. "Thanks."

"And be careful," he said, then let me go.

I got a ride partway home and started hobbling up the hill, running as best I could. I was going straight for Stewart's. I got so tired out, I thought of stopping at Ralph's for a lift, but the Camaro was gone. Mom, of course, was at the barracks, miles away, so I pushed on. The whole time I kept praying that Stewart was home, that maybe he'd even come around, that he'd listen to me. He *had* to listen to me. I'd listened to him, followed him all these years, and now it was my turn. My turn to be Don.

I'd passed my house and reached the edge of Shangri La Road when Stewart's car came flying around the bend. It took me a second to figure out it was him—the front of the Volvo was covered by a metal frame with a 55-gallon drum lashed to it.

"Oh shit." I recognized the frame—I'd caught a glimpse of it a couple weeks ago in the Bolgers' garage.

I barely managed to jump out of the way as he hit the brakes and skidded to a halt.

"Where are you going, Stewart?" I yelled, running up to the driver's side door as he rolled down the window.

"There you are, Sancho!" He broke into a smile. He was still in full regalia. Only his eyes were different now—dark with exhaustion. "I was just about to leave without you."

"What did you do to your car?"

"My steed has been modified. Altered to suit my needs. All part of the plan, Sancho. You'll see."

"What plan?" Then I looked into the car and my stomach flipped.

The whole backseat was loaded with tanks, with Mr. Bolger's tanks—oxygen, acetylene, propane—the ones he used to fuel his torches. Stewart had piled them up. From the way his car sagged, I guessed he had more in the trunk.

It all clicked. After weeks of watching Don charge his hated windmills on the stage, I suddenly knew what Stewart was planning to do. Project Quixote was coming to an end.

"One last adventure, old friend. You were right, you were right. There's no running, no escape. We can only go through. I'm going through."

I started to feel dizzy now, like I'd entered a dream. This was all happening in some alternate world, not this one.

"No, Stewart. You can't do this."

"It's already done."

"Get out of the car, Stewart."

His grin faded. He drew back from the window.

"Get out of the fucking car!" I grabbed at the handle, but he'd locked the doors. "You can't do this, Stewart. This isn't you. I told Bryant that this isn't you. You want to make me a goddam liar?"

The car continued to run, its exhaust curling in the frigid air. For a moment we stared at each other.

"Get out of the car," I pleaded, coming up close to the window and leaning in.

"A clever ruse," he said at last, his voice all thick and strange. "You've taken many shapes, but I never thought you'd have the nerve to become my dear Sancho."

"Stewart, I'm not the Enchanter. There is no Enchanter. Look at me. Look at me, Stewart."

He wouldn't look, so I reached in to touch his shoulder. As soon as my hand brushed him, he recoiled. Then he hit the gas.

I took off after him, waving my arms, screaming for him to stop, but he just turned the corner and sped off down the hill with me chasing him.

He disappeared around the corner, but I didn't stop. I kept on running, grateful for the downhill momentum that carried me all the way to my driveway and into the house. I burst inside, grabbed the phone, then hesitated. I almost called the police, wondered in those horrible seconds if I should. Then I tried to imagine Stewart—alone, confused, ready to explode—confronted by a score of cruisers. I knew I needed to get to him first. I needed to be the one to save him. Because I could.

I dialed Kaela's cell, praying she'd pick up. For once, I caught a break.

"Is this the famous actor?" Kaela's voice, playful and coy, sounded in my ear.

"Kaela, you have to come pick me up at my house. Something's happened. Something with Stewart."

"What happened?"

"Please, Kaela. Just come. I need you."

"I'm already on my way."

I hung up the phone, but I didn't wait. I tore out of the house and kept on going down the hill, half running, half limping. Anything to meet her sooner, anything to get me to the only place Stewart could be going.

⣠⣼ CHAPTER TWENTY-NINE ⣧⣀

"You can't blame yourself, Frenchy," Kaela said as we made our way up Wind Farm Road, skidding around one switchback after another. She was already driving ridiculously fast, but I wanted her to go faster.

"He kept saying he was taking care of it." I slammed the dash.

"How were you supposed to know what he meant?"

"I just should've. Stewart's clever. He never means exactly what he says. I should've guessed that he was planning something like this."

"You sure he's going to blow them up?"

"He's going to try," I said. "He's been wanting those things down from the beginning, long before Quixote came along."

"But do you think he can? I mean, they're so goddam big."

"If anyone can figure it out, it's Stewart. You know how smart he is."

We were approaching the top. I could see the gate. It was open. My stomach clenched even tighter.

"So what's the plan, anyway?" She pulled to a stop.

"The plan? I don't know what the fucking plan is, Kaela. Stewart's always the one who had the plan. Not me."

"Forget about that." She grabbed me as I started to jump out. "The play's over. You're not Sancho anymore. You're a smart, tough guy, Frenchy. You can figure this out."

"Let's hope you're right," I said, trying to muster a smile. She patted me on the cheek and let go.

We got out and looked up at the towers rising above the trees. They were still standing. No smoke, no sound—the blades were still.

"Maybe we should call someone," she said, drawing close to me and squeezing my hand.

"You mean like the police? Yeah, get a SWAT team up here. That'll really help. Besides, we don't know how much time we have. We might not have any."

The two of us passed through the open gate and set out.

"Are you positive this is where he'd go?" she said as we hurried along the service road.

"He's here."

Sure enough, there he was, standing on the roof of his car at the top of the rise, where the road peaked before heading back down toward the row of wind towers. From here, he wasn't much more than a silhouette against the November afternoon sky, with his cloak spread out behind him, one hand resting on his hip, the other holding his sword as he looked away from us toward the turbines, preparing for one last battle.

Turning to Kaela, I put my finger to my lips. She nodded, her face white and full of fear.

I took off along the road, quiet and quick, sneaking toward him like I would a deer, the way my father taught me. No more fucking around. I was going to take him out before anything could happen.

I had only twenty yards to go when he turned and caught sight of me. With a curse, he tossed his sword aside, hopped down off the car, armor rattling, and jumped inside, slamming the door and starting the engine as I came upon him.

"Open the door, Stewart!" I banged on the glass.

He turned and looked at me through the window. His face was white and streaked with tears. He looked more terrified than I'd ever seen anyone look, worse than at the smoking rock, even worse than last night. His mouth moved, but I couldn't hear the words behind the glass.

I tried the door. It was locked. I knocked on the window again, but he only looked away, back toward the towers. I'd never felt so helpless in my whole life. Not even when I'd heard the shot in the middle of the night and come out to find Dad there on the bathroom floor. Then, there was nothing to be done, nothing to stop. Not like now.

Think, Sancho, I told myself, then grimaced. *Fuck Sancho.* Kaela was right. Being Sancho wasn't enough.

I reached down and grabbed the sword, then ran around to the front of the car and pointed it right at him. The cap on the large metal drum was sealed with duct tape. A rubber hose lay on the ground beneath it. I didn't know what was in that drum, but I knew Stewart was sharp enough to have figured something out. He'd turned his car into a bomb, an exploding steed, and he was determined to charge it right into the base of the wind tower and take it out, Quixote-style, even if it meant taking himself out with it.

He revved the engine, then honked the horn a few times. I stood my ground.

I could see him frown. He rolled down the window and stuck out his head.

"Get in, Sancho!" he hollered, his voice cracking as the tears continued to flow. "Come with me!"

"I'm not Sancho, Stewart. And I'm not the Enchanter, either. I'm just Frenchy, that's all. And you're just Stewart."

He shook his head and gave a bitter laugh as snow started to fall.

"Laugh if you want, but it's the truth. It's real. And if you do this, Stewart, you're going to die, and that's real too. This isn't a play or a movie or a book. You're not going to come back!"

"I don't care!" he wailed.

"Just stop the car, for chrissake!"

His face darkened. "Get out of the way, Sancho. I'll run you over, I swear."

"Go ahead. Go ahead and do it!"

He started to roll toward me. I braced myself. At that point, I didn't know who was crazier—him or me. I just knew I wasn't going to let him do this to himself. I wasn't going to let him do it to *me*.

He laid on the horn, a loud, steady rip as the car moved closer. The noise triggered something in me, and all of a sudden I found myself raising the sword above my head, ready to come down on the barrel as hard as I could. I took a deep breath and closed my eyes.

"Don't!" I heard him scream.

I opened my eyes. The car had stopped moving. Through the windshield I could see the confusion on his face. I lowered the sword.

"Listen to me, Stewart. For once, just listen!" I called out. "You said you couldn't be Don Quixote without me, and so I did it. I became Sancho for you. But I need you now, Stewart. We can figure out what's real and what isn't later on. Right now, I need you to stay."

He started to cry again. Then he began to shake his head, and yell, and beat the steering wheel, and all I could think was that this was it, this was the end. I glanced over at Kaela, watching me from the edge of the clearing, her arms wrapped around herself against the snow.

When I looked back, Stewart had slumped forward, his head down on the steering wheel. And then the car began to roll.

Dropping the sword, I ran around to the driver's side door, reached through the open window, and popped the lock. I managed to open the door and haul him out by his armor just as the car went over the crest toward the base of the first tower.

We hit the ground with a thud, rolling a few times before coming to a stop. Stewart just lay there, limp and dazed, as I struggled to my elbows and turned toward the tower, watching as the car moved silently down the incline, rolling faster and faster through the snow as it closed the gap between us and the base of the turbine, sailing closer, closer, bouncing over the uneven ground.

It took one particularly hard bump and left the ground entirely. For an instant it seemed to float there in space—a silver form hovering above the ground, glowing as the late-day sun reflected off the windows—a moment of perfect silence. Then it fell, its front end tilting toward the dark ledge rising from the snow.

The explosion ripped through the afternoon gloom, a combination of sound and light that knocked me on my back. I rolled over to cover Stewart and shut my eyes as the flames crackled and debris fell all around us. When I managed to sit up again, the Volvo was nothing more than a blackened frame burning thirty feet from the tower, its plume of dark smoke rising up to mingle with the still blades.

Stewart moaned, then started laughing and crying at the same time. I reached over and put my hand on his shoulder.

"Did I do it, Sancho?" he gasped. "Is it done?"

"It's done, Stewart."

He nodded, opened his eyes, and looked at me. "I'm so tired. I just want it to be over."

"It is," I said. "Project Quixote is finished."

Then Stewart closed his eyes again and smiled.

EPILOGUE

"Finally." Stewart nodded toward the Bolgers as they stepped out for a private meeting with the doctors. He leaned back in the leather chair with a sigh. "Hope they didn't drive you too insane on the ride down."

Hearing him use that word made me wince a little. I tried not to show it, but he caught me anyway and laughed.

"Don't worry," he said. "It's a running joke around here. Gotta have a sense of humor in the ward, you know."

I smiled, getting up from the bed to remove my peacoat. I wandered over to the window. It was snowing again, heavy now, so that I could only just make out the Christmas lights on the trees around the parking lot of the Wilmington Retreat.

"Gets dark early now," I said, turning back.

He shrugged. "Tomorrow's the solstice. After that, it'll start getting brighter."

I nodded, looking around the room at the wood paneling, the flat-screen TV, the quilt on the bed, the leather chair.

"Pretty nice place."

"Not bad for a nuthouse," he said with a grin. "Beats the state hospital, anyway. Lucinda and Phil spared no expense. Nothing but the best for Stewart Bolger."

It felt good to hear him use his real name. And to see him grin. It made him seem more like himself, the way he used to be. It had only been a month since he'd been committed, but I noticed he looked different as soon as I walked in. He'd cut his hair, for starters. But it was more than just that. It was his smile, the way he sat, the way he turned to stare out the window. He was calmer, more subdued. I mean, he didn't seem drugged out or anything, but the edge was gone, the sharps a little flattened. I didn't know if it was because it had been a while, or because of the medication, or if maybe I was just different.

"Things good with Kaela?" he asked. His gaze lowered. I watched him pick at a few loose threads on his jeans before finally smoothing out the leg, something I'd never seen him do before.

"Yeah," I replied. "Real good. Too good, maybe. I'm a little scared."

He looked back up. "Fuck that. You deserve it."

"Thanks."

"And good old Ralphie?"

"Still around. All excited about going back to school. He's cleaned up his act, you know. A total update. Two point oh, I call him. He doesn't know what the fuck that means, but it beats me calling him a douche bag." Stewart laughed.

"I mean, don't get me wrong," I added. "He's still a douche bag. But he's all right. Mom's happy."

"That's all that matters."

I nodded. "What about you? Things okay here? You on an even keel?"

He looked down. "I still have my days, but yeah, it's better. Schizophrenia's a real bitch. But the meds started kicking in a couple weeks ago, so that's good." He looked back up. "Things have quieted down."

"Looking forward to coming home, I bet."

He shrugged. "Yeah, well, it's going to be another month, maybe two. I'm not even sure where I'm going after this. Everything's up in the air still. Of course, I've got court waiting for me."

I laughed. "You really did a number up there."

"I guess. It seems so long ago, like some dream I only half remember. Especially those last couple days."

"Don't worry. I remember well enough for both of us."

And believe me, I did. Turns out it was a good thing I didn't whack that barrel with the stupid sword after all. Stewart had filled it with acetylene from one of his father's tanks just before Kaela and I got there. The gas is pretty safe in the tank, but once it gets out, it's volatile as hell. One good spark or jolt was all it would've taken to crisp both of us, and that didn't even count the tanks of propane and pure oxygen Stewart had loaded into the Volvo, all meant for the tower. Of course, the Volvo never made it that far. The bumps had seen to that.

But that wasn't why Stewart was being taken to court. The Volvo may not have done any damage, but Stewart had done plenty before that afternoon. He'd been sneaking up there for a while, ever since I'd come across him at the smoking rock and he'd promised to "take care of it." All those sleepless nights and lonely Sundays, all those times he'd been keeping to himself, he'd been up there, walking around, testing, figuring out angles and thicknesses, or he'd been in his father's shop, learning how to work the torches. And then the cutting started—midnight trips in the cold, ripping away at the base in a shower of sparks. He'd hoped to send one into the next, domino style. Take them all down at once. He'd made some headway—enough so that the power company had had to shut down the first tower indefinitely—but not enough to really do the job. And so when he'd finally hit bottom, he'd decided to finish what he'd started.

"Don't worry about court."

"Yeah, I guess I have a pretty good defense, don't I?" he snorted. "That's what my lawyers say, anyway."

He grew quiet for a moment. .

"I never thanked you," he said, his voice cracking. "Last week on the phone. I meant to."

I waved it off. "Fuck that. It's all part of the deal."

"Still." His eyes started to water. "I didn't treat you right. After everything you'd been through. It wasn't fair."

"It was an adventure, Stewart. The play—me being Sancho, you being Don—it changed both of us. I needed it. And it had a happy ending, right?"

He gave a weak smile. "It doesn't ever end, Frenchy. But we manage, don't we? We get by."

"I can live with that." I looked down at the watch he'd given me. It hadn't lost its shine.

"They'll be back in a minute," he said. "These things don't take long."

I nodded, then pulled the box from the pocket of my coat.

"Merry Christmas. I did the ribbon myself, believe it or not."

His eyes widened at the sight of the present, then his face went red as I put it in his hands.

"I didn't get you anything."

I laughed and shook my head. "Just fucking open it."

He undid the ribbon, opened the lid, then froze a moment before lifting the medal.

"This is a Purple Heart." He stared up at me.

"Yeah, that's right."

"I can't take this, Frenchy."

"Don't worry," I said. "It's from Desert Storm. I got the newer one at home."

He nodded, his eyes welling with fresh tears.

"Besides," I said. "You deserve it."

He laughed at that. His parents came back. Then it was time to go.

He hugged me before I left. It was good not to feel the armor on him, no matter how thin he was. He held me for a moment, then let me go.

"Good-bye, Old Friend," he said, his smile tight and thin. I gave him a quick salute.

"Farewell, Your Grace."

Nobody said much of anything on the way home. It was still snowing and slow going, so I just sat in the back of the SUV, pressed my head against the glass, and stared out into the darkness, trying to tell myself that it had been a good visit. And it *was* good to see him more like himself, to see he'd managed to find at least some sort of peace, some refuge from all that suffering.

But it was tough to leave him, to look up at that window on the way out and see him standing there, watching us go without him. All through high school I'd never felt freer than when I was with Stewart, and seeing him confined in that place, nice as it was, made me realize just how limited my own world would have been without him in it. The best people in life make the world a bigger place, then help you grow to fit it. Stewart had been that person for me, and now he was stuck. Left behind.

He said it would be a few months, but who really knew? All I knew was that he had a long, hard road to travel, one whose end he might never reach.

Then again, the same could be said for me, though for the first time since last spring, I actually felt like there was some hope of making it through. My mother was starting to smile more and cry less, Ralph wasn't quite so much of a douche bag, and I even had a cool girlfriend who was smart enough to have fun with but not too smart to realize she was dating an idiot whose idea of a hot date was bowling and ribs. I was even starting to look at a few colleges for next year. Ones with a good theater program. All in all, things were moving in the right direction.

It was the play that had really done it. Even in the midst of all the shit with Stewart and my father, the experience of being part of something bigger than myself, of surprising myself along with everyone else with a talent I never knew I had, had changed me in ways I never would have imagined. And I owed that to Stewart as much as anything else—that one last bit of Quixote magic.

And that's why—as we rounded the last bend on the interstate and I watched the wind tower lights hovering in the distance, turning the snowy night red—I missed Stewart more than ever and wished he was by my side to see how it was all turning out. But I guess in the end, there are some journeys you have to make alone.

Acknowledgments

One of the great things about teaching in a high school like Lyndon Institute is having access to so many talented people from different backgrounds. Several colleagues helped make this book possible.

I'd first like to thank theater director Erin Galligan for the time she took to answer all my questions about the life of a high school musical production and for allowing me to sit in on so many auditions and rehearsals.

I'd also like to thank welding instructor Larry Kirchoff and physics teacher Kevin Hickey for helping me work out the logistics of blowing stuff up.

Most of all, I want to thank counselors Don Hunt and Steve Berman, not only for their expertise in the field of mental illness, but also for their compassion and dedication to helping others—young people especially—deal with life's many struggles.

Finally, I'd like to thank Chronicle editor Julie Romeis for seeing the promise of this book and for all her help in making it better.